A WILDERNESS WITHIN

Unlikely Heroes - Book 2

EMMA CASTLE

EMMA CASTLE
Dark and Edgy Romance

ISBN: 978-1-947206-70-0 (ebook)

ISBN:978-1-947206-71-7 (Trade paperback)

IMPORTANT NOTE FROM THE AUTHOR

I know what you're thinking...this book sounds like the Covid-19 pandemic. Now you're thinking maybe I, the author, wrote on purpose about the pandemic while it was occurring and was inspired by real life events.

That is exactly why I had to update and revise this book to include this note so I hope you'll keep reading —because I wrote this book *before* the pandemic. It was published in June of 2019 before there was any discussion of a virus in China.

A Wilderness Within was conceived early in January 2019, long before the world knew Covid-19 was on the horizon. I've always been obsessed with viruses. I grew up watching movies like Outbreak and later on films like Contagion. In January of 2019 I had this sudden thought that no one had written a real pandemic romance. There were a lot of virus zombie stories that sometimes had romances. But no one had really tried to write a realistic romance novel set during a pandemic (at least from what I could find—there may be some out there and I'm sorry if I missed them!).

I spent the early part of 2019 researching viruses, epidemiology, Ebola, viruses, reading chronicled accounts of Marburg viruses outbreaks, cholera, and I also began watching the CDC twitter feed to see how they commented on virus developments around the world. I did what I believed was a simple thing. I made an educated guess as to what I believe a realistic pandemic might result from. It came down to these four things:

- It would start in a wet market in China.
- It would come from animals being too close together which shouldn't be.
- It would an influenza-like airborne strain with a high transmission rate.
- Lastly...we'd never see it coming (despite scientists predicting this was only a matter of time).

When I began writing the story of Lincoln and Caroline, I thought of what I wanted this book to accomplish. I didn't want this book to scare readers, but I wanted it to be real, yet I wanted it to be a book about hope. They say the darkest hour is just before dawn. After all that I've seen this year in 2020, I believe we are facing our darkest hour...and I have faith our dawn is coming.

I know you might be afraid to turn the page, afraid to read a scenario that feels so close to our own harrowing year. But reader, take heart. As you read about Caroline, know that she is just like you and me... and she is the real hero of this story, not the dashing, sexy delta force soldier who I do promise you will enjoy. *wink.

So take heart. This is a story of love, a story of hope, a story where a woman saves the world.

--Emma Castle

PROLOGUE

@CDC: We have been made aware of a small outbreak in Beijing created by an unknown disease. The situation is being contained and monitored.

—Centers for Disease Control Twitter Feed
November 3, 2019

February 2020
Omaha, Nebraska, undisclosed location
The underground bunker had been compromised, and death now stalked the halls, moving invisibly beneath the flashing fluorescent lamps. Lincoln Atwood leaned back against the concrete wall inside the tunnel that would lead to freedom...and likely more

death. He couldn't breathe, his lungs strained for air, but with each panicked gasping inhalation, he smelled the sickly-sweet cloying scent of decayed and mummified flesh.

Much farther down the hall, he could see the shadowy outlines of bodies. It had been seven weeks since those men had collapsed and died where they lay. Seven weeks and the virus that had ravaged their bodies had mummified them. Another two months and there would be nothing left but stark white bones. Before he'd been assigned to the bunker, he'd seen the disease destroy the world, the final tsunami of a pandemic storm that had started four months ago.

He and the other survivors below ground hadn't wanted to touch the bodies at first, but over the last three weeks as the sickness spread, he'd realized to his horror that he was immune. He could walk among the remains, touch them, inhale the infected air. There was nowhere to lay these last few men and women to rest. So they'd remained where they'd fallen, leaving him almost completely alone with the virus.

The CDC had named the virus Hydra-1. Much like the mythological creature of many heads, this virus was an unstoppable killing machine. Victims bled out and then dried up, but rather than be preserved, the mummified remains quickly turned to dust or washed away in the rain, leaving behind only bones.

"Lincoln..." His name came through the small

walkie-talkie clipped to his hip, the sound scratchy and tinny as the signal struggled against the concrete barriers. Lincoln raised the walkie-talkie to his mouth, holding the button down, his hand shaking.

"Yeah?"

"It's time."

Those two words hung in the air, sizzling with dread like a live wire in a raging storm.

He stood. "I'll be there in a minute."

For a second, a wave of dizziness swamped him. Was it Hydra, or was it the low-protein diet and tiny rations from the food in the bunker? It didn't really matter. He wouldn't survive long once he ran out of food and water. He had been in the company of the shadow of death far too long not to fall prey to it. The men in his unit used to joke about death being an old friend, one who would greet them and walk them into the black sands of eternity.

How wrong they'd all been. Death was an uncaring assassin, a complete bastard who stole everything and gave nothing in return, not even comfort.

Lincoln started down the hall, toward the bodies. He paused in front of the first door on the right and entered. It had been his room for the last few months, not that it had ever been home. The peeling white paint on the walls exposed the concrete, and the metal-framed cot was worse than most prisons.

Lincoln began to pluck the photos he had taped to

the wall, one by one. He slid them into a plastic bag and put them in his sand-colored army-issued backpack. He had everything he needed to survive in that bag, or so he told himself. A compass, space blanket, knives, metal wire, rope, two guns, as much spare ammo as he could carry, bottled water, a filtration straw, a medical kit, and a dozen other items.

He picked up a paperback copy of *The Great Gatsby* and his solar charging battery pack and added them to his bag.

"Time to go," he whispered to the empty room. He had been living in the cramped space for months. He was the last person alive down here...except for Adam Caine.

It was Adam who needed him now.

Lincoln paused by the door, startled for a moment by his own reflection. His instincts were razor-sharp now, and every movement had him tensing. The bearded stranger, hand resting on the doorjamb, didn't look like Lincoln anymore. The young, happy face of his thirty-five-year-old self was gone. Hard-edged, cold, hollowed out, his brown eyes were dark with ancient sorrow. He looked like a man lost, who'd stepped into the deep woods of his own soul and had never been seen again, not once the wilderness within had swallowed him whole.

"Lincoln...please hurry." Adam's voice echoed in the small room from the walkie-talkie.

Lincoln's shoulders dropped as he walked the rest of

the way down the hall. He didn't even see the bodies as he passed anymore. Over the last seven weeks, they had ceased to be there in his mind and were almost now as invisible as the concrete walls. To survive, he'd learned to tune out the horrors of the dying world around him.

Look away... The ghostly whisper in his head made him shudder as he reached Adam's room.

Adam was lying on his cot, dressed in his best navy-blue suit, his bright red and white striped tie in a neat Windsor knot. Lincoln lifted his gaze up to his friend's face, forcing himself to see the man and not the dying body. Adam managed a weak smile. His eyes were hollow and ringed with purple bruises, and sweat glistened on his skin, which had turned a sallow yellow.

"Thought maybe you wouldn't come." Adam's sigh carried a hint of a death rattle.

Lincoln wanted to smile, wanted to give his friend some kind of final reassurance. But he couldn't. Pain tore at him, and it took every ounce of strength to fight back the sting of tears in his eyes. He swallowed hard, and it felt like glass shards were tearing up his throat.

"Here..." Adam patted a stack of photos sealed in a bag on his chest. Lincoln picked them up. Familiar faces, old places... All of it only made this worse.

"Ten years," Adam said. "Long time to serve together, brother."

Lincoln nodded, still unable to speak. They weren't brothers by blood, but they had been brothers in arms. Adam had taught him everything he knew. He was thirty-seven and had led their unit on over a hundred missions, saving the world a dozen times—not that it mattered now, because no one would be alive anymore to hear or care. Humanity was all but wiped out. Nature had reclaimed its bruised planet, and soon humanity would be but a dim memory in Earth's history. Perhaps one best forgotten.

Adam coughed, a light dotting of blood covering his lips as he gripped a handgun. He tried to lift it, but his arm collapsed back to his chest.

"Afraid you'll have to do the honors." Adam managed a wry smile, but Lincoln shook his head.

"No...I can't..." He'd had to do this for too many others, but for Adam, he couldn't stomach it.

Adam's gray eyes hardened. "You can. You have to." He drew in a shaky breath. "You owe me. I don't want to waste away like the others. Don't make me pull rank."

Lincoln's eyes snapped back to his friend's face. The last two years they had been in Washington, DC, while Adam had moved up in the ranks and politics. It was how they had ended up here in the bunker after all. Not that it had saved them. But Adam always joked about pulling rank whenever Lincoln tried to resist orders.

"Don't you fucking bring that up now," Lincoln said. His vision blurred as he tried to swallow down the knot of emotions raging inside him.

"You have your orders, Major." Adam shifted the gun on his chest.

Lincoln reached out and took the gun, checking the chamber. The action was instinctive after so many years, but a chill crept over him when his brain caught up with his actions and the significance of what he was about to do became clear.

Adam watched him, the war of fear and sorrow on his face now softened to a peacefulness Lincoln hadn't ever seen before.

"You know what to do, Lincoln."

But he didn't. No one had ever trained him to kill his best friend.

"Once I'm gone, get out of here. Don't stay in the bunker. If you want to die, die in the open with the sky above you. At least topside, you've got a chance to survive." They'd talked about it, the way they would end it, if it ever came to that. The blue sky above would be the way to go, not trapped here beneath the ground.

"I could take you up there." Lincoln tried not to choke on the words. "Before..."

Adam shook his head, the faint move barely there. "No. I'd only spread the disease. Better to seal me down here with the others."

Lincoln nodded numbly. Adam had stayed here, manning the communication room as other outposts dropped off the comms one by one, everyone hoping a cure would be found before the end came. Last week Adam had started showing signs of infection. They had believed they were both immune since the last man to die had been five weeks ago, but for whatever reason,

Adam had fallen ill. But he'd stayed on the radio each day for just a few minutes, broadcasting when he could, listening for any other signal. He'd never given up hope. But Lincoln knew there was none. After this, he would be alone.

Adam's face contorted with pain. "Better do it now." The virus inside him would bleed him out, then dehydrate what was left. It was an agonizing death.

Raising the gun, Lincoln aimed it at Adam's head, but his hands started to shake. Adam closed his eyes.

"Do it!"

The harsh military tone snapped Lincoln into focus, and he pulled the trigger. The loud report made his ears ring, and the heavy silence that followed grew into a deafening roar. The tiny red, white, and blue flag pinned to Adam's chest gleamed in the light. Lincoln removed the pin, slipped it into his backpack, and laid the pistol on Adam's chest. There was no need to bury him, no need to remove him from this final resting place. Lincoln stood to attention as he saluted Adam one final time.

"It has been an honor to serve and protect you, Mr. President." He knew those may very well be the last words he would ever speak to another person. He should have said them before...but if he'd dared to, might not have had the strength to pull the trigger.

He stood there for a long moment, his mind mercifully blank with grief, and he let the dark, agonizing emotion rip through him like a tidal wave. The silence haunted him, whispering softly in his head about the days before...the days when the world was still alive, when he could see children play and the bustle of the cities and the sunsets on farmhouse porches. There had been so much to love, so much to enjoy.

Now it was all gone and so was Adam, his brother in arms, his best friend. Hope's last wellspring had vanished with him.

There's nothing for me in the world now.

But a man couldn't die from grief alone, no matter how hard he might want to.

He turned and walked away.

At the bunker's exit, he climbed up the steps and cranked the wheel that released the seal and locks on the latch and pushed it open. Bright sunlight poured into the darkness of the bunker. Lincoln shielded his eyes for a moment as his eyes adjusted. Fresh air surrounded him, the scent of prairie grasses and trees teasing his nostrils. He climbed out and closed the hatch behind him. An open meadow stretched endlessly in one direction, and a light wooded area spread in the other direction. Prairie wind rustled the grasses, and he suddenly felt homesick in a way he hadn't in years.

But home was gone, as was everything else. It was possible he was the last man on earth, and it was only a matter of time before death claimed him too.

He started walking, the distant vision of the cityscape far ahead of him. Would there be any other survivors? Would he even be able to help them? He'd

9

killed his best friend, the last leader of the free world. Whoever might be left in this dying land wouldn't want his help. He was a murderer of a good man, a lost soul. Lincoln let go and chose to embrace the wilderness and the darkness inside him.

It would be the only way to survive now.

※ I ※

@CDC: The virus in Beijing has been identified as a new disease named Hydra-1. The World Health Organization (The WHO) is monitoring the situation closely. We believe it is contained and there is no cause to worry.

—Centers for Disease Control Twitter Feed

November 10, 2019

March 2020

Caroline Kelly crouched in the shadows outside the old supermarket on the outskirts of Omaha. Night was creeping closer. Usually she hated the dark, but tonight it was her friend. Whenever she entered a store or any dwelling, she knew she ran the risk of running into survivors. Ever since H–Day, as she called it, the day everyone truly realized there was a contagion sweeping over the world, people went insane.

Common decency and the humanitarian spirit had been destroyed. Knowing they had nothing to lose, many had reverted to barbarism, violence, greed, and lust. The last legacy of a dying species. And those few who had survived hadn't been much better.

Caroline shuddered and pulled her coat tight around her body. She scanned the darkened entrance to the grocery store. The chances that anything edible was in there were slim, but she had to look. She would eat just about anything right now. Last week she had found a stash of canned sardines in someone's house and had a feast that any cat would envy. Then she had thrown up because the oily texture of the tiny fish had made her nauseous. She'd never been into seafood, but starvation was still starvation.

She checked the straps on her backpack, making sure they weren't loose. Whenever she had a chance to fill up with supplies or food, she needed to make sure that the bag stayed tight to her body. She had already lost one bag when she was running from a man who tried to corner her inside a drugstore last month. The bag had been too loose and heavy. When she rounded a corner too fast, the momentum from the bag swung so hard it knocked her onto her ass. The man caught up with her and tried to grab it. She had to abandon it or risk him catching her. She knew all too well what would have been next if that had happened. In the early days of the contagion, she'd tried to trust other survivors, believing that they could work together to survive. That had been a mistake, a nearly fatal one. She still believed deep down that humanity could survive this, but as the dark days stretched on, her hope was dying, like a candle sputtering in a violent wind. All too soon it would be snuffed out.

The store had been quiet for the last hour. She had been hiding in the shadows across the street, and once darkness fell, she inched her way toward the store, using abandoned cars as cover. But she didn't go inside, not yet. Someone was out there. She could feel their presence somehow, like a sixth sense warning her of danger. She couldn't wait forever. Hunger and desperation would force her hand sooner or later. If she was being watched, she would have to brave it and just go.

Caroline moved toward the door. The glass had shattered long ago, and all that remained was a metal frame laced with jagged edges. She didn't bother to open it but instead slipped through where the glass had once been. Her boots crunched on the broken shards, but she couldn't help that. Some things were unavoidable. She squinted at the signs hanging overhead, trying to see what was in each aisle.

If she had been more certain she was alone, she would have pulled out her flashlight, but that would be a shining beacon to anyone close by. So she wandered down each aisle, careful to avoid any shelves that had toppled over. The stench of rotten produce a few aisles over made her eyes water, so she stayed closer to the center. The majority of the edible food was gone, but not all of it.

When the virus had swept through the major cities like this one, it had killed so many so quickly that people didn't have time to loot stores. People were too busy dying to steal TVs. There had been some looting, but not as much as she had expected. Not that it mattered without electricity. She couldn't benefit from most of the things left behind. She would love a giant flat-screen as much as the next girl, but what would she do with it?

Caroline passed by the empty canned food aisle. The items that could last the longest had been taken first. So she focused on other items like cereal. The easily reached shelves were bare, but she thought she saw something up top. She carefully scaled the shelves, praying they wouldn't fall down and crush her. She reached her hand along, trying to search for anything that might've been left behind. Her fingers brushed along the dust-covered surface of the shelf. They bumped into something. She reached, clawing at the object, and closed her hand around it.

It *moved*. The furry thing squeaked and bit her hand.

Caroline screamed and toppled backward, landing hard on her back. The air whooshed out of her lungs, and she choked on a sob. It was a damn rat. She hated rats. Pain radiated through her as she struggled to catch her breath. She'd missed landing on a bunch of broken jars by mere inches. After a long moment, she stifled a whimper as she rolled onto her side. She got up and wiped the dirt and debris off her jeans and checked her bag. She'd been smart enough to put it down while she'd been searching the shelves. She knelt down and caught sight of several boxes of granola bars at the back of the bottom shelf.

"Yes!" She grinned as she pulled them out, squinting at them in the dim light. Peanut butter and chocolate. Her favorite. She opened the boxes and dumped the bars in her bag to save space. Then she zipped the bag shut and slung it over her shoulder before searching the other aisles. She passed by the frozen foods section and saw the now hardened pools of melted sugary liquid that once had been ice cream. In the shadows they were dark, like blood, and the sight made her stomach churn.

The pharmacy was mostly cleaned out, but she did find some Tylenol and multivitamins. She also discovered a few small bottles of Pedialyte. The salty liquid didn't taste that great, but she could power through days of little to no food with it. Her personal record so far was four days. Not that she wanted to brag about that.

She was almost done browsing the pharmacy when she heard the faint sound of glass beneath boots. But not *her* boots.

Oh God.

Her unseen watcher had decided to show his or her face, but Caroline had no plans on sticking around to see who it was. She waited, listening to the sounds around her, ears straining to pick up every little sound. There was a distant scrape from the opposite end of the store. Caroline exhaled slowly, her heart pounding. They were moving away from her. She still had time to escape. She crouched over, using the shorter shelves in the store's pharmacy section to shield her while she slipped her backpack back on. The harsh grinding sound of the zipper teeth locking into place seemed far too loud to her. Then she swung it over her shoulders and secured it to her waist with straps.

The sound of a can rolling in the distance made her tense. When she peered around the edge of the nearest shelf, she saw a tin of baked beans flash in the moonlight that poured into the grocery store's high empty panes. That was too good a find to ignore. There might be a way to grab the can as she left the store. Whoever was here was still in the far end of the store and might not see her.

Already tasting the beans in her mind, she left her spot behind the shelf and started to crawl forward slowly on hands and knees toward the can. She bumped against some broken glass and stopped. She was only inches away. She reached out, her hand brushing the metal rim of the can when a booted foot materialized from the shadows. It stepped on the can, pinning it in place.

A scream froze in Caroline's throat, and she threw

her head back to look up at whoever had discovered her.

A tall, well-built man with broad shoulders stared down at her. He was wearing a thick gray sweater, one that looked military, and he had a thick beard that covered his chin and mouth, making his expression impossible to read, but it leaned toward menacing.

"Easy, beautiful." His deep voice was a little rough, as though he hadn't spoken in days.

She knew all too well what that sound was like. How long had it been since she'd actually talked to someone? Shouting at them to leave her alone while she ran away didn't count. It had been at least two weeks. The rare times she came into contact with other survivors, it was a hard scramble, like animals fighting for survival. A person had but a few seconds to measure up the other survivor, to see if they were friend or foe. Could they be trusted, or would they be dangerous? She'd always tried to talk to them and try to calm them down. It never worked. A woman she'd run into last month had pretended to be nice, but then she tried to stab her when Caroline turned her back to help her lift a box of bottled water off the ground. Caroline had the scars to prove that trusting people wasn't worthwhile, no matter how much she wanted to.

She glanced up at the man looming over her. "You can have whatever's left in the store. I don't want any trouble." She released her hold on the can and slowly sat back on her heels. This guy, whoever he was, was definitely not someone she could trust. He was a mass of muscle and intimidation. A mountain man who likely only thought of base instincts. If she could get him to think she was helpless and weak, she could buy herself time to attack and escape because he'd lower his guard. In seconds, she could rock up fully into a standing position and run, but he didn't know that. Speed was one of her advantages. She had gotten really good at running since the virus had spread.

"What if I want *you*?" Rather than menacing, the man's deep voice sounded gentle and melodic. Hell, in another world she would've called it seductive.

But luxuries like love and other complex emotions had perished in the night, along with baser feelings like hope. She was going to die, not from Hydra but from this man.

Her hand by her knee brushed against a piece of glass. She curled her fingers around it as she met his gaze. His eyes were black in the darkness. He seemed in that moment more shadow than mortal flesh. Nightmare rather than reality.

I don't want to die. I want to live.

Even this cold, empty world still called to her. She would not go down without a fight.

"Go on and stand up," he said more brusquely, as though frustrated by her silence. "I want a better look at you." At first she thought he'd reached out to grab her, but he didn't. He just held out his hand, a gesture so normal in this abnormal world that she nearly laughed. She rose, her knees knocking as she tried to control the surge of adrenaline inside her. Every sound, every breath, every move seemed slower in time. Caroline kept the shard of glass loosely balanced on her partially curled fingers to conceal it, waiting.

When she raised her gaze to his face again, she could now see the handsome features partially hidden behind the mountain man beard. He was a little older than her, early thirties maybe? The beard made it hard to tell.

"Fuck, you're gorgeous," he growled. "I couldn't tell when I first spotted you a few hours ago. I only saw you from behind and at a distance." He seemed to be talking more to himself than her.

Shit...he wanted her. That wasn't good.

"Just let me go," she said again.

"No can do." He bent to pick up the can of beans and slipped it into the pack on his shoulders. Caroline almost made a run for it, but he was too close and would easily grab her before she got far.

"I'll give you my bag," she offered, hating that she would do just that if it saved her life. She had gotten far too used to starting over. Losing everything she had the moment she started to get ahead.

The man sighed. "I don't want your bag." He held out his hand to her again. "Now, come on. Let's go someplace safe to talk."

Caroline knew her chances were better if he never saw the attack coming. She placed her hand in his. The flare of heat between that single connection rocked her to her core. She hadn't touched another person in so long, she was surprised by the warmth she felt. For a moment she imagined that this wasn't the end of the world and she was just walking hand-in-hand with a sexy man.

I cannot be feeling anything. It's just shock from touching another person after so long.

He led her toward the front of the store. She walked along beside him, still holding his hand. When they were within feet of the exit she lunged, stabbing him in the shoulder with the glass shard. The glass cut her hand, but she pushed harder. He grunted and released her as he tried to pull the glass out of his shoulder.

She sprinted around him, running for freedom, but with a panicked cry she twisted her right ankle, coming down on it hard as she collided with a shelf. The structure wobbled, and she looked up in terror as the metal shelves teetered and fell right on top of her. She blacked out and crumpled to the floor in sheer agony as the metal hit her body. A moment later, she was conscious again. She breathed in heavy pants as she tried to claw her way out from under the shelves, focused on the only thing that mattered—escape.

Metal creaked and groaned as it came off her body, and she dragged herself free of it. Then the metal crashed back down, and the bearded man stood there, breathing hard as he watched her. She closed her eyes, praying death would be swift if that was her fate now.

A pair of hands slid under her body, lifting her up effortlessly. She cried out in fear, clawing at the man as he held her against his chest.

"Easy, beautiful, easy," That gentle rumbling voice of his made her restless panic ease, but only for a fraction of a second. The pain in her ankle was so great she could barely think. She closed her eyes, breathing in and out, her hands fisted in his thick sweater.

Stay alive. That was all that mattered. Whatever he wanted to do to her, he wouldn't do it here and not right now. She could fight him off and escape as soon as her body stopped hurting.

He stepped through the doorway and carried her into the street, bold and unafraid. She'd run from car to car to get here, hiding like a mouse. But he strode out like a god of war. For now, she belonged to him. That seemed to be the way this dead new world was going to work. Ten thousand years of civilization was gone in less than four months. Whatever rules humans made now would be hard and cruel. Caroline shivered as that burning hope for mankind shrank even more.

Even with his wounded shoulder, the man carried her half a block as though she weighed nothing at all. Then he stopped in front of a black Ford SUV. He shifted her in his arms as he opened the back door and settled her into a passenger seat. Fresh pain shot through her ankle, and she lay uncomfortably on top of her backpack, like a turtle flipped onto its shell.

"Please... Don't..." She whimpered as she saw him

digging around in his own backpack. She couldn't escape; she couldn't fight him off.

He pulled out a syringe with a mean-looking needle and ripped the cap off.

"No!" She kicked at him, but he anticipated the blow. Her foot barely made contact.

"Stop it. I'm not going to hurt you." He grabbed both of her legs with one hand and pinned her down. Caroline screamed in pain. The man hissed and pulled up her sweater, jabbing the needle into her side just above her hip.

She moaned and thrashed. Her leg hurt so badly that she had no strength left. She rolled onto her stomach, trying to drag herself through the vehicle, her fingers scraping over the nice leather. Whatever he'd given her was moving through her veins, dulling her senses, numbing her all over. Tears leaked out of her eyes as she struggled and fought. Strains of the last address on the radio by the final president of the United States came back to her.

"We shall not go quietly into the night. Stand together, stand strong..."

And just like the radio, the lights around Caroline went dark.

@CDC: Hydra-1 update: There have been many rumors and speculation about the disease. It is believed to have originated in a wet market where live and dead animals were sold out in the open with no sanitary control. We have traced its origins to a wet market in Guangzhou where horseshoe bats were caged too closely to palm civet cats. Much like the way SARS developed, Hydra-1 jumped species and is moving to humans. The CDC is analyzing samples to begin developing a vaccine.

—Centers for Disease Control Twitter Feed

November 13, 2019

L incoln tossed the empty needle to the ground and stared at the unconscious young woman in the back seat of his car.

Somehow he had fucked up, *bad*. She'd been terrified. He knew better than to approach a civilian like that. She was frightened out of her mind. He should have followed her and waited until morning to approach her. Sneaking up on her like that had been cruel. She didn't know that he wasn't like the other monsters out there, the men who would have raped and killed her. She was attractive—he wasn't going to lie to himself about that—but he wasn't a rapist.

It was just...well, he couldn't let her go on her own. He'd been following her discreetly for a day now, trying to assess her. She had developed some survival instincts, but she clearly wasn't military. It was a miracle she'd made it this long without someone watching her back. The fact was she needed protection. She was young, probably in her early twenties. So whether she liked it or not, he was going to look out for her. It had been two weeks since Adam died, and he hadn't seen another living person in all that time, though he'd found plenty of evidence of the kind of people who might still be roaming the cities. He'd seen smoke from fires, heard gunshots. Enough to know that the people still out there were dangerous. In all his years as a soldier, he'd seen hellscapes before. Men roving in gangs, killing and raping. People turning on each other for a scrap of food to survive. And that had been in war-torn areas, just small pockets of chaos. But now the entire world was in chaos.

Lincoln closed his eyes for a brief second, his breath slowing as he remembered seeing this girl for the first time yesterday and how it had been like seeing the sun after months of clouds.

He'd been sleeping in one of the military vehicles parked in the woods close to the underground bunker. He heard her footsteps as she passed him on the road. He'd sat up just enough to catch a glimpse of her. He'd lied to her about only having seen her from behind. He'd gotten a damned good look at her through his long-range binoculars as she'd turned around to scan the road. But he hadn't really believed what he'd seen. She had long, coffee-brown hair that glowed beneath the afternoon sun, and her eyes, a rich hazel green, made him feel strangely homesick for a home he'd left a long time ago. She was a tiny woman of only five foot four, and when he had taken one look at her curves, something inside him demanded he pursue her. Pursue and protect and maybe one day...

He shook himself. Two weeks out of the bunker and he was already thinking like a barbarian. He wouldn't allow that. The country he'd defended might not exist, but he could still defend its ideals. Still, he couldn't help but dream, imagining a connection forming between them, and maybe one day he would get lucky enough to know exactly how she felt in his arms when her eyes were bright with passion and her lips were hungry for pleasure. But that wasn't in his control. The only thing in his control right now was protecting her. Two people together had a better chance of survival than one alone.

Lincoln walked around to the driver's side and

climbed in. He had plenty of gas for now. He was one of the few survivors still using vehicles. Quite a few of the stations still had gas, but only older stations off the beaten path still had pumps he could start without paying. But he was also pretty good at siphoning gas. Special forces training had come in handy during the end of the world.

As he drove down the road to the house he'd been using as a base of operations for the last week, he noticed the twilight slash across the sky as a deeper purple bled into it and the moon rose even higher. He stared at the endless neighborhoods of eastern Nebraska, stunned at how empty it all seemed without people.

Life after us... Is it really life?

Since he'd left the bunker two weeks ago, he had been lost. Not literally, but figuratively. There were no more missions. His best friend and former commander —the last president of the United States—was dead. There were no terrorist cells to track down, no hostages to rescue, no tyrannical governments to topple. It was all over. Everything he'd done in the last decade of his life had become meaningless on the whim of some microbial virus. For as long as he could remember, he'd been a kid with a plan and then a man with a mission. Now it was just about surviving.

But surviving for what? What was the point of all this? For a man who didn't like dwelling on philosophy, he'd become far too comfortable with existential thoughts these last few months.

Lincoln could still taste the bitterness when he thought back to that first night after he left the bunker, how he'd sat by a small campfire deep in the woods and watched the firelight play upon the barrel of his gun. It had felt heavy, a solid weight that was almost comfort-ing. The bullet in the chamber promised an end to his worries.

He'd nearly put the gun to his temple, his hand had even lifted an inch or two off his lap, but something had stopped him. Some damn internal instinct to survive. He'd seen a flash of the old lake cabin his parents used to take him to during the summer when he'd been a kid. The quiet still water, the blue sky above and the wooded hills reflected on the perfect mirror surface of the lake. Then there had been a flash, just an instant of light in his head and a whisper...one word...*hope*.

The vision had been so clear, so powerful that he'd dropped the gun back to the ground, his heart pounding wildly as he gasped for breath. He couldn't go through with it now even if he wanted to because every time he thought about it, he heard that word in his head again. *Hope*. But how could he have any hope left? It hadn't been possible.

Until he had seen her.

He would have to figure out what her real name was. She probably wouldn't like being called *beautiful*. She probably already thought he was some crazy, insane creep who just wanted to use her and kill her. But he'd show her he wasn't like that. They were in this together now, and he had a strong desire to believe in her, if he couldn't believe in anything else right now.

Lincoln pulled into a neighborhood of expensive houses and drove down a series of streets. It seemed that looters didn't like driving through a maze of complex neighborhoods and hit the easier targets in town. It was safer to embed himself deep into a neighborhood instead of choosing a house close to a city street.

He parked the car and killed the lights. He left the woman in the car while he unloaded a month's worth of supplies.

On his last trip he had found a decent haul of medical supplies, food, and camping gear. After he put away all the supplies, he returned for the woman. She was still unconscious. Good. He'd given her a powerful cocktail of painkillers. She would probably hate him when she woke up in a few hours, but she needed pain relief for that ankle and for any pain she had from when the grocery shelf had collapsed on her.

He carried her inside the house and up the stairs to one of the bedrooms. His room. Not because he was going to do anything he shouldn't. He simply needed to keep an eye on her while she slept. She was a fighter, and no matter how badly she was hurt, she would try to escape, and he couldn't have her getting hurt again. So the closer she was to him the better.

Unluckily for her, he was a light sleeper by nature and by training.

Lincoln set her down on the bed and turned on one of the camping lanterns. Bright light blossomed through the room, creating an eerie sense of daylight tinged with shadows on the edges. He moved one lamp closer so he could examine her leg. Carefully, he pushed her jeans up to her mid-calf. If she'd been awake, she would've been in agony. Her ankle was already swelling. He'd seen this type of injury before. A man in his unit, Jenkins, had been forced to jump out of a second-story window to escape enemy fire. He landed badly and popped his ankle out of place and popped it back in a second later when he righted himself. Their medic had later told him it would have been less painful to simply break the bone.

Pressing gently around the woman's ankle, Lincoln felt no evidence of a fracture. But until he could get the swelling down, he couldn't be sure if there was a break or not. Christ, he wished he had a bag of frozen peas to lay on her ankle. He would have given anything for that. The best he could do was a cold towel. He'd broken into a sporting goods store last week and found a set of exercise towels that turned cold when drenched in water to a chemical reaction. He'd seen the genius of it and grabbed three of them.

Lincoln went into the master bathroom and to the sink, where he soaked one of the blue towels. Although the power was out in this area, the water was still running. He'd have to set out some barrels to catch rain soon just in case the water stopped running. Then he returned to the bed and removed her boot and sock before he wound the towel around her ankle. Then he slipped her backpack off, which was lying lopsided beneath her. After a quick check for weapons inside, and finding none, he set it on the floor near her. Then he peeled off her coat and covered her with several thick blankets. March in Nebraska was not usually warm, the temperature would fall to fifty-five degrees inside the house tonight.

Lincoln checked her palm next, the one she'd cut when she'd stabbed him in the shoulder. It was a shallow cut, but he didn't want her to get an infection. He retrieved some antiseptic cloths from his first aid kit and thoroughly cleaned the wound before he used a wound sealer like superglue to bind the cut together, and then he wrapped it securely with some bandages. As long as she was careful, she wouldn't need stitches. He'd have to track down some antibiotics in a day or two to battle any potential infections.

Once he was certain he left her in as comfortable a position as possible, he grabbed one of the lanterns and headed back into the bathroom. He set the lantern on the counter and tried not to grimace when he caught sight of his face in the mirror. He hadn't shaved in at least three months. He looked like a fucking bear. No wonder she'd screamed when she saw him.

He winced as he removed his sweater and turned his

back on the mirror. He glanced over his shoulder. The piece of glass she'd stabbed him with had fallen out during their struggle. It hadn't been deep, but blood dripped down his chest and was drying in dark black streaks. He cursed, grabbed a bottle of rubbing alcohol, and dabbed some over the wound. He let loose a string of curses his mother would have smacked him for, but he muttered through gritted teeth so he didn't wake the woman in the bedroom. He worked quickly, cleaning the wound with antiseptic wipes and covering it with antibiotic cream. At least it wouldn't need stitches.

He pushed a single finger through the place in his sweater where his little beauty had stabbed him. Dried black blood had ruined the expensive fabric. It had been one of the last few military-issued pieces of clothing he'd taken with him, aside from his boots and shoulder holster. He pressed his palms on the counter for a moment, praying this all hadn't been a huge fucking mistake. No, this was right—he needed to help her. She was a survivor like him, and she wasn't one of those bastards he'd heard from a few nights ago who were firing shots off in the nearby woods. He'd steered clear of whoever that had been.

Lincoln brushed his teeth and drank a glass of scotch from a bottle he'd found in the basement. Then he lay down in the bed beside the woman and closed his eyes.

God, he needed to sleep. Whenever he closed his eyes, all he saw was Adam's face before he pulled the trigger, and then the ruins, the bodies, the empty world left behind.

He didn't want to think about the two graves he had dug in the frozen backyard that contained the two bodies he'd found in the car in the garage. The house's owners had killed themselves rather than face the agony of dying from the inside out. He had cleared out the garage, carefully moved the people to the backyard, and buried them. Two simple wooden crosses marked their graves. He'd never been a religious man, but he'd looked up into the cold, wintry gray skies, listened to the sound of wind whistling down empty roads nearby, and whispered a prayer.

The home they'd left behind was a good one. Two main stories and a basement that opened up to a backyard that sloped down to a creek. It wasn't a bad place to settle temporarily. He would have to move out eventually, but for now, he could make trips deeper into the city and still find decent supplies. He'd found his beauty, after all. She had been worth the risk. He didn't have a clue what to do with her once she was healed, but he didn't want to let her out of sight. It wasn't safe out there.

Lincoln slept fitfully for a couple of hours, then headed downstairs to the kitchen and grabbed a few bottles of water. When he returned, he set them by the side of the bed closest to her. The meds he'd given her would dehydrate her. Then he lay back down. Waiting.

Waiting for her to wake up, waiting to fall asleep... waiting for this nightmare to end.

Nightmares had to end eventually...didn't they?

―――――

November 2019

Caroline was trapped.

She stood in line at the Chicago O'Hare airport, trying to find out why her flight home to Joplin, Missouri, was canceled. All around her people were shuffling in lines or were camped out in the uncomfortable rows of connected airport waiting area seats. The man behind her coughed, and she winced. If she got a cold now, she would be super pissed. She'd spent the last week practically bathing in hand sanitizer at work to keep from picking up the illnesses her boss usually brought. Her advertising firm sometimes felt like a petri dish of bacteria and viruses.

Her boss, Jill, had three kids ages three, five and nine, which meant at least two or three times a year Jill became what was jokingly called by her coworkers a carrier for the "super cold" that her kids picked up at school. Caroline tended to catch them most because she worked in a small cubicle just outside Jill's corner office. Close proximity to the boss did her in every time.

"Passengers of flight 1502 to New York, we're sorry

to inform you that the flight has been canceled. All flights to and from LaGuardia are grounded until further notice. Please see your gate attendant to schedule a new flight." The employee who made the announcement sounded mildly stressed. Carolyn didn't blame her. Dozens of flights had been delayed or canceled in the last three hours, and people were getting restless.

The woman in front of Caroline turned to face her.

"LaGuardia's closed? You suppose they had a terrorist issue?" The woman slung her Prada purse over her shoulder and peeked around at the other passengers nearby.

"Could be." Caroline set her heavy backpack down, placing her feet on either side of it while she stretched her neck. This line wasn't moving at all, and she'd pinch a nerve in her neck if she had her backpack on for another ten minutes.

"I'll google it." The woman began to type on her phone. Caroline was sure the news wouldn't report anything about a terrorist threat until it was dealt with and everyone was safe.

The woman cleared her throat, tucked a strand of hair that was threaded with silver behind her ears, and the color drained from her face. "Oh..."

Caroline leaned forward, worry starting to form knots in her gut. "What is it?"

"Um..." The woman scrolled down on her phone, her lips moving slightly as she silently read the article.

She slowly raised her head, her gaze sweeping the somewhat cantankerous crowd of people around them.

Caroline reached out and touched the woman's arm, trying to get her attention. "Is it bad?" The touch seemed to electrify the woman. She pulled away from Caroline, grabbed her bag and purse, and abruptly left the line at the gate. She practically sprinted down the terminal and vanished.

"So much for airport camaraderie," Caroline muttered, but her chest was tight with worry. The woman was clearly spooked by something.

Caroline inched forward in the line, nudging her backpack forward with her boot before she retrieved her own cell phone so she could look up LaGuardia on the internet. The headline that jumped out on the first page of results startled her:

Man on Paris Flight Collapses at LaGuardia Airport. Signs of Infectious Virus Reported.

She read further on, seeing that the terminal was closed and a medical team had been brought in to examine the man. The passengers at the terminal were currently quarantined. Caroline scrolled past some annoying pop-up ads about kitchen utensils. The rest of the article discussed how the airport was going to close down the other terminals, and all flights would soon be grounded. There were no comments as to what the virus was.

Maybe it was Ebola? The 2014 scare had been a little frightening. A girl who worked with Caroline had been on a cruise with a nurse who had treated an Ebola victim in Dallas. The nurse had then gone on her vacation. Once it was revealed she was on a cruise ship, the CDC had contacted the ship and requested the nurse quarantine herself inside her room. The entire ship panicked, but the cruise company offered free drinks and when that didn't work, a full refund to all passengers. The Ebola scare ultimately calmed down and seemed to be neutralized, at least in the United States.

Caroline wondered if the man in New York who had fallen ill had come from Sierra Leone, Ghana, or South Africa. It shouldn't be cause for concern, though. They'd stopped him from getting on another flight, so he shouldn't have infected anyone, right? Unless...

Caroline didn't want to think about "unless," but her brain couldn't stop itself.

What if it was already too late? What if he had met and touched a bunch of other passengers on his flight, and then they had boarded planes an hour or so before this man collapsed? Those other people could be going anywhere.

The terminal suddenly seemed very stifling. The man behind her coughed again, and Caroline fought to banish a wave of panic.

"Next!" the gate attendant called, Caroline rushed forward, desperate to get away from the man behind her.

"Name?" the woman asked.

"Caroline Kelly."

"Headed to Joplin?" the attendant asked.

"Yeah."

"Okay..." The attendant perused her screen for available flights. The PA crackled, and the voice from earlier came on over the sound system.

"Code Bravo. Repeat, Code Bravo. Employees, please make your stations ready."

The woman behind the blue-and-white striped counter froze for a split second. Then she very calmly looked up at Caroline.

"I'm so sorry. The terminal is going to be shutting down. Please find a seat nearby. We'll be making an announcement soon." The attendant placed a *Closed* sign next to her post and hurried down the crowded terminal to an office about fifty feet away.

"Hey, what the hell?" the man behind her snapped.

Caroline turned, picked up her backpack, and tried to get around him. He coughed right in her face. She wiped her face with her sleeve, trying not to freak out. Maybe they were closing the terminal for some other reason. She went straight to the bathroom to wash her hands and pulled out a travel-size bottle of hand sanitizer. She applied the sanitizer to her hands so she could smear the sanitizer around on her face.

Maybe I'm just being super paranoid.

But she wasn't. Two hours later, the man who'd been behind her in line collapsed, and everyone at Chicago O'Hare was trapped. The man who had fallen ill had come in on a flight from LaGuardia. When he was carried away on a stretcher, the paramedics wore masks and thick gloves. Police officers, also wearing masks, blocked anyone from leaving after they had removed the ill man. Caroline had collapsed in a corner, clutching her backpack, and pulled out her phone to call home. Her older sister, Natalie, answered.

"Caro, what the hell? Shouldn't you be on a plane?"

"Yeah, I should." She sighed, the sound a little shaky. "Is Mom or Dad there?"

"Uh-huh. What's going on, sis? You sound funny." Natalie, her older sister by four years, always knew when something was up with her.

"Well, they closed down O'Hare. I'm stuck here." She tried not to let her sister hear the fear that was radiating inside her.

"What do you mean, *stuck*? They won't let you leave?"

"Yeah. No one can leave. A man got sick, and they shut everything down."

"Caro. Wait..." Her sister paused, her voice lowering on the phone. "Is this connected to the man at LaGuardia? Rick saw it on the news. He and Dad have been glued to the TV all morning." Natalie's husband was a news junkie like their father.

"I think so, but I'm not positive. They're not telling us much."

"Oh God, Caro, this is so scary. I'll have Rick figure out what's going on. He has a friend that works in airport security in Kansas City. He might be able to learn what's happening up in Chicago."

"Don't let Mom and Dad freak out, okay? Once I have a chance to leave, I'll rent a car and drive." That was assuming they'd let her leave the airport...and right now that felt like a really big *if*.

"Sure, got it. We'll be waiting. I can't wait for you to meet Ellie. You're going to love her."

Ellie, her sister's baby, had been born two months ago, and Caroline hadn't been able to leave work to fly to Missouri and see the new addition to the family.

"Can't wait," she said, her throat tightening as she fought off a fresh wave of anxiety.

Everything was going to be okay...wasn't it?

———

Caroline woke as the last bits of the dream faded around her. Her cheeks were wet with tears, her head felt foggy, and for a moment she didn't remember where she was or how she'd fallen asleep. She was warm, not toasty, but she wasn't really cold. Not like she had been in a long time. It was dark, and when she shifted, she felt a pillow, an honest-to-God pillow behind her head. She moved her hands, which were tucked beneath the thick fleece blanket. She was lying on something soft, and she could hear the cold wind whistling from outside. She wasn't sleeping outside?

She struggled to sit up and bit her lip as pain shot up her leg. Just like that, the memories from the grocery store came rushing back. Blood pounded in her ears as she turned her head and saw a man lying in bed beside her. His body was more shadow than anything else in the dim moonlight coming through the wide windows opposite the bed.

Oh God, he had drugged her and probably brought her here and raped her. She touched her clothes. Her jeans and shirt were still on. Had he put her clothes back on after assaulting her? Surely that would have taken too much effort.

Her wounded ankle felt cold, so she carefully pulled the blankets back and saw something blue and damp wrapped around her ankle. Some kind of compress. The man had treated it?

Caroline was confused. Why had he tried to help her? No one did that anymore. The kind people, the ones who thought of others, were long dead. They had been the first to go because they had rushed to help the sick or stop the looters. She'd seen many of them killed on the news, either by the disease or by other people who thought they needed to kill to survive. Now only the immune who were violent and tough survived, at least so far as she could tell. But she ran into so few survivors these days, and the ones she did meet scared her. There had to be good people still left in the world. Statistically it had to be possible, right?

I'm not tough, just immune. She had been inches from

the man who died in O'Hare. He'd coughed right into her face, and yet she was fine. The employee who had worked the desk had been rushed from the airport only two hours into the lockdown. That was how the world ended.

She'd never heard where the man from Paris had caught it, or if it originated from China like the CDC said. The CDC hadn't revealed any information, assuming they even knew. Not that it mattered now. Hydra-1 was unstoppable except to a small portion of the population. Caroline tried not to think about that most days, but now she was facing it. She was more alone than ever, despite the shadowy stranger lying beside her in bed. She curled her arms around her body, hugging herself as she tried to dream of better days. But all she could see was the bearded face of the man next to her, and she worried about her future and the future of the other survivors.

@CDC: We have confirmed that the virus in Beijing has spread to Shanghai and New Delhi. Two WHO workers did not properly dispose of their working clothes and have carried the virus out of Beijing. The CDC and the WHO are trying to trace all movements of these two individuals in order to determine where the virus may spread. Sign up for alerts on Hydra-1 via our website.

—Centers for Disease Control Twitter Feed
November 16, 2019

C aroline couldn't escape in the morning. Her ankle wouldn't let her, nor would her body. After that shelf collapsed on her, *everything* hurt. Each little move forced her to groan, but she couldn't stay in bed next to that...mountain man. Any movement she made where she put weight on her ankle shot pain straight up the rest of her leg. She valiantly attempted several times to get away from the bed. Each time she crumpled, the mountain man's strong arms lifted her up and carried her back to bed.

"I'm not going to hurt you," he murmured as he settled her back onto her side of the bed and covered her with blankets.

"Then let me go."

"No." He sighed and closed his eyes again. "Now go back to sleep. You need to rest your body after that fall."

By the time morning sunlight was streaming through the windows, she had given up. She lay in bed, feeling the heat of the sun on her face, trying to make sense of what had happened. After her last attempt to escape, the man seemed to realize she was done with her efforts and had risen from bed and left her alone to sleep a little longer, but she was too nervous.

She could hear soft domestic sounds from the kitchen downstairs, the murmur of water moving through pipes in the walls, the occasional bang of pots or pans. And then she heard something else. Music.

Caroline stared at the ceiling, mystified. *Music.* How was that possible?

Determined to get to the source of the noise, she got out of the bed again, but this time she gave her predicament some thought. She hopped on one leg, using the wall for support. Silly, yes, but far less agonizing. She reached a short stairway that had one small landing before the stairs turned perpendicular. She scooted down the steps on her bottom with her bad leg aloft, careful not to bump her ankle. When she reached the bottom, she slowly started to limp toward the kitchen. She froze when she caught sight of her mysterious mountain man in the early sunlight.

He was just as tall as she remembered. Well over six feet and muscled. He was built like a rock, with broad shoulders that led down to a narrow waist and hips. He wore jeans and a gray sweater with the sleeves rolled up. He should not have looked sexy to her, not under these circumstances, but there was something about the way the sun hit his arms and how his muscles flexed that made her want to reach out and touch him.

On the counter he was cooking something in a pot on a small camping stove. A delicious smell rolled through the kitchen toward her. She focused on his face. The noble profile was somewhat hidden by the scruff of his beard, but she could see he was totally gorgeous. Caroline swallowed hard. Damn, did her captor have to be completely hot as hell?

Beside the stove, a smartphone sat on the counter, connected to a battery pack and a portable speaker. She'd had lost hers when she'd had to give up her last bag.

The sound of 70s rock 'n' roll came through the phone's speaker. After months of silence, the music sounded like heaven. She'd thought she'd never hear any of it again, the drums, the harmonic voices, the guitar riffs. Who would compose music now that the human race was drawing its last breath?

Her lips trembled as she listened to the sounds, emotions riding through her like a summer storm. Whoever this man was, he had brought music back to her world.

"Stay right there," the man said. She jolted, unaware that he had known she was in the room.

"I"

"I'm going to carry you to the couch." He looked at her and then waved toward a nook with two couches set perpendicular to each other with a large ottoman in between. He paused in front of her, and she swallowed hard at his massive size and how small and fragile he made her feel. She wasn't all that short, but she'd never been aware of anyone like she was of him and his towering height right now. His eyes were just as dark as before. Dark pools of rich brown that seemed to draw in the light rather than reflect it. Her skin flushed with heat as his gaze swept slowly over her, taking her in.

Then, without a word, he scooped her up carefully and carried her over to one of the couches and laid her down on it. Then he covered her with a blanket.

"*Stay*. I've got eggs cooking and some fruit." He returned to the kitchen, leaving her to gaze after him open mouthed. She'd just been ordered to stay like some border collie. A second later, the rest of his words caught up to her.

"Eggs and *fruit*?" she echoed. Her voice was raw,

unused. How long had it been since she'd actually talked to another being? A long time.

He removed two white china plates from the cupboards and scooped eggs out of the pot on his burner onto one plate. Then he poured peaches onto it and brought it over to her, handing her a fork as well.

"I have two chickens down in the basement. They have been laying decent eggs. It's cold enough that I can leave them outside in a basket to keep them cool. The peaches... Well, the previous owners were quite the canners. The basement has a stockroom of pickled vegetables and canned fruits. Part of the reason I chose this place."

The man explained this all with barely a hint of emotion before he returned to the kitchen, where he began brewing coffee.

Caroline took a bite of the eggs, and after that first glorious swallow she burst into tears. She couldn't help herself; the sudden burst of taste had made her realize that the food was real. This wasn't some weird dream where a handsome man rescued her and cooked her delicious food. This was reality. He was by her side in an instant, kneeling down by the couch as he set her plate on the ottoman.

"What's the matter?" Worry was evident in his gruff tone.

It took her several moments to collect herself. "I haven't...had real food in weeks. It's all blurred together. Music...I never thought I'd hear songs again. It's too much. I..." She wiped her eyes and looked out the window.

By the creek, three deer wandered along the grass, dodging patches of snow as they nibbled on bushes and trees. There were two does and one fawn, old enough that the white spots were starting to fade on its coat. She watched their stately, delicate prancing walks as they studied the branches in the garden for something to eat.

The man started to stand. "We could use some venison."

Caroline caught his wrist, marveling at the strength she could feel in his arm.

"No. Please, just let them go."

She couldn't tell him, this stranger, what the sight of something so beautiful, still alive meant to her. With the harsh winter, she'd seen only a handful of crows, a few raccoons, and a couple of coyotes in the last few weeks. But those had been scavengers, signs of decay. Many of the bigger animals like horses had seemed to die along with the humans, according to the CDC. She had wondered if the Hydra-1 virus would make the jump to deer. There had been a lot of fevered panic talk in the final days about what the virus was capable of, but no one honestly knew. Seeing those deer still alive give her such hope she could barely speak.

The man shrugged off her hand. "You'll be regretting that tonight when your stomach grumbles." He handed her back the plate of food. "Now eat. You don't want to waste the eggs, trust me."

She ate the rest of the breakfast in silence and licked every bit of sugary juice off her fork from the peaches. This place was as close to heaven as she could have imagined, though her benefactor hardly seemed to be an angel. When he came to help collect her plate, their gazes locked.

"Thank you..." She struggled, hoping he would give her his name.

"Lincoln. Lincoln Atwood."

"I'm Caroline Kelly."

He nodded once, in a curt, military-like fashion.

"You live here?" She nodded at the house.

"For now." He returned to the kitchen and rested his hands on a walnut chair at the kitchen table. Caroline couldn't help but wonder why he had taken her from the store and why he was taking care of her now. It didn't make sense. Maybe he still planned to use her in some way once she was feeling better. She pushed away the thought and the way it both frightened and excited her.

"Why did you grab me at the grocery store last night?"

Lincoln returned to the kitchen and began to clean the pot he had scrambled the eggs in. This place still had running water? That meant she could take a bath? Even a cold shower?

"I saw you and I wanted you. I also knew you

wouldn't get far on your own. In this case, it was worth the risk to double our numbers."

"You *wanted* me?" The word sent a flash of fresh fear through her.

"Yes," he admitted readily. "But I won't force you."

She frowned. "You drugged me. What kind of asshole does that?"

He turned off the water and set the pot out to dry on a dishtowel. He was being so calm and domestic while he was talking about sex between two complete strangers. She could only stare at him. He was clearly insane. Lincoln came back over to the couch. Caroline wanted to shrink back, but she held her ground.

"I'm the kind of asshole who knew what pain you were in after you sprained your ankle and that shelf fell on you and wanted to help you. So I gave you the last shot I had of some of the best medicine this world will likely never see again. You're welcome."

"I didn't need your help. I had a plan, and I was doing just fine," she shot back.

"*Fine*? I checked your bag—you had no food, no first aid kit, and no weapons. You were helpless as a kitten out there."

"I was robbed a few weeks ago. I had everything I could have needed, but then some asshole cornered me and grabbed my bag from behind. I had to leave it to escape. I was working my way through the stores to restock when you found me. The smaller cities had a better chance of not being looted, and I was doing my best to get what I could."

"Yeah, well, your best wasn't cutting it, sweetheart. You would have been dead within a week."

At this she laughed bitterly. "Dead within a week? You have no fucking clue what I've been through. No clue at all. I survived the riots of Chicago. I walked out of there on my own, fully stocked and prepared for anything. I climbed the barricades with my bare hands, got through the barbed wire and all the bodies." Those were memories she hadn't wanted to relive, the smell of burning flesh, the bloody razor wire coiling in tendrils along the tops of the barricades, and the screams, so many screams, as people clawed their way up to escape. She'd helped as many over the wall as she could, at least thirty before she'd lost her footing and fallen twenty feet to the ground on the other side of the barricade. She'd looked at the other survivors around her, all standing helpless and unsure what to do next. Caroline had begged them to stick together, but they'd scattered like startled rabbits into the outskirts of the small cities surrounding Chicago.

Caroline stared hard at the man before her now, daring him to judge her weak.

"You escaped the barricades?" he asked quietly, his gaze intensifying.

She nodded once, meeting him with a stony glare.

"Humph." He made a noise of disbelief at the back of his throat and turned away.

When he stalked off, she expected to hear him stomping up the stairs like an angry child. But she heard only the barest hint of a creak of wood as he moved.

Great. She'd been kidnapped by a freaking *ninja* mountain man.

Caroline listened to the sounds of water moving through the pipes above her and let out a slow, shaky sigh. She examined the house, and then she carefully moved from the couch and made her way to the kitchen. The entire house was surprisingly sunny and warm. It probably helped that he had a fire burning in the main fireplace. The crackle and pop of the logs was a comforting sound in the silence of the house.

There was a still a hush throughout the place, like the owners had simply left for the day and would be back by nightfall. Pictures lined the fireplace, showing a smiling couple hiking in Colorado and lounging on a warm, white, sandy beach somewhere. Post-it notes clung to the wood cabinet just above the phone with numbers scrawled on them. A calendar hung from a nail by the refrigerator with holidays and birthdays written in colored markers. Caroline looked out to the backyard again. The deer had moved on now, but she could see twin mounds and a pair of rough-hewn wooden crosses. The happy, smiling couple was gone. Forever.

The world was full of ghosts now. The sighs of empty houses settling, the rasp of wind through the trees, the snow falling on graves, and the heavy, endless silence. When starved and cold, Caroline would slip into a state where she wondered if humanity had only ever been a vivid and wondrous dream. Everything bright and beautiful had vanished in three months. The earth and Mother Nature had reclaimed their world, and mankind was but a footnote in a book no one would ever write.

She explored the kitchen, careful to keep her weight off her bad ankle as she checked the cabinets. She almost squealed in delight when she found an unopened jar of peanut butter in the back of one of the cabinets. She unscrewed the lid and removed the cover. The aroma made her eyes brim with tears.

She rummaged around in the drawers for some silverware. Then, like she had done as a kid, she ate the peanut butter right off the spoon. There was a flicker of guilt at her actions, but who was going to judge her?

The depressing answer to that question destroyed the weak flutters of joy she'd felt. She heard the soft thud of a drawer closing somewhere upstairs. Caroline gazed about then, not seeing Lincoln anywhere, and approached the backpack he'd left on the kitchen table. The military backpack was a sandy brown and covered with pockets. She opened the smallest one, and her fingers brushed something hard and metallic. She pulled it out and studied it. A small flag pin, the kind a politician might wear pinned to his suit. It was such an odd thing to carry about, not that it took up any space. She tucked it back in and opened the next pocket. Small packets of birth control pills and condoms filled that area.

"Wow...a bit optimistic, are we?" She snorted and moved to the next pocket. More medicines. Acetaminophen, ibuprofen, naproxen sodium, EpiPens, and antihistamines. The pocket after that contained a Maglite, batteries, solar chargers, space blanket, rope, twine, scissors, a compass, laminated maps... Lincoln was a walking survival gold mine. She'd had all of these things in her first go-bag—well, everything but the condoms.

"Seriously?" The dark growl came from her left. She froze, hand still in the bag as she turned toward Lincoln. Then she wished she hadn't.

The man was naked except for a towel around his waist. And that towel was *barely* hanging from his hips. She blinked in a daze at the sight of the V indentations over his hip bones.

Oh boy...

She'd never seen a man who was actually that clearly muscled in her life. Did he live in the gym? Water droplets clung to his skin, and his hair, shaggy and wet, dripped onto his shoulders. He was some kind of walking sexual fantasy she'd never thought she'd experience.

Caroline pulled the peanut butter spoon clean from her mouth, and with her back still turned to him, she pulled her hand out of his bag and zipped it up, praying he wouldn't notice.

"What?" she shot back.

"You're eating it straight out of the jar. That's how pathogens like Hydra-1 spread. I'm sure you're immune by now, but seriously." He strolled over and plucked the spoon from her and set it in the sink. Then his gaze shot to his backpack on the table, and he tilted his head, studying it. She'd zipped it back up, but she must have missed something. Dread swept over her, and she backed up a step when he looked her way, one eyebrow arched.

"I'm sorry I snooped through your bag."

To her surprise, he chuckled. "I'm not mad about that. I took a shower to give you time to work up the courage to look through the bag. I want you to trust me, to know that I'm not a threat."

Caroline digested his words before replying. "So I'll sleep with you?"

"You'll sleep with me, honey. Basic biology. Once you get over the drama of how we met, you'll see me as a providing alpha male, and you'll feel the urge. When you do, I'm here."

"What the fuck?" she snapped. "I'm not some ancient cave dweller. I'm a modern human woman with feelings."

"And when you change your mind, I'll be here." He cleaned her spoon with soap and dried it off before putting it back into the silverware drawer.

"I wouldn't have sex with you even if"

"Don't say it." Lincoln cut her off. "You'll only be

wrong later." He walked past her, and damned if she didn't catch the sweet clean scent of soap on his skin. And the way he moved... Her belly quivered, and she cursed herself. Hormones be damned—she would *not* let nature take over, not when it came to this. However foolishly impossible a dream love or romance might seem now, it was still a dream she hoped for. Maybe she would die alone, but at least she would have her dignity.

The thought was not as comforting as she'd hoped it would be.

Seeing as it seemed she was free to go where she pleased in the house, she limped over to the living room, eased down on the large, black, leather sofa, and stared at the blank TV screen. She'd never been obsessed with TV, at least not the news, but she would've killed for even a faint flicker of life from that black void of a screen.

She closed her eyes, and after a while she realized she must have drifted to sleep because when she woke, she was covered in several thick blankets. Lincoln must have done that. Damn him. She didn't want him to be nice. She wanted to hate him. It was easier to not trust someone if you didn't like them.

"You can take a shower," he said.

She peeped over the top of the couch back toward the kitchen. Outside the sun was setting over a lonely winter horizon, leaving the claw-like branches of the trees to cast dark, sharp edges against the soft evening-colored skies. Time passed so quickly some days, and other days it dragged on for eternity.

Lincoln was dressed and seated at the table, a gun spread out in pieces on a cloth. He was cleaning a part of the barrel with another cloth. His large, capable hands were elegantly masculine as he carefully moved his fingers over the gun. She knew those hands were capable of gentleness too. For some reason that made her stomach flutter. Caroline forced herself to focus back on their conversation.

"I try to avoid icy baths except for every couple of days. If I can boil some water, I'll just set up a sponge bath somewhere."

"Who said anything about ice water?" he replied, still focused on his gun.

"What? This place has hot water? Are you serious?" she almost shrieked as she tried to get off the couch and went down on her bad ankle.

Lincoln was at her side in an instant, lifting her up into his arms with a smirk on his face. The asshole.

"You don't need to carry me," she huffed.

"I do when you keep flopping like a fish every time you try to stand too fast."

She didn't bother to reply, preferring the dignity of silence. He carried her upstairs to the master bathroom and set her down on the edge of the large tub by the shower. Then he let her go.

"Towels are in the closet." He nodded toward a

small linen closet nearby. "I'll wait in the bedroom to carry you back downstairs."

She waited a long moment after he closed the bathroom door before she began to undress. Part of her was convinced this was some insane dream she was having. There couldn't be warm water. There couldn't be an insanely attractive man outside the door waiting for her. She'd had a bad dream...or maybe this was a good dream. The first one she'd had in months.

Caroline shivered as she let the last of her clothes drop in a pile by the door. Then she turned on the water, cranking it hot. For a few seconds only icy water came through, and then she felt hot water burning her hand. She dashed into the stall and buried her face beneath the hot spray.

It was heaven. Forget all the food she'd dreamed about eating since Black November, forget all the little things like electricity, movies, and cell phones. Hot water was the only thing she ever truly needed to survive.

Caroline washed frantically at first but then started to take her time. She started to enjoy the experience and began to feel normal again. For just a brief instant, she could picture herself getting ready for work, seeing her coworkers and grumbling good-naturedly about their long commutes into downtown, getting home, having dinner, calling her sister, reading a steamy romance novel or a spooky thriller, and then turning in for bed. Normal life.

Then it was over, and she sat down in the shower, curled into a ball, and cried. Silent, shaking sobs racked her body until her bones hurt. When her body couldn't take it anymore, she went still as the water started to turn chilly. She stood and turned the water off. Then she retrieved a bath towel and dried herself off and reached for her jeans and sweater.

Her clothes were gone, but a fresh set was stacked on the counter just by the door. Those definitely hadn't been there when she had undressed. She examined the items. New, clean underwear, warm fleece-lined pajama pants, and a T-shirt and a fleece pullover, plus a pair of thick woolen socks. They weren't hers, but they looked like they would fit her.

It frightened her to know Lincoln had slipped into the bathroom at some point and given her the clothes. But he hadn't done anything to her. He'd left the items and vanished with her none the wiser. She dressed and then searched around the drawers for a comb. She couldn't use a dryer, but she combed out the wet strands and plaited them into a braid.

When she glanced at herself in the mirror, she was glad to see her eyes weren't red. Had Lincoln seen her crying when he had snuck the clothes inside? Unable to delay it any longer, she opened the bathroom door. Lincoln was lying on the bed, his hands folded over his stomach, his fingers on one hand tapping a tune like a drummer as he waited. Seeing him stretched out in bed, knowing how he looked almost completely naked made her blood hum with dangerous, completely foolish desire.

"Feel better?" He sat up on the bed, bracing his elbows on his bent knees.

"Yes," she grudgingly admitted. Everyone always felt more human after a hot shower. "How do you even have hot water?" she asked.

"Same way the house is still warm. It's gas powered." He sat up, his eyes roving over her, and she crossed her arms over her chest.

"But I thought all the natural gas was shut off." When the power grid had failed, so had the gas.

"Not everywhere. Somewhere close by, someone is still alive and keeping the gas running. Most likely someone who worked at the natural gas company in Omaha."

"Someone? Like another survivor?"

Lincoln rose from the bed and bent to scoop her up. She hadn't been ready for him and had to throw her arms around his neck to keep her balance in his arms.

"Yeah. There are some out there. Last I heard, less than a fifth of the population was still here. The ones that didn't die from the disease are being killed by people who are looting homes and stores. My guess is most are in hiding, which is why you don't run into them that often. Everyone is running scared these days." He didn't speak further as he carried her back down to the leather couch.

"Have you tried to find this person, whoever it is?"

"No."

"Why not?" If she'd figured out someone else was trying to get the world back up and running, she would have done anything she could have to help them.

"Didn't see a point." Lincoln's tone was gruff again.

"You don't see a point? If he's keeping the gas running, he's doing it for a reason, and not because he's bored. We could be helping him."

"I salute him, whoever he is, but it would be like finding a needle in a haystack, and he's likely just one man. What good would it do?"

"What good would it do?" she echoed, a tightness gathering in her chest. "Lincoln, this is about survival. Not just for a few but for all of us. Don't you get it? We need to be coming together."

"You ran from me," he reminded her softly.

"Because you scared the shit out of me, and I thought you wanted to rape me." She stared at his face, but he didn't meet her gaze. "There have to be good people still out in the world. Isn't it our duty to find them?"

His jaw worked as he took a long moment to respond. "I'm done with duty. I served years in the service, lost good men, and none of it fucking matters anymore. I'm looking out for just me now."

"That sounds awfully lonely," she whispered. She wondered how she fit into his world, and at the same time also wondered if she even wanted to.

They reached the couch downstairs, and he set her down with that gentleness that always surprised her.

"How long has it been since you've seen a survivor other than me?" she asked while he tried to truss her up in blankets. She swatted his hands away when he attempted to tuck the blankets up to her chin.

"How long?" He gave up when she swatted his hands away again and walked over to the window. Night had eclipsed the sky, and battery-powered lanterns lit the kitchen. She noticed he had pulled the curtains on most of the windows. Was that to hide their presence? A prickle of fear rode beneath her skin. Was there something out there he feared? Or was she the one who should be afraid that he was hiding her away?

"The last person I saw a few weeks ago was infected. He died."

"Did you know him, or was he a stranger?"

"I knew him," Lincoln said. "He was a good man."

"I'm sorry," she whispered. He glanced away. She wished she could read his expression, but it was hard to tell because of his beard.

"What about you? When did you last see someone?" he asked.

"About two weeks ago. I saw this woman walking down the street, holding a bundle...a baby. But..." Caroline choked down the rising horror she felt as the awful memory came back. "But the baby was gone. Dead. It was turning to dust and bones in her arms, and she was too far lost in her grief to notice when I tried to talk to her. I've...I've never seen anything like that before. A grief so deep that it embedded itself inside your mind. It's worse than any virus. It kills hope...kills *everything*."

Lincoln dragged a hand through his hair and stared out through the one curtainless window. "Almost everything is dead now. We are but the ruins left behind."

4

@CDC: Our researchers have traced the Hydra-1 virus back to a microbe found in horseshoe bats in China. Bats have unusual immune systems. Their hollow bones, like those of birds, don't produce immune cells in their marrow like other mammals. Therefore, they can carry exotic and unique microbes that sometimes merge with ones found in mammals and can mutate into pathogens that can be transmitted to humans.

—Centers for Disease Control Twitter Feed
November 19, 2019

Lincoln suppressed a shudder at the thought of Caroline having witnessed something so awful. He'd seen terrible things, things that would give even the devil himself nightmares, but he had been trained to deal with them. Soldiers were no stronger than civilians like Caroline. They reacted the same inside to anything awful, but they were trained to push aside any feelings until it was safe to deal with them, long after the threat was over. But nothing in his years on Delta Force had prepared him for the end of humanity.

During a supply run a few days ago, he'd passed by the stadium that hosted the College World Series, and he'd seen the small city of medical tents and stretchers. The endless rows of bones and mummified remains covered the field where the Red Cross and FEMA had tried to set up triage stations. He'd seen the bodies in the streets, the bodies in cars in the middle of the freeways, in the hotel rooms, and in houses. The looks on the faces of the ones who still bore a passing resemblance to people were emotionless, their slack features empty in a way that would haunt him forever. As he'd stood watching the wind whistle through the medical tents on the baseball field, he felt something fracture inside him. He'd given up. He had let go of his hope forever...until he had seen Caroline.

In the midst of all these endless wintry skies, Caroline had burst into his life like a bright beacon of hope that poured in through the clouds, like brilliant and defiant sunlight. She was his hope, his only hope which meant he could never let her go. He'd protect her from the world. She'd likely hate him for trying to protect her, but he wasn't going to back down. Like a wild wolf who'd come across a helpless kitten, he'd somehow defied the urge to be a predator and instead would protect her like the sacred discovery she was.

He hadn't known what to expect when he'd come to the surface, but to see humanity had vanished had frightened the hell out of him. Any survivors he could only assume had lost their compass of morality, leaving them directionless resulting in lawlessness. This new world would have only one rule: fight for survival, fight for your needs to be fulfilled, whatever those needs were. Hunger, thirst, lust, greed. He'd expected to come across a war band straight out of *Mad Max* rather than someone like Caroline.

We had so many warnings...so many trumpets sounding that the walls of Jericho were tumbling down. Epidemics had struck before, but nothing like this. The proverbial levee had broken, and the floodwaters were rushing over it with no end in sight.

We will all succumb and drown in the darkness of our hearts.

He glanced over to her now. She was watching him, and her hazel eyes were almost brown in the dim lights.

She looks so young, so innocent. How the hell has she survived this long?

"Where were you when it started?" he asked.

She didn't immediately answer, but the shadows flashing across her eyes warned him that whatever answer she was about to give him wouldn't be the full story. The horrors she'd seen would stay inside her.

"I was in Chicago. The airport. I got trapped there trying to get home for the holidays."

"Trapped?"

She nodded. "Yes. There was a man who came in from La Guardia who'd shared a plane with a man from Paris who they think might be patient zero or close to." She shivered and looked down at her hands. Her fingers plucked the decorative fringes of the blanket wrapped around her.

"You're truly immune then?"

She nodded again. "He coughed on me. I left the line, and he infected the woman at the desk. She collapsed within a few hours. It was terrifying. We were trapped like rats, falling sick by the dozens while they sealed us off from the rest of the world. I understand it, I do. But they sentenced us to die." Her voice cracked with emotion, and Lincoln knew she was close to breaking. He wasn't used to sharing his own stories, but what did it matter now if he talked? She needed to know she hadn't been alone in her fear and her suffering.

"I was in Turkey when I heard the rumors of the virus in China and Pakistan."

Her gaze focused back on him as he sat down on the opposite end of the couch.

"Turkey? What were you doing there?"

For a moment he didn't answer. He was conditioned not to speak of his missions under any circumstances. But it didn't matter now. None of it mattered. The country he had protected and fought for was an empty shell now. The halls of the White House were empty, and the chambers of the Supreme Court were vacant. The Capitol Building was gathering dust. Everything, the good and the bad, was all gone.

He cleared his throat. "I was in the First Special Forces Operational Detachment, what you probably know as Delta Force. We were trying to find a way into Syria to kill their president. The people up top were sick of them gassing their own people, and he wanted that monster gone."

The faces in the pictures on the walls witnessed his confession, but their lips were sealed, their graves topped with snow.

"Delta Force? That's top-secret stuff, like the SEAL teams?"

"Yeah, the SEALs are navy, Delta's army. But similar. We do covert missions, things that, if done right, the world never knows about."

Caroline shifted on the couch, moving closer to him. "I thought you might be military."

"Oh? What gave me away?" he asked, genuinely interested. Not that he had been hiding his military position, but he was certainly curious to know how a civilian would view him.

"Aside from your clothes, it's how you move. The way you looked around when we stepped outside of the store. What do you guys call it, situational awareness?"

Lincoln scratched his beard, thinking back to last night. He'd had one mission. Secure the girl. Protect the girl. Nothing else mattered. There had been no fear except in losing her.

"So what are you doing here?" she asked. "I mean, how did you get from Turkey to Omaha?"

Lincoln wasn't sure how much he should tell her. Adam's loss was still too deep and fresh, too much of a nightmare. That was a burden no one else should have to carry.

"I was assigned to presidential detail and flew back with my team. We met the acting president in DC and then flew to Omaha. It's not much of a secret these days that we had a huge bunker here."

"The president is dead, isn't he?" She bit her lip and said, "Both of them, I mean. I remember when President Whitaker died. I heard on the radio that Vice President Adam Caine took over. But if you're here, he must be gone too."

"Yes." The single word cut his throat to ribbons.

Caroline continued to stare at him. Misery twisted an invisible knife in his chest. He didn't want to talk anymore.

"You should probably sleep now. To mend your ankle, you need to rest. I'll rub on the tendons around your ankle bone to keep any scar tissue from knotting around it, or you'll never regain your full strength and mobility."

He knew she wanted to argue, but he saw the weariness overwhelming her. There were lines carved into her face, her pain exacting a toll upon her. For an instant he tried to imagine her laughing and carefree, no ghosts lingering in her gaze, no sorrow furrowing her brow, her lips no longer wilted in a frown. Grief and loss had made a mirror of her beauty, a darker version, yet he sensed that her joy, if she ever claimed it, would make her stunning beyond imagining.

He stood, collected her and the blankets in his arms, and carried her once more up the stairs to the master bedroom. He'd left a battery-powered lantern up there by the nightstand.

"Turn it off and on with this button." He showed her the button on the base of the lantern.

"Thanks." She settled deeper under the blankets, and he walked to the door and had nearly closed it when she spoke.

"Lincoln..." Hearing his name on her lips made his body tense. "Thank you for finding me."

"You're welcome," he said.

"But seriously, I'm not sleeping with you." The light, almost playful petulance in her tone cracked a smile on his face.

He chuckled. He suspected that in time instincts would take over. It was all humanity had left. Drives and hungers. The chemistry was there. He had seen it burning in her eyes when he'd come down in a towel after his shower. She'd looked at him with that ancient animal magnetism reflected in her gaze. He would wait as long as it took, but he knew she would succumb sooner rather than later. They might well be the last two people on earth someday. And it would be awfully lonely if she denied her body what it wanted, what it *craved*.

He closed the bedroom door and returned to the kitchen to collect one of his lanterns. Then he checked the locks on all the doors, and finally, only then did he trust himself to sleep. He didn't want to tell Caroline that he had seen fires on the horizon tonight. They weren't campfires—they had been the fires of burning houses. Those kinds of fires meant men were nearby. Dangerous men. They'd have to move if he saw fires any closer. And they would keep moving until he found a safe place for her to rest and recover.

But they would never be truly safe, never again.

@CDC: *We have received thousands of messages asking us to explain how viruses like Hydra-1 mutate. When humans reproduce, we share genetic material vertically from parents to children. Microbes share genetic material horizontally. They exchanged genes laterally when they bump against other viruses. These exchanges or mutations happen in microbe-rich, fecally contaminated environments. The Hydra-1 virus developed in a wet market in China where horseshoe bats and civet cats defecated in the shared space. Their fecal matter merged, and the microbes of different viruses were able to mutate using each other's genetic material. The WHO has cleared the area and quarantined all individuals connected in any way to the market.*

—Centers for Disease Control Twitter Feed
November 24, 2019

. . .

January 2020

Lincoln and his team strode down the boarding ramp of the military transport plane in a private airfield just outside of Washington, DC. Adam Caine was waiting for him. Despite his role as vice president, he never hid from his duties. Once Delta Force, always Delta Force, he would say. Whenever he said that, the Secret Service team hovering behind him would roll their eyes before returning to their duty of scanning for danger.

"How was your flight?" Adam asked as they embraced in a brief hug and a back slap.

"Dull. Horowitz spent the whole flight telling everyone about his new kid. Man has a phone full of pictures."

Horowitz, one of Lincoln's men, shot Lincoln a dirty look. "Fuck you, Atwood. My kid's amazing."

"I'm sure he is," Adam said, grinning as he waved the team forward. "Come on, let's get you inside." Adam gestured to three black SUVs. Lincoln nodded at his men, and they divided up between the vehicles. Adam and Lincoln rode together in the middle SUV.

"Dare I ask how Turkey was?" Adam asked once they were in the car and the driver was pulling out of the airfield.

"Bloody. Everyone wanted a piece of us. The Russians, the Syrians, you name it."

"He who controls Turkey controls the gates to the

Western world," Adam muttered as he looked out the window. "I miss it. I wish I was back in field."

Lincoln smiled. "You are where you need to be. Whitaker needed someone like you. No bullshit, no politics, just someone who gets shit done. That's what the country needs right now."

"I hope so. No one believes in us anymore. It's easy to criticize the system when you're seeing only one side of it. But if people looked at the big picture, they would see..." He sighed, as if collecting his thoughts. "We fight for what's right, for the betterment of everyone. At least, we try. But everyone's got an agenda, including us. Like this damned virus in China and India. We've been trying to work with a network of foreign governments and health organizations. China thinks *we* planted the virus, and they won't let our teams into the infected areas without putting up a hell of a fight. Russia's using it as a bargaining chip, hinting they'll make things difficult if we don't make some concessions on nuclear disarmament in Syria. Our second team of CDC specialists was stuck in an immigration hellhole for over a week before we twisted China's arm to get them released. By that point, the virus was already devastating several of the villages outside where we think it originated."

Lincoln had heard the rumblings of discord while he and his team had waited for their transport plane to arrive.

"Adam, what is this thing, really?" He hadn't forgotten the 2014 Ebola scare, the way the world had overreacted. Ebola, as far as anyone knew, could only be transmitted by exchanging bodily fluids with a victim or somehow consuming infected vomit. Bottom line, it didn't transmit easily. Yet individuals were forced into quarantine just for having been in the same *city* as a victim being treated for Ebola.

"Hydra-1, as the CDC is officially calling the virus in their memos, dehydrates the victims. All soft tissue eventually dries out, and the cell walls break down. The usual process of decay doesn't seem to occur, and the normal preservation you'd expect to find on a desiccated corpse doesn't either. The cells are so devastated by the virus that they literally turn into dust. It's the scariest thing. Eventually, you have nothing but a damn skeleton where a body once was."

"Jesus," Lincoln said. "No wonder people are talking about it being a bioweapon. It sure as fuck sounds like one."

Adam nodded. "It's part of the reason China is so paranoid. But that's not the worst part. It's airborne. The strands, as far as we can tell, can be turned into an aerosol when someone coughs. If you're too close to a victim or you're in a place where airflow is strong, you can catch it. We haven't had a new airborne pathogen with a mortality rate like this in a long time." Adam met Lincoln's gaze. "If we can't control it, the r-naught rate is high. Too high."

"The r-naught rate?" Lincoln had heard the term, but he didn't really know what it meant.

"If you have the virus and you infect, say, two people, the r-naught rate is two. Ebola has a typical r-naught rate of two, but something like measles is much higher, however, less fatal."

"What's the Hydra-1 r-naught rate?"

Adam swallowed hard, fear showing in his blue eyes, and Lincoln felt his skin ripple with his pulse.

"Hydra-1 has an r-naught of six. Six victims for every single infected person. Combine that with the projected mortality rate, and the CDC says it has the potential to wipe out the world. The virus is a 'race killer.' Unless we can find a cure or create a lasting vaccine..."

Adam didn't have to finish. Lincoln knew what he wasn't saying. The end would come. Humanity would die out.

"What's the plan?"

"The plan for now is containment. But..."

"But?"

"If that fails...Omaha."

Omaha. The word sent a bolt of dread through him. Omaha was where the secret bunker for the president and other key staff would be housed in the event of a disaster or a massive attack.

"So we hide, like cowards?"

Adam frowned at him, the reprimand clear in his gaze. "You think I want that? I don't. But what the hell are we supposed to do? You can't shoot viruses. The country will need to have someone leading it while everything goes to hell. It's our only chance. So if we have to sit in a concrete cell twenty goddamn feet belowground, we'll do it."

"What about placing cities under quarantine?" Lincoln suggested after a moment's thought.

Adam shook his head. "It's part of the overall strategy, but it won't work. Quarantines cause riots, fires, death, and large-scale destruction. People always find a way through the walls. Nothing can ever be truly bottled up. The CDC is still trying to figure out the incubation period and infection rate. Some victims are hanging on for up to a week before the last stages set in and they die. If we have thousands of infected victims loose, it's only going to spread faster. I just don't know how we can effectively trap it or even bottleneck it in any of the major cities."

Adam didn't have to say it, but Lincoln could hear it in his words. Nothing can ever be truly contained. Which meant there was no stopping Hydra-1.

"There's really nothing we can do?" Lincoln whispered as he stared out at the city as they drove through it. He could see groups of tourists like colorful birds as they flocked toward the entrances of museums and national monuments. For every one infected person, six more would catch the disease—and pass it on to six more each before they died. Whole cities would perish, states would empty out, and the world would go dark in a way it hadn't since the middle ages.

He'd read about the Black Death when he'd been a kid, and the idea of a plague wiping out entire populations had been fascinating back then. The tiny bacteria had spread on the backs of fleas clinging to the fur of rats as they traveled in the bellies of ships and crouched in the corners of medieval hovels. That epidemic killed 25 million people and wiped out entire cities.

He'd even been interested in the Ebola virus. Scared shitless, but still fascinated. The virus had emerged from the remotest corners of Africa, pooled in the cold-water ponds inside Kitum Cave, where elephants scraped at the walls with their tusks looking for salt deposits and panthers trod underneath bats and monkeys. It was an ancient weapon that mankind was struggling to defend against.

And now, from somewhere in the Far East, this new virus had emerged, one that made Ebola look like the common cold. And it had its microbial sights set on humankind.

"You should call your family," Adam said quietly.

"Will you tell the others?" Lincoln looked away as he imagined making the call to his mother. She'd try to get him to talk to his father, and that was the last thing he wanted. Even the end of the world didn't make that necessary. When a man repeatedly knocked his kid around, the kid didn't ever want to see him again.

"I'll tell the rest of the team soon, once I know more." Adam pulled back the sleeve of his suit and checked his watch. "POTUS is having a briefing at the White House in fifteen minutes."

By the time they arrived, reporters were gathering

around the gates, which usually wasn't allowed for security purposes. But no one was paying attention. The world was facing a bigger threat than any terrorist group. Even those dirtbags were hiding in their holes, shaking with fear. A virus could get them anywhere, and they knew it.

Lincoln followed Adam and his security detail through the White House corridors before they entered a briefing room. Adam motioned for Lincoln and his team to stand at the back. The large conference table was full of generals, economic advisors, diplomats, and several people who wore WHO and CDC badges.

Adam took a seat beside President Whitaker. The man was in his late fifties, but he was toned and fit. His expression was solemn as he surveyed the room, even meeting the eyes of Lincoln and his team before he spoke. He was good leader and a man to be respected. Adam wouldn't have agreed to run as his VP otherwise, which meant Lincoln trusted Whitaker too.

"We're facing a crisis. What is spoken of in this room today *must not* leave this room. We can't have the country falling into chaos, not before we can present a solution."

———

L incoln banished the memories from his mind as he stared into the darkness of the back-yard. Those men and women were gone, ghosts who lived only in his memories.

Death was a funny thing. It robbed the dead of their blood, their breath, their very existence, yet within the mind of another person, they still somehow went on, even if they were faded copies, muted and limited. Flashes of Adam's face, his sunken eyes pleading for the end, would never stop haunting him.

I did my duty. I did what was required of me.

But he could still feel the blood on his hands, invisible, yet there, burning into his palms like fire. He rubbed at his right hand, massaging the muscles, and tried to focus on Caroline. She needed him now. The past was the past, and he couldn't undo any of it.

He wearily climbed the stairs and headed for the master bedroom. When he opened the door, Caroline was passed out, her lantern still on. She had either forgotten to turn it off or she had needed the comfort of a night-light. Either way, he could hardly blame her.

During those first few nights in the bunker, he'd listened to the sounds of the other men settling in the next room, making tense jokes and hearing the creak of metal cot frames as they all tried to get to sleep. He'd never been afraid of the dark until that first night. With twenty feet of earth and concrete between him and the sky, he'd felt like he couldn't breathe. He was buried alive. They all were. His vision had blurred, and he'd struggled to get air into his lungs. He'd fallen off his cot, clutching his chest as panic got a death grip on his throat.

Then his door had opened, and Adam stood there, a camping lantern hanging from one hand. He'd set the lantern on the bedside table, touched Lincoln's shoulder where he knelt by the bed, and then left the room without a word.

Seeing the light, knowing he wasn't in a tomb, had given him back his ability to breathe. After a moment, he'd gotten back into bed, rolled onto his side, and closed his eyes, the light of the lantern illuminating the backs of his eyelids. In time, he managed to sleep.

Now Lincoln stared down at Caroline, hoping she didn't suffer the same nightmares he had. They were free, aboveground, with the moon and the wind outside. Perhaps it was the emptiness of the darkness that scared her rather than the suffocation of it. He reached out and brushed a lock of hair away from her forehead. Her lips curved suddenly, just the slightest bit, as though she was dreaming of something nice. Thank God she still had good dreams. God knew he sure didn't.

What the hell are we supposed to do, honey?

The virus hadn't taken either of them. What was next? He sat down on the edge of the bed, removed his boots and reached for one of the extra blankets. When Lincoln started to reach over Caroline to turn off the lantern, he stopped. The thought of darkness swallowing them up tonight didn't seem right. From the moment he left the bunker, he'd had nothing to lose. But now? He had Caroline. And he wanted to fall asleep looking at her.

When he started to slide down in the bed beside her, he heard a distant *pop-pop-pop* and then silence, followed by another *pop-pop-pop*. He reached for the lantern and slammed his fingers down on the button. The light vanished. He'd crushed Caroline in his effort to kill the light, and she woke with the start of a scream. He covered her mouth with his hand, and she tried to scream even harder.

"Shut up!" he hissed. "Listen! Someone's shooting nearby." He held still, keeping her pinned beneath him. She froze, and he wished he could see her face. He could only feel her, her mouth against his hand, her body warm beneath his. More pops, farther away this time, which made Lincoln relax. He let go of Caroline's mouth and rolled away from her. Then he slid off the bed and crawled over to the window, pulling the curtain back a few inches.

The silence in the bedroom seemed to thicken until finally she whispered, "Do you see anything?"

"No, but there's barely a sliver of moon. I'm not sure I could see anything out there if there was something to see."

He continued to stare into the blackness beyond, searching for any hint of danger. But when he heard nothing more after several minutes, and saw nothing, he finally crawled back to bed.

"I'm sleeping here tonight," he said, then pulled back the blankets beside her and settled in. He expected her to try to leave or possibly to punch him, but she didn't. Maybe she was actually starting to trust him.

"You have a gun here, don't you?" she asked, her warm breath so close that he felt it. Something about that made his chest ache. The feel of another person so close while darkness and danger ruled the night... It gave him a sense of comfort he wasn't sure he deserved.

Lincoln shifted, sliding one hand under his pillow and curling his fingers around his Glock.

"Yes." With that single word, he was making a promise that he would protect her.

"Good." She turned on her side to face him. She was a dark outline between the pillows and blankets, yet he could feel her gaze upon him.

"Good night, Caroline," he whispered, hoping she would fall back asleep. It unnerved him to think of her watching him back. He preferred to see and be left unseen. While she was in his care, she would see more of him than anyone else had, maybe even more than the men from his unit, even Adam. He dreaded to think of what would happen when she saw too much and ran away from him.

"Good night, Lincoln."

D awn arrived, and Lincoln watched the sky, still black with fires. But this time he couldn't hide them from her.

"The other survivors are setting fires?" She joined him at the windows. She barely limped and no longer needed him to carry her about. She needed to be mobile, just in case things went south and they had to run.

"Men like to watch things burn," he said and sipped his coffee. He'd gotten used to making his own coffee ages ago.

"But why? There's so little left. We should be rebuilding, working together to save one other." Caroline's hazel eyes were more of a soft green rather than brown in the pale gray today. For a moment, he was lost in the fracturing splinters of the colors blending in that worried gaze.

"You still haven't lost faith in humanity, even after everything you've seen?" He couldn't believe it. Was she that naïve?

"No, I haven't." She met his astonished stare and half smiled. "I'm not stupid—I know people are running scared, that they're doing terrible things. But someone has to find a way to reach them, to remind them what we used to be. The world wasn't perfect before Hydra struck, but humanity isn't without hope.

As long as there are people who believe in goodness, there's always hope."

Lincoln wanted to believe her, to trust that burning certainty in her eyes. She wasn't naïve—he could see that now. She was a crusader, a person who would never stop fighting for what she knew in her heart to be right. It was a damned brave thing in this brave new world. But he had to make her face the fact that the world she wanted to save might be unsavable.

"Mankind has always felt the need to control its environment. When we lose control, our fear overpowers us. Fear makes us do anything we can to feel like we're in control again." He knew what he was telling her might frighten her, but these were truths she needed to know. The civilized world was gone. People as she understood them had changed. Law-abiding citizens, governments, rules, police, all those protections put in place over the past hundreds of years were gone. Animal instincts were all that was left.

"I fought men overseas, all afraid of what change would bring. Groups of men who believed that different beliefs halfway across the world spelled doom for their own religion. I fought governments who believed women were property and should have no control over their own lives. I've seen corruption take root like rot in the trunks of ancient trees and how it spreads through the ranks of soldiers until no man is left untouched. All of them have one thing in common. They will destroy what threatens them, what is out of their control or beyond their understanding. A quickly spreading illness turns us against each other rather than unites us. So..." He met her gaze again. "Men burn things to ash rather than stand together. It's one of our greatest failings."

He could feel the weight of the Glock where it rested at his lower back, tucked into his jeans. The sweater was loose, and he covered it from Caroline's view, but he felt the weight of it all the same.

"I wish..." She pressed a palm against the wide window, still looking over the yard below. "I wish the world didn't have to burn." She curled her fingers into slight claws against the glass. "I just want to find my family. I just want to go home."

Lincoln nearly told her that her family was likely dead, had to be. But then he considered, if she was immune, maybe her parents or siblings were too. A slim chance, for sure, but still a chance.

"Where is your family?" he asked after a moment. They probably had to leave here soon, and he preferred to have a destination in mind ahead of time.

"Missouri. Joplin," she said and looked his way again. Her eyes burned with sudden hope. "Will...will you help me get there?"

Right now, he would follow her to the ends of the earth. But telling her that would only scare the shit out of her.

"Look, I know we didn't get off to the best start, you kidnapping and drugging me"

"And you *literally* stabbing me in the back." He

almost chuckled, but he didn't want her to think he thought it was funny. He did not want Caroline thinking it was okay to run around stabbing him with whatever was at hand because she thought he was tough enough to handle it.

"Please, Lincoln. Help me find my family, and I'll..." She paused, and he hung on that word, wondering just what she would offer him. She ducked her head, face flushing red, and he couldn't resist tilting her head up with his hand under her chin.

"I...I'll give you what you want."

"And what is that?" he asked, his gaze fixed on her lips. She looked so sexy and sweet, with plush, soft, pink lips, dark lashes fanning down as she tried to hide those lovely eyes from him.

"*Me*—you said you wanted me." She was now staring at his mouth, and a bolt of arousal shot straight south to his groin, and he nearly moaned. She knew just how to test his control.

"You would give yourself to me?" he asked, his voice low and rough even though he knew he wouldn't let her do it. He wasn't a barbarian, no matter how good it would feel to strip her bare and pin her down on the bed and take her until they both were too exhausted to move. But it didn't stop him from seeing how far she'd try to go before he stopped her from offering herself to him.

"Y-yes."

He stroked the pad of his thumb over her bottom

lip. "Prove it. Kiss me like you want me," he said in a gruff whisper. One kiss was all he would take from her. Just one, one that would likely haunt him with its fiery sweetness until he died. He wanted her more than his next breath, but he wasn't going to take her when she wasn't truly willing.

Caroline's eyes flashed with a fury that made Lincoln want to laugh in delight. She was a fighter, and that was good. Only fighters would survive in this brave new world.

She reached up and gripped the collar of his sweater and jerked him down to her. Their lips met in an explosion of fire.

Fucking Christ.

6

@CDC: We urge you not to panic. Hydra-1 outbreaks have been reported only in India and China. Until we learn more about its ability to infect humans, there is no need to fear. The White House is working closely with foreign governments to install measures to control the spread of the virus. There will be checkpoints on roads and warnings issued to travelers in affected areas. Aid workers will be present to help diagnose people who believe they may be infected with Hydra-1. If you show any of the symptoms listed on our and are currently in India or China near the affected areas, please visit the camps set up by the WHO and the CDC.

—Centers for Disease Control Twitter Feed

November 26, 2019

.   .   .

Damn, *he tastes good.*

Caroline wanted to hate Lincoln, but she couldn't. The second she grabbed him and pulled his head down to hers, she was lost. He'd been right about the chemistry—it had been there from the moment she'd gotten her first real look at him the morning after he'd taken her from the grocery store. He was the kind of guy she had fantasized about her entire life, and now it seemed the universe had dropped him right in her path to make of it what she would. She wanted to kiss him, felt insane for suggesting it, but she did truly want to taste him, to feel something, anything, after so much cold and darkness.

The haze of his kiss, the way their mouths moved together, the way his beard tickled her skin... made her feel alive in a way she'd never been, even before the world had crumbled to dust around her. His large hands gripped her by the waist, lifted her up and carried her to the wall, pressing her against it, making her feel wonderfully small trapped in his arms. These last few months she'd felt so dead inside, and now all she felt was him...and her own body coming alive beneath his kiss and his touch.

She was on fire. Her skin burned with desire, and she wrapped her legs around his narrow hips and clung to his shoulders, feeling his muscles move beneath his sweater like shifting tectonic plates. He was hard everywhere, except for his mouth. He knew how to kiss, conquering her lips in a sensual, playful way. She couldn't catch her breath, and she didn't want to.

The world spun wildly around her as she parted her lips to his exploring tongue. He thrust inside her, playful and dominating, showing her an all too tempting glimpse of what it would be like for him to take her. She arched her back as a lusty warmth stole through her, muddying her thoughts. But she didn't care, not while he was kissing her like this.

How long had it been since she had been kissed? Forever, it seemed. She had broken up with Jackson, her boyfriend, a month before Hydra-1 struck. Months... months since she had felt any intimacy with another person. But Jackson had never kissed her like this. She and Lincoln were strangers, two animals desperate to survive. Now she understood what he had meant, damn him. She *did* want him because her instincts told her she needed him, needed him to survive. She was drawn to him because he was a survivor. The thought horrified and fascinated her. What if this dark, intense man was one of the last men on earth? What did that mean?

He threaded a hand through her hair at the nape of her neck, tugging lightly so she tilted her head back. He trailed kisses on the exposed column of her throat until she whimpered beneath him. She could feel the hard press of his arousal against her, and he rocked into her, faintly, as though restraining his desire to fuck her right there against the wall. The image made her burn even hotter, but she struggled for control.

"Lincoln..." She gasped his name, and suddenly he was moving, setting her back down on shaky legs.

She touched her bruised lips and panted hard as he turned away from her, drawing in a slow breath. She couldn't deny the warring emotions within her. Relief that he'd let her go, that she had a minute to think over what she'd just foolishly promised, and how disappointed she was that he'd stopped. Caroline couldn't tie herself to a man. Not now, not like this. She needed to focus on her family, not her hormones.

His jaw clenched as he gazed out the tall windows, his hands on his hips in a pose of restraint and power.

"I'll help you find your family, but you're not a commodity to offer in trade. I told you, you'll want me in time, of your own free will. Just basic biology. Till then..." He walked toward the door to the basement and left her alone, confused and trembling with interrupted desire.

When the afterglow of that kiss finally receded, she was able to focus on his promise to help her. They were going home.

Mom, Dad, her sister, her niece, and her sister's husband. Joy surged through her, chasing away the lingering shadows that the previous night had left behind. They wouldn't stay here, where men burned things just to feel better. They would move south, they would find her family, and she would feel safe again, wouldn't she? She had to. She wasn't going to think about anything else except the plan. Find her family, and then she'd figure out the next step from there.

The muffled flutter of wings and an excited clucking from the basement told her Lincoln was checking on the chickens. She walked over to the open basement door, peering down into the darkened stairwell and listening to him speak to the birds. He was sweet-talking them, telling them what lovely ladies they were to lay such big eggs for him. Caroline's lips twitched in a smile. She hadn't expected that from him. Lincoln was a fascinating blend of intensity and serenity. She had never met anyone like him before. She likely never would again, come to think of it.

She gazed out through the wide windows in the nook, studying the winding streets in the distance and the hundreds of homes. What had this place been like before the virus? Had people sat out on their decks, grilling steaks and sipping beers while they talked about the future of the University of Nebraska's Husker foot-ball team? What would become of this neighborhood now?

What happened to a world where people vanished almost overnight? She remembered seeing an article once about places in certain cities that suffered from urban decay, and she'd clicked through a slideshow of photos showing abandoned train stations, empty shop-ping malls, crumbling opera halls. Each picture had held a quiet, melancholy majesty.

Beauty within decay and emptiness. Beauty within

sorrow of an ended age. Perhaps someday a new species would take over, and it would marvel a thousand years from now at the crumbling superdomes and national monuments the way humans had done when they'd set foot in the ruins of castles in Scotland or the skeletal remains of the Roman Colosseum.

With a shake, she pulled her focus away from the windows and tried to busy herself with other tasks. It was so easy now to lose a sense of time and drift away in dark thoughts.

She put away their dishes after washing them, then sat down at the table and rolled her ankle around. It still hurt a little and was stiff, so she'd been massaging it a little every few hours. If they left tomorrow, she would be able to travel, just so long as she didn't have to sprint.

Lincoln stayed down in the basement for a long time. It was eerie being alone upstairs, so she carefully came down the winding carpeted basement steps. To her surprise, the walk-out basement which opened up to the backyard was homey. A small bar was at one end and a family room with a TV, and a gas fireplace was opposite the bar. Next to the back door were two dog kennels stuffed with hay. Two red-and-brown chickens clucked contentedly as they sat in the kennels.

"Dog kennels?" she asked Lincoln.

He shrugged. "It's the only thing I could find."

Lincoln leaned against the pool table, his back to her as he watched the wintry landscape of the backyard and the creek beyond. She couldn't help but admire his strong body, the way he seemed to fill the room with this quiet, brooding presence. He had a predatory and animal intensity, yet she'd seen flickers of compassion in him. He wanted her to think he was a solid wall, impenetrable, impassive, unyielding, but he wasn't made of stone.

There was something about him, a melancholy perfection, a tortured beauty to him that warned her he had seen and caused pain to others in this world and that those actions still haunted him. He wanted her to think he didn't believe that there was still good in the world, but deep down, he had to have hope or else he never would have helped her. He would have taken her, used her and left her to die. Instead, he'd helped her, and he hadn't taken advantage even when she'd offered.

He remembers what it was like, how good people can be when we work together. I won't ever give up, and I won't let him either. She made the silent vow to herself.

Caroline joined him by the pool table and watched the clouds slowly circle in cold patterns above the leafless trees. Without the buzz of cell phones and the constant noise and bustle of her old life, time had slowed to a trickle. It had only been a few months since this nightmare began, but it felt like she had been on the run for decades. Those first panicked and frightening moments in the airport seemed like a lifetime ago. The woman she had been then was gone. Dead. A ghost. Now she was the woman who had spent a week helping others in her apartment complex find food, shelter, and medical supplies. She was the woman who'd lifted people over the Chicago barricades to help them escape. She was hardened but not broken. She was steel but not unbending.

"What do you miss most about the way things were?" she asked as she slid closer to him. Their shoulders touched, and she could feel the heat of his body from that single point of contact. He didn't pull away, and her heart gave a hopeful, stuttering staccato of beats.

"I miss knowing where I belong," he replied, his voice a little gruff. She studied his bearded face, wishing she could hear his thoughts.

"Where you belong?"

"Before the contagion, I knew what my job was, what my purpose in life was. I knew where to go and what to do. I had my unit. Horowitz, Phillips, Holt, Finch, Norton. They were my men, my friends. My family." His voice roughened as he spoke.

"What happened to them?" She reached over and covered his hand closest to her with her own, but he still didn't look at her. The brown of his eyes was lit by the overcast winter sky, and the color was softer, darker, like the wood of trees in an ancient forest.

"Horowitz and Finch were with me here in Omaha. We stayed in a bunker. Philips, Holt, and Norton were sent to assist in escorting key government personnel to safe locations."

"Safe locations? Like the bunker you were in?" She'd heard rumors over the years that there was a bunker in Omaha for the president if the United States was ever invaded.

"Yeah."

She hesitated, thinking of the American flag pin. "Were...you with President Whitaker in the bunker?"

For a long second he didn't reply, but a tic worked in his jaw. At last he said, "Yes. Whitaker died only two weeks in. One of us had carried the virus into the bunker, but we didn't know it until it was too late. It killed everyone...except me."

"Oh my God," she whispered, only too able to imagine the horror he must have endured. She could see he wasn't going to talk about it anymore. Not right now. But after a moment he looked her way.

"What do you miss about...before?" he finally asked, his voice softer, but still gruff.

She took her time in answering. There were hundreds of things she missed—hot showers, warm beds, pizza delivery, even her email. But there was one thing she missed more than anything.

"People. The feeling of knowing that our world was full of people. I swear, some days I could almost feel the collective creative energy as they worked, played, laughed, and cried, as they *lived*, you know? I don't think it occurred to me until recently just what Hydra-1 has taken from us. It killed blindly, without thought, without discrimination. It took our dreamers, musicians, artists, engineers, lawyers, doctors, farmers... The virus stole our future as well as our past." She had to wait for a moment before she continued. "Who is left among us now to create a life for those born after us? We have nothing left...*nothing*. This can't be the end, can it? We can find a way to rebuild, can't we? I mean... we have to...right?" The bleakness of the world seemed to close in on her then, crushing the last bit of her hope. She shut her eyes, choking down an agonizing sob as it knifed the inside of her throat.

Lincoln's arms wrapped around her, holding her tight, absorbing the trembling of her body as she cried. It felt good to let it go with someone around, to expel the negative surge of energy that was trying to drown her and to know that someone was there for her. Lincoln held her through it all and rocked her in his arms. In that moment, she started to realize how lucky she was that he'd found her. Underneath all that cynicism was someone who cared. He was like her own personal sun, one that burned through the gloom of this dark world.

Sniffling, she pulled back to look up into his fierce face and saw a deep need there. Not one of lust, but one of the heart. A need to no longer be alone.

"It isn't true," he said softly, his rich voice rumbling.

"What isn't?" she asked.

"That we don't have anything left. As long as there are two of us, two who can remember the world before, we won't let it die. When I saw you that first time, you reminded me that this isn't the end. I was trained to fight until my last breath, and I forgot that, until I saw you. But now...now I'm fighting not just for my country —I'm fighting for the world." When he said this, she couldn't help but feel he'd almost said he was fighting for her too, and she shivered and leaned close to him again, burying her face against his chest.

"*We* are fighting for the world," she said and smiled when he chuckled. "You're not the only hero out there."

"No, I'm certainly not. You're the one who believes, the one with hope. I'm believing in *you*."

They stayed like that for a moment longer, sharing the warmth and comfort that only such an embrace could give before she turned her thoughts toward finding her family.

"When do we leave for Missouri?"

"The day after tomorrow," Lincoln replied. "We need supplies. More maps, food, water, and gas."

"What do I need to do?" She hoped he wouldn't leave her here. What if he never came back? What if he got hurt? What if...? She didn't want to think about it anymore. "Food's on short supply inside the city, but I know of at least one place where we can fill up the gas for the SUV."

"Good, we can start there." Lincoln nodded in approval. "We'll go together, but if I tell you to stay in the car at any point, you do it. Got it? I'm in charge now, kid." His stern expression firmed his mouth into a hard line. For some reason, after having kissed that mouth, she wasn't quite as afraid of him when he looked so grave. She raised a hand in salute.

"*Sir, yes sir.*"

"Smartass," he growled, but she could see him smirk.

"That's Captain Smartass to you."

His lips twitched. "Then I'm afraid I outrank you, Captain, seeing as I'm actually a major."

At this Caroline laughed. "Okay you got me there, Major Bossy." God, she hadn't felt this good in months. It was the first time she'd felt safe—well, *safer*—and she had hope for the future.

"So what are we going to do until nightfall?" she asked.

"Clean my guns. You know how to shoot?"

Caroline shook her head. "Not really. I played paintball once with some friends from work for a team-building exercise."

Lincoln rolled his eyes.

"Hey! It could be worse. At least I didn't say I played laser tag or something."

"God help me if you had." His grumble was good-natured as she followed him toward the basement stairs.

"Come upstairs and I'll show you how to clean the guns. I'll walk you through the basics of gun safety, but we won't fire anything. I'm worried those men we heard last night are still nearby. If they hear us firing shots, they might come sniffing around."

Lincoln headed upstairs, and she followed behind. She didn't like guns, but right now guns meant safety. If he could teach her, she'd feel a hell of a lot better going to sleep at night.

Two hours later, she sat back exhausted in her chair at the kitchen table. Six different guns, including handguns and even an assault rifle, lay spread out on a beach towel covering the wood surface of the table. Lincoln had walked her through all of them until she understood how to clean and load each one, getting the feel of their weight and how she should stand to fire them. It was unsettling to hold them in her hands, to feel the life-ending power under her fingers. She could see why some men loved guns. But her? Knowing with one tiny squeeze she could kill a man was not a happy thought.

"You hungry? It's around dinnertime, isn't it?" she asked as she pushed the last gun away on the table and heaved a sigh.

Lincoln chuckled. "Is that your way of saying you like my cooking?"

She couldn't deny she felt spoiled by the fact that he was able to make a decent meal out of what he had on hand. She was terrible at cooking at the best of times and was next to hopeless without stocked grocery stores.

"It's better than my diet of Hostess cupcakes and saltine crackers." She had discovered early on that those two products had a long shelf life.

"Jesus...tell me you weren't really eating those. Even the rats don't eat that stuff." He was laughing now, and she couldn't help laughing too.

"They never expire. Don't judge me."

The corners of his eyes crinkled, and he smiled as he got his laughter under control. "How about mac and cheese?"

"I might kiss you again if you make that." She was teasing, but she saw the heat in his gaze in response, and her own body began to hum. Whenever he looked at her like that, like he wanted to devour her, she seemed to vibrate like she was a wineglass half-full and he was stroking his fingertip around the rim, making her sing.

"Promise me that kiss?" he asked. His low, rumbling voice was whiskey rough. Her throat burned as she imagined that kiss.

"You make the mac and cheese? Then yes."

His smug, cocky look was one of a man slowly winning an argument she didn't even know they were having.

"Go stretch your ankle some more. I'll handle dinner."

He turned on a few lamps and drew the curtains tight around the kitchen as darkness descended on the landscape. She walked over to the stairs and stood so that the balls of her feet were on the bottom step, doing the poses he'd shown her earlier that morning. Then she lowered her body so her heels sank below the lip of that stair. It stretched her calves and the tight knot around her ankle. She repeated this stretch a dozen times.

As she stretched, she listened to the comforting

sounds coming from the kitchen, the water running, the clang of pots, and the music. Lincoln always seemed to play music when he cooked. Tonight it was classical, soft and melodic. He had a lot of music on his phone. And for that she was truly grateful, because music for a brief few moments each day drowned out the silence and killed the weight she carried on her shoulders.

She didn't want to interrupt Lincoln, so she explored more of the house after she finished her stretches. There was a small office that had a desk littered with papers, a laptop, and a printer. More happy family photos decorated the walls.

Caroline reached out and touched the edge of one picture frame, sending up a silent prayer to whoever these people had been. She glanced about the room and saw the black upright piano in the corner by the window. She lifted the lid off the keys and pressed down on the middle C. The note rang in the air, slightly off-key. She'd had piano lessons along with her sister as a child, and she could still remember a song or two, but it felt wrong to play now. Like it would disrupt its resting place in this family's tomb.

"Dinner's ready." Lincoln's voice startled her so much that she jumped and clutched at her chest. He was right behind her.

"Jesus, warn me next time, Delta Force, or I'll tie a cat bell on you." His lean, muscled form was filling the narrow doorway. His arms were crossed, not in a way that suggested he was mad, but rather relaxed. She had begun over the last few days to piece together more and more of the puzzle that was Lincoln Atwood. There was something to be said for having no modern-day electronic distractions. She realized she actually could decipher more of him because watching Lincoln was one of the few things she could do. And he was damned fascinating.

"Mac and cheese?" she asked.

"You bet, honey." He winked and then turned his back on her as he headed into the kitchen. She tried to ignore the way her stomach fluttered when he called her *honey*.

He had set up the table for two, clearing away all the guns. There was candlelight and even two glasses of white wine.

"Wine?" she asked, nodding at the bottle. He picked it up and waved a hand at the label like a sommelier at a five-star restaurant.

"I believe this pinot grigio brings out the best tastes of the artificial cheese sauce and shell pasta." He winked at her, and she laughed as she sat down. When he'd seated himself opposite her, she raised her glass in the air.

"A toast," she suggested. When he clinked his glass against hers, she continued. "To saving the world."

He echoed the words, but she didn't miss the flickering shadows in his eyes. She wasn't surprised. Everyone was dead. Almost everyone, anyway. But she had to keep hope alive.

"You think you can really save it?" he asked. His tone was soft rather than hard and mocking like she might have expected at first.

"Maybe. If we can get enough people in the right place, at the right time, with clear heads, we can work on restoring power, gas, water...and from there we start spreading it outward. Once we restore the necessities, we can restore the structure, government, law and order. It won't be easy, but I think it could be done." In the hours she wasn't thinking about Lincoln or her family, she'd been making plans, thinking over how she'd go about resurrecting society if she ever had the chance. She wasn't naïve enough to think it would be easy, but if she saw a window of opportunity, she'd leap through without a second thought.

She took a bite of the shell mac and cheese. It was as good as before, maybe better. "Do you still have family?"

"I... did. My mother and father." He didn't volunteer any more information.

"Do you know if...?"

"Gone. I'm pretty sure."

"Where do they live? We can go check on"

The decisive look on his face warned her not to push any further.

They ate their meal in silence, and she finished her glass of wine, grateful for the distraction of a slight buzz. She helped Lincoln wash the dishes and almost giggled. It was like they were an old married couple—

dinner, dishes, wine, and candlelight, along with very little conversation.

"Could we listen to some more music?" she asked. She expected him to say no, that they needed to conserve energy, but to her surprise, he agreed.

"Anything in particular?"

"Surprise me." She wiped her hands on the dish towel and finished putting away the glasses in the cupboards while Lincoln turned on his phone. Seconds later "Stand by Me" began to play.

"I love this one!" Caroline exclaimed, and she couldn't resist humming along.

Lincoln started loading his guns into a black duffel bag on the sideboard table by the kitchen. Caroline watched him, her heart hammering as she debated with herself. She did like him, even though he had infuriated her when they first met. His intensity still scared her. But she *liked* him. She liked the way he always tucked her beneath the blankets, how he'd taken care of her ankle, how he cooked for her, the way he looked in the early-morning light when she caught sight of the faint freckles on his nose and cheeks, and the way he held her when she felt like the world was disintegrating around her.

"Er...Lincoln?"

"Hmm?" He didn't look at her as he continued to load the last of the spare ammo into the heavy-duty duffel bag.

"Would you dance with me?"

He paused in the act of zipping up the bag and looked at her.

His eyes smoldered, and she knew asking him to do a simple thing like dancing could lead to so much more. But this was the end of the world, at least the human one. Did she really have anything left to lose?

"I don't really dance, honey," he said softly, but she could feel his gaze, like a tangible caress as it swept down her body.

"I find that hard to believe. Please. Just one. Just so I can feel normal for a while." She didn't like begging, but if she got to dance, she'd forget this hell for just one minute, and it would be worth it.

Lincoln abandoned the bag and came over to her in the wide space between the couch and the TV. He looked uncomfortable.

"What? They don't teach slow dancing in Delta Force?" she teased, hoping to put them at ease. He continued to stare at her like he was trying to figure out how to defuse a bomb, not slow dance with a girl.

"I know two hundred ways to kill a man, but I never did get those dance lessons my mom always wanted to take me to."

"Your mom was into dancing?" she asked, genuinely curious and hoping he would tell her more. She wanted details about his life.

"Yeah. She was a ballet dancer when she was young. Nothing major, but she did perform with a North Carolina company for a few years."

"Really? That's amazing. I love ballet. I used to go see the ballet in Chicago."

Lincoln flashed her a crooked grin. "Let me guess, you danced as a child?"

She blushed. "Yes. I was okay, but my mom ended up putting me in gymnastics when she realized I was a little too tall and muscled for ballet."

Lincoln placed his hands on her waist, tugging her close as that dark, clean, woodsy scent enveloped her.

"You're not tall and muscled." He playfully pinched one of her biceps.

"Hey," she laughed. "I was tall and muscled as a kid compared to the other girls. And I *am* strong. I stabbed you with that glass shard."

"You did. But you were lucky. We're going to have to work on your self-defense." He brushed his hands underneath her sweater just above her waistline, and she giggled as it tickled her.

"And you're ticklish," he mused. His brown eyes twinkled as he teased her. For a second she forgot about the world outside, and she was just here with Lincoln, flirting like she would on a first date. But the wind whistling in the fireplace brought her slowly back down from the cloud she'd been floating on for that brief moment.

She wrinkled her nose. "We can work on self-defense tomorrow. But tonight we are dancing. Eyes up here, soldier," she reminded him when his gaze dropped to her breasts.

"Yes, ma'am." Lincoln's eyes slid languidly up from her breasts to her mouth. She placed her hands on his shoulders as the next song started: "At Last" by Etta James.

"Now, follow my lead." She took a step toward him, and he took a step back. "Just do that in a slow circle, and I'll follow you as you lead."

His face was full of concentration, but his hold on her body was loose and relaxed. "Got it. I think."

And he did get it. Whatever his protestations about not having taken lessons, he didn't need them. Caroline leaned into him, absorbing his warmth and his strength, wishing that this was a normal date with a normal guy. She wanted to close her eyes and see herself in a nightclub in Chicago, or on a balcony outside a fancy restaurant.

When she had first seen Lincoln, she had thought him wild, untamed, and maybe he was, too. Maybe they both were. But how did one escape the new wildness they found themselves in? Or was it better to just let go? To surrender to that primal urge inside her to give herself over to him in hopes that he would do the same?

"I can feel you thinking," Lincoln murmured as he laid his cheek against the top of her head.

"I do that sometimes. Think too hard," she admitted. "My dad always teased me about that. He said it would give me wrinkles someday, but then he'd laugh and tell me to smile more."

"Your dad's right. You get this little wrinkle between your brows."

"Hey!" She laughed a little before settling back in against him.

"Just let go. Feel my heartbeat and measure it against your own." His soft voice was hypnotic as she pressed her cheek against his chest. Beneath the warm wool of his sweater, she felt the slow, steady *thump-thump*, as dependable as a grandfather clock.

They danced to "Smoke Gets in Your Eyes" and "Bitter Fruit," sharing nothing but breaths and matching heartbeats as darkness claimed the world outside. The single camping lantern cast slow-moving shadows upon the walls. She watched as their two distinct shapes blurred together into one being.

I am not alone. Not anymore. It's me and Lincoln against the world.

She almost smiled. There was some comfort in that thought. Caroline lifted her gaze when the last song ended, and silence fell around them. He looked down at her, his hand still on her waist, and she saw tenderness and animal hunger warring upon his features. Driven by a sudden urgency to be closer, she stood on her tiptoes and kissed him. Slow, lingering, hot. Their tongues sweetly dueled, and she pressed her body flush to his. He cradled the back of her head with one hand.

A slow, delicious tingling built deep in her belly as he deepened the kiss, turning the experience raw and carnal. God, she liked that. He kissed her like he wanted to brand her and never let her forget how well he could kiss. She liked the bold, aggressive way he captured her mouth. He wasn't afraid or timid. A bold warrior. A soldier. Nothing frightened him. She knew it was silly to feel like this with him, because it was just her hormones talking, but she liked this and him all too much, and she did feel safe.

Maybe love wasn't possible in a world like this anymore, but she didn't want to give up the possibility of it.

Lincoln explored the hollow of her back with one hand, sliding his palm up beneath her sweater and brushing against her bare skin. The simple contact almost burned, it felt so good. She teased the strong hardness of his lips and moaned in delight as he kissed her in gentle demand, her blood humming in her veins with a song as old as time itself. He held her close, his entire being focused on kissing her, and she melted against him.

Her knees buckled a little as a delightful dizziness washed over her. When they eventually broke apart, their harsh breathing mixed in the silence. There were a thousand things she wanted to say, but none of them seemed right. She was clinging to a stranger in the dark because she had no one else. That was the reality of the moment. Nothing she could say could fully explain the sexual and emotional hunger and confusion she felt, of wanting more and fearing more, which melded together inside her.

She blushed and ducked her head.

"I think that," he said at a slow pace, "I earned my mac and cheese kiss."

He trailed a fingertip down her nose, and then with one more sexy bedroom look that made her almost forget her name, he let go of her.

She let out a husky laugh. "Yeah, you did."

"We should get to bed. We have a lot to do tomorrow."

He headed for the stairs, carrying the lantern with him. She watched his tall, lean figure and couldn't help but wonder if the real danger was here...with him. If there one was one thing she'd learned, it was that anything you depended on or cared about could be destroyed or taken away. And not everyone was what they appeared to be.

7

Here, where the world is quiet;
Here, where all trouble seems
Dead winds' in the spent waves' riot
In doubtful dreams of dreams.

—"The Garden of Proserpine"
by Charles Algernon Swinburne

Caroline watched out the window of the SUV as Lincoln drove them into an outdoor shopping mall complex. There were dozens of abandoned cars and storefronts with broken windows, but this one didn't look as savaged as other parts of Omaha.

"Strip malls are usually better for supplies. People

forget them because they're farther out," Lincoln said as he parked the car amid the abandoned vehicles.

"Why park here?" she asked.

"I don't want anyone passing by to notice us. We want people to think this is just one of the abandoned cars out here," he explained and held out her backpack. She slung it around her shoulders and zipped her coat. He put his own bag on. They'd both agreed not to leave their packs in the car unless they were in the car with them. If they had to leave the vehicle, they needed their gear.

"I'm going to test a few car batteries nearby and scavenge what I can. I'll also collect any extra fuel these cars might have. You go into that sporting goods store and collect what you can on this list." He handed her a list of items on a piece of notebook paper.

She nodded and headed across the parking lot for the sporting goods store. Caroline kept a careful eye out for movement. When she reached the entrance, she carefully climbed through the broken glass doorway, her boots sliding and crunching on the shards, but she kept her balance. The interior of the store was dimly lit from the skylights three stories up. Her skin crawled as she worked her way through the overturned display stands. Exercise clothes and pale, naked mannequins littered the aisles. Caroline squinted at the list.

"Hand warmers, space blanket, batteries..." She navigated her way back to the camping section of the store and used the small flashlight Lincoln had given her to locate what she needed. She shoved them into the big gear bag Lincoln had given her and looked at the next part of her list.

"Rope, carabineers, and wool socks." She meandered down more aisles and grabbed a spare pair of wool gloves for her and Lincoln and a pair of wool caps. Hers was a cable knit hat with the poufy faux fur ball on top, and his was a dark gray one lined with fleece. She finished packing the items into her bag and turned to search the aisles for anything else that might be useful, but then someone moved behind her. She froze.

"Hands up, turn around. Slowly," the hard voice demanded. Heart pounding, she fought off a wave of terror and set her pack down and raised her hands in the air as she turned around.

A man in his midfifties had a shotgun aimed at her. His hard blue eyes were cold.

"Please, I just need some supplies…"

The man stared at her without speaking, and she waited for him to shoot her.

"You alone?" he asked.

Caroline wondered how she should answer—lie to give Lincoln the advantage, or tell the truth in the hopes it would make him think twice about doing anything to her.

"Not alone, then," the man muttered to himself when she took too long to answer. "Pick up your bag, but no sudden moves."

She bent, grasped the straps of her bag, and slowly

straightened. He clicked on a flashlight, shining it brightly in her face. She winced and half shut her eyes to block out the blinding beam of light.

"Where are the others with you?" the man demanded.

"Here," Lincoln said behind him.

The man whirled, and he grunted as Lincoln slammed a fist into his solar plexus. "Fuck!" The man doubled over and fell to his knees. Caroline, rooted in place, watched as Lincoln raised a gun to the man's head.

"Wait!" she gasped, at last finding her voice. She rushed to stand behind the stranger and looked at Lincoln. "He didn't hurt me."

Lincoln didn't look at her, his face a mask of hard lines. She couldn't be sure what he was planning to do, but she feared the worst.

"Please, Lincoln." The man who'd danced with her last night was tender, merciful. But right now she didn't know this man, didn't want to know him.

"You alone?" Lincoln asked, echoing the man's question.

"Yes."

Lincoln cocked the hammer. "That's a lie."

"My wife, Joanie, she's in the back. Please, don't hurt her." The man's voice dropped to a broken whisper, and his head lowered in defeat.

"We won't," Caroline said more loudly and reached out, pushing Lincoln's hand with the gun down to point to the floor. "Right, Lincoln?" She tugged on his sleeve, and he looked her way at last.

"We'll see." Lincoln nodded for the man to get to his feet. He turned to Caroline and saw the look on her face, and for a moment, where there had been deadly focus, she saw hesitation and doubt. He turned back to the man, a hint of a relaxed smile on his lips. "You'd make an awful Walmart greeter."

"These are different times, son. Not easy to know who to trust."

"But it has to start somewhere," said Caroline. "This is Lincoln, and I'm Caroline."

The man smiled hesitantly. "I'm Glenn."

"Nice to meet you, Glenn."

The man took a deep breath. "Sorry I scared you. My wife and I have been here for a few weeks now. I thought we were finally safe, but then I saw your car pull in and got worried. Bands of men have been roving around, some shooting people, others taking whatever they wanted." He shuddered. "Last month, I saw a group of them execute a kid. A *kid*. They threw his body in a ditch. He couldn't have been more than ten." Glenn's voice grew rough with emotion. "I didn't want folks like that finding us."

"And I'm sure Caroline here just struck terror into your heart," Lincoln growled, holstering his pistol.

"We can't be too careful," said Glenn. "Mean comes in all shapes and sizes."

"We're doing the same, avoiding people like that," Caroline reassured him.

"Let me introduce you to Joanie. She would love to have someone to talk to."

Glenn used his flashlight to guide them to the back of the store where a sort of small town had been built up using shelves. Inside were a couple of tents and quite a bit of stockpiled food.

"Joanie, we've got guests," Glenn called out. A woman emerged from the tent nearest them, a gun raised as she assessed the situation.

"Joanie, hon, we're fine. Put that away."

Joanie slipped a hand through her long black curls, eyeing them carefully before she set the gun down on top of the cooler beside her tent.

"This is Caroline and Lincoln." Glenn nodded at them.

Caroline smiled at Joanie, and to her relief the woman smiled back.

"Sorry, can't be too careful these days."

"I get it. I was robbed of everything not long back. It's hard to know who to trust." Caroline glanced at Lincoln. He was standing silent and serious, his hand close to his hip where he could reach his pistol.

"You two are welcome to stay here for dinner, if you like," Glenn offered.

"We can't stay the night," Lincoln said. "Got a lot of miles to cover."

"How about lunch?" Caroline suggested. He answered with the barest hint of a nod.

"Lunch it is." Joanie waved to Caroline. "Want to help?"

"Sure." Caroline followed her toward the back of the couple's small indoor camp, where they started sorting out canned vegetables. Lincoln stayed with Glenn, but she could still feel his eyes on her.

"Glenn said you guys have been here for a few weeks?"

"Yep." Joanie handed her a can of creamed corn. "We came here from Blair. We thought a big city would have more supplies, but we soon learned we were better off on the outskirts. What about you?"

"Chicago. I'm from Missouri originally, though."

"And Lincoln? Where's he from?" Joanie asked.

"He is...well, North Carolina is where his family is, but he's sort of from all over the place. He was coming back from Turkey when Hydra struck. He's..."

"A soldier?" Joanie offered.

"Yes. How did you know?"

"Not many men can sneak up on my husband. He's a hell of a hunter. Stalks bucks for days like a ghost."

"How did you know Lincoln snuck up on him?"

"Because Glenn wouldn't have brought you back here unless he felt he had to," Joanie said more quietly. "We both know about the roving gangs. He wouldn't put me at risk like that, which means your man caught him off guard. But he seems to trust you right now, so I'll do the same."

"Thank you," Caroline whispered, unable to stop thinking about how Joanie had called Lincoln *her* man. "It's so nice to see someone after all this time. Well, someone normal. I only met Lincoln a few days ago. Before that..." She trailed off.

Joanie patted her hand. "Lonely. I know. Even with Glenn, I still feel alone. We all do." Joanie collected some plates, and they settled down by a gas-powered stove. Joanie and Caroline open the creamed corn and poured it into the pot. Caroline sought out Lincoln in the small space Glenn and Joanie had created. He was standing beside Glenn. Their guns were out but set on the table as the two seemed to be comparing weapons. Glenn said something, and Lincoln suddenly laughed. The sound made her heart flutter wildly as she watched him, seeing him again as the man she'd danced with last night. There was something about that beard and those muscles and the intensity...she just couldn't help but get lost in fantasies.

Joanie nudged Caroline in the ribs. "Only a few days, you said?"

"Hmm?" She turned back to Joanie, not understanding the woman's question.

"You said you've only known Lincoln a few days?"

"Yeah."

Joanie's eyes twinkled, and she brushed her curly hair back.

"You've got it bad, hon."

"Got what bad?"

"For that man. It's all over your face—and his, once you get past the beard." Joanie stirred the creamed corn, her expression full of amusement.

"We've only just met, really."

"Sometimes that's all it takes. You two look like you could start a fire with the sparks between you. He barely takes his eyes off you."

Caroline looked back to Lincoln, and she realized Joanie was right. He was focused on his discussion with Glenn, but his eyes still turned to her every few seconds. And that single look made her body flush with feminine awareness. He looked damned sexy standing there, his tall muscled body relaxed for the first time since she'd met him.

"Well...he's protective. It's dangerous out here."

"Uh-huh... Men protect only what they want to protect. He's not being noble. He wants you."

She knew that—he'd said as much—but Caroline didn't want to think about it right now.

"Well, I don't know if I want him," she replied, even though it felt like a lie. After that kiss last night, she'd been forced to admit, at least to herself, that she wanted him bad.

Joanie didn't argue, but her face said she didn't believe her. Caroline didn't either. Her body wanted Lincoln, wanted to be claimed, protected, mated, but her rational mind reminded her that they weren't wild beasts. They were human, and she was going to cling to civilized behavior as long as she could before it was ripped away from her.

"Food's ready!" Joanie called out. The men turned and came over. They all filled plates with creamed corn. Joanie produced a box of Twinkies, and Caroline laughed at the look of horror on Lincoln's face. She hadn't been the only one to discover the shelf life of Hostess products was forever.

"So where you all headed?" Glenn asked as he opened some beers that had been cooling outside.

"South," Lincoln replied. Caroline frowned at him and clarified.

"Joplin. I'm trying to see if my family is still alive. They were there when I last spoke to them. I was supposed to be there for Christmas." Her throat tightened as she thought of them, wondering if any of them were still alive.

Glenn and Joanie exchanged a worried glance.

"What is it?" Lincoln asked.

"But that's so far south," said Glenn. "The roads are dangerous. What if your family is gone? Maybe you should stay with us. We'd be safer in numbers. Got a decent setup here in the store. It keeps the bad weather out, and there's plenty of supplies."

"For now." Lincoln set his clean plate down on the ground and rested his forearms on his knees. He looked so rugged, and a little scary. "You'll run out of food soon. There aren't likely to be any more places nearby that haven't been heavily raided. You'd be wise to move south until you can get to warmer weather to start farming and irrigation."

"I'm a hunter, not a farmer," Glenn replied.

"Hunting alone won't cut it. The only people who will survive the next year are those who adapt." Lincoln stood and looked at Caroline. "We'd better go. We have more stops to make." He focused on their host again. "Thank you for the food and rest."

"Yeah, of course." Glenn offered a hand, and Lincoln shook it.

Caroline didn't want to leave, but she had to stay with Lincoln. She stood and hugged Joanie and shook Glenn's hand. She wrote down her parents' address in Joplin and gave it to them.

"If you can, join us in Joplin," she said and hugged Joanie a second time.

She didn't want to leave—it felt wrong to walk away from them like this. She wanted to be with other people. It was important to remind the other survivors that they were all in this together. People were not the enemy, the virus was, and those of humanity still left were possibly immune, the lucky few who had a duty not only to survive, but to rebuild their world.

The one thing humans had that set them apart from other animals was the ability to build communities, to delegate responsibilities, and share in the work of not just getting by but developing and thriving. Caroline knew that if she could just get enough people together where they could work alongside one another, it could be a new beginning. That was why walking away from Glenn and Joanie made her heart ache.

"Goodbye, hon." Joanie squeezed her hand. "Take care with that one," her new friend said with a wink. "He still has that untamed look about him."

Caroline nodded, her eyes burning with tears. It was crazy. She had known them only a few hours, but already it felt like she was abandoning lifelong friends. Glenn helped them load the rest of their supplies in the SUV before they waved goodbye and left the strip mall.

"I didn't want to leave," she said.

"I know, but the more time we waste, the more we risk not finding your family. We can't operate off the assumption that all survivors are immune. There could be pockets of people who have escaped exposure, and *if* that's the case...we need to find them and assure their survival," Lincoln said, keeping his eyes on the road. She didn't miss the way he'd stressed the word *if*. He didn't believe they were still alive. His lack of faith shouldn't have hurt—it was pragmatic, logical. But it did hurt. It left a burning ache inside her that only seemed to grow as they put miles on the road. At his heart he was still a cynic, believing the worst in things, even now.

She hoped it hadn't been a mistake to trust Lincoln.

———

Lincoln knew he was a fucking asshole. He could see how much Caroline was hurting inside. But they couldn't stay. Glenn and Joanie were facing hard times, harder if they didn't move south like he said. Everyone had their own choices to make.

And my choice is protecting her at all cost.

The house they'd been staying at deep in the neighborhood was much safer than a strip mall. After he had talked with Glenn, Lincoln had realized that the other man was afraid to leave the store. He'd made a good little space for himself and his wife, but he didn't want to leave it. Glenn didn't understand that the lights weren't coming back on, and the world wasn't going to come back to the way it had been. Not for a long time. Maybe not ever.

We're in the wilderness now. If a man couldn't face that, he wouldn't survive.

"Do you...do you really know how to farm?" she asked, sniffing a little.

Lincoln refused to look at Caroline. Crying women set his teeth on edge, and if she was crying, he'd really be fucking pissed knowing he had caused it.

"I have had some training. I worked on a ranch as a teen."

"North Carolina?" She perked up at this. Her eyes were red-rimmed from tears, but she wiped the tears away. It was a punch to his gut see the evidence of the pain his decision had caused. So he kept talking. She seemed to like to hear him talk about himself. He wasn't used to that, but if that's what she wanted, he'd talk until he lost his voice.

"I worked summers at old man Peterson's ranch. He lived on the outskirts of the city. He knew my father and offered me a job baling hay and breaking in geldings." It had been hard work, but he'd loved it all, from the blisters and exhaustion to the feel of a horse coming to trust him so that they became one unit. He'd grown into a man on that ranch.

"I worked at the vet clinic one summer," Caroline said, but her tone was tinged with sorrow.

"You didn't like it?" He was surprised. She was so sweet and caring; the animals had to have loved her.

She shook her head. "I wanted to be a vet. I love animals. But I figured out after just a few weeks that I couldn't handle it." She studied her hands in her lap, and he refocused his attention on the highway, careful to dodge any abandoned cars. Fortunately, most were on the shoulders of the road.

"What couldn't you handle?"

She didn't answer at first. "The dying. The suffering. Seeing the pain of a dog as it struggled for breath. It..." She swallowed. "I used to cry every night after work. I wasn't strong enough. I'm not strong enough now."

Lincoln pulled the car over to the side of the road, more out of habit than anything. He could have just stopped in the middle of the road. He leaned over and cupped her chin.

"Look at me," he commanded, but he kept his tone gentle.

She raised her gaze to his, and he sucked in a breath. Fuck, she was so damn beautiful, and she didn't have a clue what she did to him. Her dark hair hung loose around her shoulders, and he wanted to fist his hands in it and drag her to him.

"Strength isn't the absence of pain or fear. It's about facing it head-on and staying alive. You're strong, Caroline."

Tears glistened in her eyes, and he couldn't stop himself.

"Fuck it." He pulled her close and slanted his mouth down over hers. She tasted sweet, and her lips were so soft. He parted her mouth with his tongue and fisted a hand in her hair as he stroked her tongue with his. Kissing her was like touching a live wire. It was a violent shock to his system that made his ears ring and his blood roar through his veins. He could've kissed her for days, but he had to stop.

He pulled back, all too satisfied with the dazed expression on her face. He brushed the pad of his thumb over her lips. "Anyone still alive in this fucked-up world is strong. You got me?"

"Yeah." She reached up and touched her lips. A blush stained her cheeks.

"We'll meet people the more we travel, and they

won't all be nice like Glenn and Joanie. You have to be prepared, okay? We can't save everyone, and we can't be friends with everyone. Just be prepared."

"I am prepared. I've seen the best and the worst of what we can be in the last few months." She paused for a moment and licked her lips nervously. "We are a team, aren't we?" she asked, worry in her eyes. "You won't abandon me if I don't fit your plans?"

"No," he promised. She *was* his plan. Nothing else in this world made sense anymore except being with her, protecting her. He started driving again. Neither of them spoke until they reached the familiar place they'd been secretly calling home the last few days. It seemed abandoned, and it was far enough from anywhere that it might be untouched.

"Remember to pack everything of value. We'll load it and the chickens in the car tomorrow and leave at first light."

They entered the house, him first and her behind. But it took only a second to realize that they had made a mistake. The creak of floorboards, the rustle of cloth, the click of a trigger being pulled...

"Run!" he bellowed to Caroline, shoving her back into the yard.

Pain exploded in his shoulder, and he stumbled back, smacking the doorjamb. Caroline screamed, and he struggled not to fall. If he fell, he might not have the strength to get back up.

"Lincoln!" Caroline screamed. He looked deeper

into the house as three men approached him, all dressed in military gear, armed to the teeth.

Fuck. How had he been so stupid? He should have left her in the car and checked the place himself first. *Shit, shit, shit...*

"Caro..." He growled her name and tried to look over his shoulder, but one of the men grabbed him and swung his fist right into Lincoln's face.

❧ 8 ❧

I am weary of days and hours,
Blown buds of barren flowers,
Desires and dreams and powers
And everything but sleep.

—"The Garden of Proserpine"
by Algernon Charles Swinburne

January 2020

Adam threw himself into his office chair, and Lincoln followed, lingering just inside the door. The briefing with POTUS hadn't gone well. Everyone was terrified of Hydra-1 and everything it represented.

"Dr. Kennedy at the CDC is doing her best to develop a vaccine, but they can't seem to grow a live virus in the lab. It kills the host cells too quickly for them to learn much, and it won't grow in isolated dormant cells."

"Adam," Lincoln said, clearing his throat. "Mr. Vice President. What can I do?" There had to be something, a mission, a race to find the right scientist, something. He couldn't stand feeling this helpless.

"What you can do is call your parents, Lincoln." It was the second time Adam had told him this, and knowing what Adam really meant chilled him to his core. They weren't going to win this fight.

"Do it here, my office." Adam nodded toward the black leather chair in the corner by a wall of bookshelves.

Lincoln sat, shifting his weapons, and pulled out his phone. He hadn't dialed that number in over a year. His heart raced as he put the phone to his ear and listened.

"Hello?" His mother's voice came through.

"Mom." He almost had to repeat himself, the word came out so rough.

"Lincoln?" Her joy at hearing his voice stung him with guilt. He loved his mother, but as long as she was married to his father, he couldn't talk to her without having to think about or interact with *him*.

"Mom. Listen, are you at home?"

"Yes, why?"

"Sit down, okay?" He waited until she confirmed she was sitting down. "Something bad is coming. You've heard about the virus on the news? It's going to spread.

Things are going to get bad. Real bad. You need to buy bottled water, canned foods, bullets for Dad's rifles. And you need to move to the cabin by the lake. You understand?"

"My God, Lincoln..." His mother, a true mother to a soldier, knew better than to ask a million questions or let emotions run away with her. "Where are you?"

"DC." He glanced to Adam, who nodded. "With Adam. It's bad, Mom. I want you to stay at that cabin. Do not go into the city, do not go looking for your friends. You have to close yourselves off. Do you understand?"

"I...I understand." Her voice trembled. He hated having to deliver such an awful warning to her, but it was the only way he could give her a chance.

"Mom..."

"Yes?"

"I love you."

She sniffled. "I love you too, Lincoln. Do you want to speak to your"

"No." He cut her off. Even if the world burned down around him, he wasn't going to talk to that man.

"But"

"Tell him that if he gets stubborn and doesn't do what I just said, I'll kill him." Then he hung up before she could say anything else.

"'I love you, Dad,' might have been more appropriate," Adam said with chuckle.

Lincoln clenched his cell phone in a white-knuckled

grip. "We both know I wouldn't mean it, so what's the point?"

"Fair enough." Adam stood and walked to the window overlooking the street outside. For a long moment neither of them spoke. They'd worked together for years, had been friends even longer, and their silences often said more than words.

Lincoln stood and joined Adam at the window, staring at the White House lawn covered in snow.

"It feels like someone stepped over my grave, you know?" Adam raked a hand through his hair and glanced at him. "I hate feeling this powerless."

Lincoln understood. Whenever he cleared out a village run by insurgents, he would kill them, but he had to leave behind the women and children knowing that more would come after Lincoln left and sooner or later those innocents would be tortured and killed.

Hydra-1 was worse than any tyrant, worse than any terrorist group. It had the ability to destroy everything, and there was no way to stop it. There was no playing the hero, not this time.

"Maybe it's time," he muttered.

"Time?" Adam turned, confused.

"Time to wipe the slate clean. Humanity gets a chance to start over—assuming any of us survive, that is."

Adam faced his desk and leaned over it. He pressed his palms flat against the wood. He looked world-weary for a man in his mid-thirties.

"Don't ever forget what our purpose is, Lincoln. We may not be bound to win, but we are bound to be true. We may not be bound to succeed, but we are bound to live up to what light we have."

Leave it to Adam to quote President Lincoln at him, the sentimental bastard.

"What's *your* light, Lincoln?" Adam's face vanished, and his voice seemed to soften to an eerie whisper as though from a vast distance in the dark.

What's your light...?

Light danced across the backs of Lincoln's closed eyelids as he struggled out of unconsciousness. Deep voices came from somewhere above him, dark laughs and mutterings. Where was he? A floating pain beat behind his eyes on invisible drums.

"That car was loaded. Looks like they were going somewhere."

"Well, they aren't anymore," someone said, and the others laughed.

Every muscle inside Lincoln tensed as he remembered. Caroline...the house...a bullet tearing through his shoulder. He kept his body relaxed as he listened to the voices. Three men. *Three.* He almost laughed. He could handle three. He moved slightly, tensing his wrists as he tested for restraints. He wasn't bound. They must have thought the blow to his shoulder would immobilize him after they knocked him out.

Whoever they were, they were amateurs. Rule

number one—when you incapacitate an enemy, always make sure they are restrained or put down.

"We'll find out what this one knows first," one of the men said. "They came from the city. Might know where others are."

"And the girl? It'd be nice to have a piece of ass around for more than just a few hours."

"You want another mouth to feed just to have something to fuck?" one of the men snapped.

"She's small. She probably wouldn't eat m—" The sound of a fist hitting flesh cut off that reply. He heard a grunt of pain.

Lincoln almost laughed, and his stifled snort silenced the room. He listened to the boots entering the carpeted area where he lay. He could feel the thick shaggy carpet against his cheek and knew which room he was in. He pictured the living room in his head, the couch, the chairs, and the kitchen table behind it.

Seconds before they reached him, he rolled onto his feet and lunged. He caught the man around the waist and tackled him into the couch. The second he had the man on his back, he swung a fist hard against his jaw. Then he dodged back, avoiding the other two men, who tried to grab him from behind. The one on the couch bellowed as he clutched his broken jaw.

Lincoln vaulted over the L-shaped couch, ignoring the pain in his shoulder. He had to let the adrenaline carry him through this. He sprinted for the kitchen counter and grabbed the nearest weapon, a kitchen knife. He stabbed the man nearest him. The man hissed and wheezed as the blade punctured his chest, and in a fluid motion, Lincoln drew it back out and drove it up into his neck. The man fell over with the knife still lodged there, and blood frosted his lips.

"You fucker!" The second man fumbled for his gun at the same time Lincoln grabbed one from the table. Lincoln was quicker. He shot the man in the center of his chest twice, then again between the eyes.

The man he'd punched lumbered into the room and froze at the sight of the two bodies lying dead at Lincoln's feet.

"Where's the girl?" Lincoln demanded.

"Upstairs. Tied to the bed."

Lincoln could barely keep his control as a red haze of hateful fury descended over his eyes. "Did you touch her?"

"Does it matter? You're going to kill me either way."

"True." Lincoln caressed the trigger, his body tensed for more killing.

"We didn't, though," the man said, his words slurred from his fractured jaw.

"Good." Lincoln squeezed off a shot, and the bullet tore through the man's skull and embedded into the wall behind him. The TV screen spiderwebbed with fractures outward from the two bullet holes. Sucking in a breath, Lincoln lowered the gun and then almost collapsed. Blood soaked his shoulder, and his vision was swimming in and out. Lincoln staggered out of the kitchen and toward the stairs.

"Caroline?" He called her name and heard a muffled cry. He climbed the stairs and searched the rooms until he found her. A dish towel was stuffed in her mouth, and her limbs were tied spread-eagle to the bed. She was still clothed and shaking violently as she saw him.

"It's okay, honey," he whispered as he untied the knots and freed her. She jerked the towel out of her mouth.

"It's not okay! I'm... Oh my God, you're bleeding!" She grasped him by the shoulders, and he let loose a string of profanities before she released him.

"Sorry!" she exclaimed, her eyes darting over his face and shoulder.

"Do you see an exit wound?" he asked, turning around to show her his back.

"Yes. There's a bloody spot on your sweater, and it's torn."

"Good...you won't have to dig out a bullet, but you will need to clean the wound. I've lost too much blood. Grab my medkit from the bathroom. Use QuikClot—it increases...clotting."

Lincoln sank off the bed and onto the ground, leaning against the edge of the mattress. His head was already spinning.

"Tell me what to do," Caroline said.

"You worked at a vet's office... It's all the same." Those were his last words before he passed out.

Caroline was paralyzed with fear. It rooted her to the bed for far too long. But when she got herself back under control, she had an idea. She ran to the bathroom and got a cup of clean water and soap, along with the medical kit he kept on the counter. She rinsed the wound with soap and water after she cut his sweater off. Then she dressed the wound with the QuikClot gauze she found in the kit and secured it with bandage tape. Then she kept him upright and in a seated position and waited for half an hour, checking his vitals. His pulse remained steady and strong, so she took a chance to leave him alone for a minute.

When she went downstairs, she saw the blood...and the bodies.

The three men who had broken into her temporary home and ambushed her and Lincoln were lying dead in the kitchen and the family room. The solemn sanctuary of this empty house seemed to have changed. It was violated by violence and death, which now settled like a black shroud over the once peaceful refuge. In that moment Caroline felt a surge of hatred inside her. How could they do this? These men... How could they take her home, her safety, almost take her and Lincoln's lives?

She was glad they were dead. These weren't survivors—they were predators. Parasites. She wouldn't mourn these men; their stories were over. All that mattered now was getting them out of the house and taking care of Lincoln.

She dragged the bodies outside one by one and down the upper deck stairs and left them in a pile by the creek, where the scavengers could handle them. She didn't have the time or energy to dig graves. Her back ached and her muscles cramped with the effort, but when she was done, she wearily climbed the porch steps and headed back to the guest room.

Lincoln was still okay, as far as she could tell. But she couldn't just sit there, watching him and worrying. She had to stay busy, so she returned to the first floor and mopped up the blood. There was no saving the expensive white carpets. Pink stains remained, despite her scrubbing for what seemed like an eternity with a cocktail of different cleaning solutions.

When she was finished, she sank down against the door leading to the porch. Her back was knotted with pain, her clothes were stained with blood, and she suddenly had no strength left.

Tears ran down her cheeks as she struggled to cope with what had just happened. If Lincoln hadn't killed those men, she would've been raped by now. Probably dead. And he had almost died protecting her. She wasn't sure how long she sat there, exhausted, crying, frightened. Finally, she dragged herself back upstairs to check on Lincoln. He was sleeping, the soft rhythmic sounds of his breath were calming. She lay down beside him, curling her hand through his before she let sleep claim her. For now, this was comfort.

She woke a while later, darkness thick around her.

"Caroline." Lincoln's rough voice stirred her more fully awake.

"I'm here," she whispered and squeezed his hand.

"Water," he rasped.

"Hang on." She left the guest room and fumbled in the master bedroom until she found the camping lantern and then turned on the water and filled him a glass. Then she returned and put the cup to his lips. He drank the water greedily.

"You okay?" he asked once it was empty.

"Yeah, how about you? I did my best to patch up the wound."

Lincoln checked her work. "Not bad."

More than ever she wished she had actually been a vet rather than an advertising specialist. She would have felt more useful. With the internet gone, her job was obsolete. Her specialty was useless.

"Lincoln." She studied his face, his piercing eyes and the proud chin covered by his thick beard.

"Yeah?" He looked at her, the light from the small lantern creating shadows on his face, making him look world-weary.

She kept her hand curled around his. "Thank you for saving me."

"You're mine, honey, and I protect what's mine."

She didn't argue with him this time. In a way, she did

belong to this man. In that same way, he belonged to her. Not as lovers or friends, but something else. She couldn't quite find the right word. She felt like she understood what ancient men and women felt when they dwelt in the wilderness when those ancient forests were still young and the hills were full of a thousand dangers. Those men and women had formed a bond that kept them together. They'd survived by sharing their strengths and trusting one another.

"I kept your upper body elevated, but I think you can lie down in bed tonight," she offered.

"That would be nice." He started to get up, and she threw his good arm over her shoulder and helped. They walked back to the master bedroom, where she removed his boots and his pants. She blushed when she saw his briefs, but he didn't say anything. Then he collapsed into bed, and she covered him with blankets.

Afterward, she undressed and climbed into bed beside him, tucking herself against him, careful to avoid touching his shoulder. Three days ago she would have fought this moment of intimacy, but now she craved it.

"I'll handle the bodies tomorrow," Lincoln said, sighing heavily in the darkness.

"I've already handled them," she replied, listening to his breath.

"You didn't have to"

"I did. Rest. I've taken care of it."

He chuckled and then cursed. "So you're giving the orders now, huh?"

"Consider yourself temporarily relieved of duty, Major."

He snorted a laugh and then winced.

She didn't like admitting that she felt safer when he was in charge, but it was true. He knew about surviving in the wilderness. She would be glad when he was up and feeling better. Until then...she would take care of him.

9

@CDC: We know people are concerned about the spread of virus Hydra-1. It is important to remember to work with each other. If cooperation among nations and peoples fails, pandemics occur. When we think only of ourselves and not of others, we provide contagions with the opportunity to transmit and spread. Save each other and we save the world.

—Centers for Disease Control Twitter Feed

November 29, 2019

I n the weeks that followed, Caroline kept Lincoln in bed as much as possible. It was like trying to soothe an angry bear whenever she insisted he stay in bed. She took over making the meals and tending to the chickens, whom she had named Narcissa and Persephone. Not that Lincoln had found her naming them all that amusing.

"When we eat Narcissa someday, you will regret naming her," he grumbled.

"Actually, we should focus on finding a rooster so we can breed more chickens." She had to admit she would have loved some grilled chicken, but she couldn't look at the two chickens in their nests when that thought strayed across her mind.

"That's a good idea. Once we settle down again, I'll find us one."

Caroline spent her days exploring the house, looking at old photos and papers tucked away in drawers, trying to piece together the lives of the people who had built and lived in the home that now felt like hers. But by the end of the third week, she couldn't keep Lincoln resting any longer.

"We need to move," he said over breakfast. "It's time we headed to Joplin."

"But your arm..." She nodded at the sling she had found after running to a nearby drugstore.

"Food is running low, and I don't want to spend any more time here. The longer we wait, the longer it is until we find your family."

The need to see her parents and her sister was over-whelming, and she nodded as her throat tightened. How were they surviving? Were they able to find food? Did they have running water or gas-powered hot water tanks? How was her sister's baby? Caroline couldn't wait to see them. It felt like a lifetime since that phone call from the airport. And in that time, small doubts had started to creep in. It was entirely possible they were gone, that they weren't immune like her, but as naïve as she knew it was, she needed to believe they were still alive.

"Then let's go." She collected the dishes and washed them before putting them back in the cupboards.

"What are you doing?" Lincoln asked. He leaned back against the unusable dishwasher, studying her. His lean form was so close, and it always made her body heat with desire. But in the weeks since his injury, he had kept his distance, hadn't teased her or reminded her that someday she would sleep with him. He had become different, more distant and removed than usual, if that were possible.

In turn, she had become even more lonely. He had chosen to sleep in the guest room, blaming it on his bad arm, and it had wounded Caroline deeply. Their habit of sleeping beside one another, feeling each other close together, had given her a sense of safety, a sense of belonging. But with him sleeping in the guestroom now, she'd felt more alone than she ever had in her life.

So whenever he was near, whenever he was talking to her, her heart beat faster and her body ached for him, but she didn't trust him not to withdraw back into his shell.

"I just want to leave the house the way we found it." She didn't mention the bloodstains and bullet holes. "This place was home to us for a time. People lived here, and they made a place that was safe. Maybe someone else will use it someday after we're gone." She closed the cabinet with the dishes and glanced away from him and toward the window.

A tall tree, bare-branched, swayed in the breeze as goldfinches and chickadees bustled around the full bird-feeder. Caroline had done her best to keep the feeder stocked with seeds. The finches chattered wildly, chasing a poaching squirrel back down the tree limb that the feeder hung off. Her lips tugged up into a smile. Brave little birds. Seeing the cheerful gaiety of the birds despite the harsh winter gave her joy and hope. Like a tiny spark catching on tinder, she hoped to stoke it back into a burning fire of confidence.

Lincoln placed a hand on her hip, pulling her against him so her back pressed into his chest. They stayed like that for a moment, watching the birds, before she turned in his arms and searched his face, for what she wasn't entirely sure.

"We are going to find your family," he promised.

His focus moved down to her lips, and she closed her eyes, praying he would kiss her, but she felt only the briefest touch of their lips and his breath upon her cheeks before he let go of her. Her heart sank and her bottom lip trembled, but she dared not cry. She wouldn't let his rejection hurt her, at least not now where he would see.

"It's time to pack," he said.

The two of them moved their bags and supplies into the back of the SUV. They had to get on the road before nightfall to avoid driving in the dark. It was too much of a risk to move about at night without head-lights, and headlights could be seen for miles on the flat Nebraska roads. Any scavengers out there could track them far more easily at night.

"Here." Lincoln tossed her a roll of duct tape.

"What's this for?"

"The tail lights. You can't turn off like the tail lights like you can the front lights. We don't want anyone seeing us when we drive, even at dusk, and tail lights are too visible. Cover them up with the tape. Not like we need them anymore."

She did as instructed, covering up the lights while he rolled suitcases and duffel bags out to the back of the vehicle. Then she propped open the back, and they started loading the dog carriers with the hens inside.

When they were finished, she stood by the driver's side and looked back once more at the house that been her home for almost a month. She felt torn about leav-ing, and far from safe doing so. But it was time to move on. This was the first place that felt like she could stay and grow roots, and here she was aban-doning it. Her lip quivered, but she bit it hard enough to draw blood as she turned her back on the lovely, empty house.

"Come on, honey. Time to go," Lincoln's gentle voice reminded her. She wiped a tear away and pressed herself against him, not waiting for an invitation. He wrapped his good arm around her and pressed a kiss to the crown of her hair. It took a moment before she felt strong enough to pull away.

"I'm driving," she reminded him when he reached for the driver's side door.

"No, I should," he argued.

She waved the keys at him. "Not until you're totally healed you're not."

"Offensive driving might be required," he countered. "You haven't driven in combat. I have."

"You really expect the wastelands to be full of cars with spikes and drivers wearing hockey masks like in a Mad Max movie, aren't you?" said Caroline. "You got a name picked out? Loony Lincoln?"

"When my arm is better...," he growled.

"When your arm is better, *then* you can drive," she said with a laugh. "Now get in," she ordered. Despite his beard hiding his expression, she did catch him fighting off a smile.

Caroline got in, and they were soon headed onto the highway south. The chickens in the back clucked incessantly for the first hour before they quieted down. She tried not to look at the cities they passed, but it was hard not to see what was left behind. Just about every store they passed had its windows broken, from bakeries to sewing shops and hardware stores. Some were just burnt-out shells. And the bodies...everywhere...bodies were both piled like cordwood and scattered where they had fallen, all in various stages of the disease. Stray dogs roamed the streets, their eyes wild as they raced away from any sounds, especially those of cars. If there were any survivors in these places, they kept themselves well hidden.

Hydra-1 had wiped out entire cities, and no one had been able to stop it. Early on the dead had been dumped into mass graves and burned, the smoke of the fires rising for miles into the sky. There wasn't time for ceremony or respect; there was only the need to remove the bodies to try to kill the infection. But Caroline understood Hydra-1 now. It was a microscopic predator that lurked everywhere, preying on all susceptible to it. It spared no one, no one except a fortunate—or perhaps *unfortunate*—few who were left.

"Lincoln...what do you think is going to happen? To people, I mean. Will future children born from survivors be immune to Hydra if they are?"

"I don't know. It's possible that any immune survivors will have formed sufficient antibodies that might be passed down to their offspring. There's no guarantee that Hydra won't somehow mutate eventually, though. It is a virus, after all, and mutations are easy to achieve if they run across another virus and copy part of their RNA strand."

Caroline was silent a long while after that. She tried to imagine a world where she felt safe enough to have a child, or to trust a man to help her raise it. She glanced at Lincoln and then back to the road. She and Lincoln? Not likely. Yes, the man was fucking hot and kissed like out of some X-rated fantasy, but he didn't seem like he wanted to be a father. There was a shadow around him, a tragedy he didn't speak of that seemed to bleed over into his life. She wasn't sure she could ever banish whatever demon had created that shadow.

"What happened when you were at the airport?" Lincoln asked. "When you realized they weren't going to let you go?"

Caroline went white-knuckled on the steering wheel as she tried not to let the past create a fresh sense of doom within her.

"Only if you tell me something first."

"Shoot."

"Why don't you want to check on your parents?"

Lincoln growled. "Truth? My father was an abusive son of a bitch. I promised myself when I joined the army that he would never hit me again. If he did, I'd kill him. I have a feeling that if I went to visit and they were still alive...I'd end up doing what I promised."

"I'm sorry." Caroline wished now that she hadn't asked him anything about his family.

"Your turn. What happened at the airport?" he urged.

She drew in a deep breath and began to speak about the horror she had endured.

———

"You can't keep us in here!" the woman beside Caroline screamed. She and a hundred other people were pressed against the glass of the security doors that led out of the airport terminal. A row of thirty police officers stood on the other side of the glass, wearing white masks over their noses and mouths. Each officer had an assault rifle ready.

"I have a family!" someone else shouted, beating a fist on the glass. "You're killing us by leaving us here!"

Caroline anxiously studied the officers' faces. Many were impassive, but a few were wide-eyed and shifty-footed with fear. Someone broke through the police ranks and came to the glass walls. It was a woman wearing a navy-blue coat that had CDC printed on the left side.

"Excuse me! Can everyone be quiet?" the woman announced loudly. Most of the people nearest the glass barrier grew silent.

"The man removed earlier today was confirmed infected with a contagious virus. It is fatal if contracted. The symptoms are fever, thirst, and dehydration. You may experience vomiting and diarrhea." The woman searched the faces of the crowd, likely already trying to gauge the symptoms of the people nearest her.

"We will be providing water and food and any assistance possible, but you must be patient. Once we are able to determine the extent of the situation, we can find a way to start releasing you to go home."

Caroline watched the woman speak softly to a policeman behind her, and his look of pity as he glanced at Caroline and the others filled her with dread. They were being quarantined. They weren't going to be allowed to leave. The second the people around her realized that, they were going to cause a riot. She had to get somewhere safe. *Now.*

She backed up, pushing her way through the crowds until she was free of the mass near the glass security doors. Struggling for air, she slumped down in an empty gate area near the glass windows facing the airport runways. All of the planes had been grounded, and the ground crews were gone. Caroline dug around in her backpack for her phone. She dialed her parents again. Her mother answered on the first ring.

"Honey! Thank God, what's the matter? Natalie said something about you being stuck at the airport?"

"Mom... They aren't letting us go home." She tried to keep from crying. "It's bad. Really bad."

Her mother's panicked breathing wasn't a comfort. "Is it the virus from the news?"

"Yeah. A man behind me in line died today. He was infected. He coughed on me. I could be infected with it."

"Oh no," her mother said harshly. "You're not sick, you hear me? You were so ill as a baby when you came a month early, but we got through that. You'll get through this too."

"This isn't the flu, Mom. You don't survive this. The lady from the CDC was just here, and"

"The CDC? Oh my God!" Her mother's tone turned shrill with panic.

"She said it was fatal. I don't think they have a cure. They aren't letting anyone leave our terminal. It's under quarantine. I don't know how much time I have left. I"

"Caroline Marie Kelly, you won't die. When you were born prematurely, I held you in my arms, praying for you as you struggled to breathe and fought to live. I knew then that you were special and you were meant to do great things in life. Whatever this is, you will beat it."

Caroline closed her eyes, feeling more hopeless than ever. She talked to her mother for another hour, but then she heard the screams and shouts of an angry mob.

"Mom, I have to go. I love you." She hung up and crouched down.

Dozens of angry passengers were storming the shops in the airport terminal. Men and women fought over neck pillows, bags of chips, bottled water, magazines and expensive travel gear like headphones. Stunned, Caroline watched the violence, the men and women hurting each other. At this rate, they'd kill each other before the virus got them. The thought flitted through her mind on dark wings. *No one would survive this.*

Six long days later corpses were draped over uncomfortable chairs near airport gates. Bodies slumped against inside shops or restaurants. Dozens more were piled up in the restroom stalls. The thick, cloying smell of death was an invisible cloud in the terminal. Not a single body stirred, not a single chest rose and fell except hers. Caroline knew she had to be immune. She'd encountered the sick and dying hourly in the past week and hadn't been able to avoid their touch, their saliva or breath.

Now she lay alive, exhausted, inside a boarding ramp tunnel. She'd managed to break through the security door that morning, desperate to find one place where she could feel alone and breathe clean air. She used her backpack as a pillow, restlessly turning again and again as she struggled to sleep. She'd tried to read a few books and magazines, but that meant she had to wade through the bodies and feel those glassy, sightless eyes following her wherever she went to find something new to read. It wasn't worth it anymore. Nothing was.

I just want to fall asleep and never wake up.

She prayed nightly, to have her pain and fear taken away so she could just fade into nothing. Dying was easy for everyone but her, it seemed. Her body fought, drawing in breaths, refusing to give in, and she greeted the bleak winter dawn each morning with exhausted eyes and a weary, broken heart.

She was in that twilight place between wakefulness and sleep when suddenly she glimpsed the distant sway of a flashlight in the darkness.

"Anyone alive out there?" The voice seemed to come

through a distant tunnel, and for an eternity Caroline lay there, unable to move.

"Anyone alive?" The call was closer now.

"Here!" The word struggled to escape her chapped lips. Her back spasmed from long hours on the hard floor. She was weak with hunger and dehydration—not from Hydra-1 but because the food and water they had been promised had stopped arriving a full day ago after the last person expired in the terminal.

"Hello!" The call bounced off the walls of the jetway as she crawled on her hands and knees.

"He—here," she tried to shout. A beam swung her way, and she threw her hands up, covering her sensitive eyes in the dark.

"Hands down. Show your face!" the man demanded. He was wearing a hazmat suit, and his voice came through a speaker near his chin.

Caroline lowered her hands, showing him her face. She had no telltale flush, no fever... No Hydra-1.

"Step this way," the man commanded.

She followed his voice, stepping around the bodies of passengers. Her gaze drifted south, and she saw a child wrapped in her mother's arms, both dead, their faces sunken and eyes cloudy. Something inside Caroline broke then. Like when she'd once knocked over a favorite vase and the pieces scattered across the ground, too small to ever be put back together again. She could only kneel among the shards, mourning the loss, the permanency of it.

"This way. You need to be tested." The man in the hazmat suit led her through the terminal to the security exit that had once been crowded with people. A few bodies littered the area, and a man was still pressed up against the glass, but he'd been dead for days, Caroline guessed. Beyond him, through the protection of the glass, she saw the woman from the CDC and a few police officers waiting nervously.

"One survivor confirmed," the man leading her reported. "No sign of infection."

"Take her to the quarantine zone," the CDC woman said.

They led her toward a pair of distant doors that had been locked and sealed at the far end of the terminal, past the security exit. She was taken into a room where she was stripped of her clothes and belongings and forced into a chemical bath designed to kill any viruses or bacteria on her skin.

Then she was transported to a research hospital and escorted to a hospital room. A nervous-looking nurse left her a pair of scrubs on the bed before dashing out the door. A man in a hazmat suit drew a blood sample, hair sample, and saliva sample before leaving her alone with a tray of food and a few bottles of water. She ate everything and drank every bottle, to the point where her stomach felt like it would burst. Then she collapsed back on the bed and sank into a sleep so deep that not even the nightmares could chase her.

———

"Y ou are the lone O'Hare survivor?" Lincoln asked, holding his breath. He had known about that incident. Adam had briefed him about it while everyone was still at the White House.

"You heard about me?" Caroline's cheeks reddened, and it reminded him how long it had been since he'd kissed her. Too fucking long. But he'd let his pride override his lust these last three weeks. He'd been unable to protect her. He'd failed at the very mission that had kept him going. And he'd gotten shot by a bunch of fucking amateurs. There was nothing worse to a man's ego than being unable to look after himself. Caroline had handled everything, and that had filled him with a bone-deep shame. His arm was getting stronger, and he'd soon be able to protect her again and prove that he was worthy of her.

"I'd only heard there had been a confirmed survivor. The CDC worker there reported back to the vice president, Adam. She called you 'the hope for all mankind.'"

"The hope for all mankind?" She blushed again. "I'm not the only survivor. You survived too."

He shrugged. He'd been lucky, that's all. He could have died a thousand times over the years, fighting for his country secretly, behind the scenes. This was just another brush with death. Lincoln had never wanted to claim recognition for any of that. He only wanted to find peace within himself and banish the demons of his past.

"What happened after the quarantine? I remember hearing that you were escorted to the research facility for testing."

"That was the plan," she said with a sigh. "I arrived at a private research hospital just outside Chicago. But I was only there a few weeks before Hydra-1 wiped out the staff. I was abandoned. I just woke up one morning in my room and could hear machines and alarms beeping. When I went outside to see what happened, I found that most of the staff had left and the rest were dying. Someone delivering supplies to the hospital was infected and spread the disease. It happened so fast."

"I know." He thought of those final days in the bunker, the way the disease had spread until only he and Adam were left.

Flashes of being back in that hallway, of seeing the mummified bodies of his friends, his team. Then later, hearing Adam weakly call his name. The sweat on his fingers as he raised the gun to his best friend's head. He would never vanquish that demon—it would linger like a stain upon his soul forever.

"It'll be nightfall soon. We should stop." Caroline's voice broke through the rush of dark thoughts clouding his mind.

"Look for a motel off the highway," he said, glad to have something to focus on other than the past.

They watched for signs, and when he spotted a

decent-looking Holiday Inn outside of Kansas City, she took it. They parked in the lot next to the other cars, making sure their vehicle didn't stand out. Then they unloaded their bags.

"We can come back for the chickens," Lincoln said.

They took only their backpacks first, and he entered ahead of her, pistol out but not raised. The hotel was dark, the chairs in the lobby overturned, and the minibar behind the desk had been emptied. Ice cream had melted into hardened puddles on the floor. Basic medicine, razors, and shampoo bottles were still there. He touched his beard, considering shaving it. What would Caroline like? Beard? No beard?

"Let's go to the second floor," he said. He would come back for those supplies later.

"Why?" she asked in a hushed whisper.

"Tactical advantage," he explained. "We can still leave quickly if there's a fire, but we aren't as vulnerable as we would be on the first floor. Most scavengers look for a quick and easy hit. Break into the ground floor, check those rooms, and move on."

"Oh, got it." Caroline adjusted her backpack and followed him as he led them to the staircase used by employees.

He found an empty room and checked the door adjoining to a neighboring room was locked on their side. Then he went back to their door and checked the sliding bolt lock.

He noticed her watching and cocked a brow. "What?"

She grinned. "Nothing." She shrugged casually, which would have pissed him off if it had been anyone else. But with her it was actually kind of cute, not annoying like he thought it would be. He didn't press her on what she was thinking. He just liked knowing she was acting, well... normal. Normal, considering. Like a normal woman would when she teased a man.

"So this is our place tonight, huh?" The way she said "our place" made him grin back at her.

"Yeah." He nodded at the two twin beds. He had hoped for a king, but he didn't want to kick down every door in the place looking for one.

Caroline collapsed onto one bed and dropped her bag at her feet. "God, I wish we could watch TV right now." She flopped back onto the bed, presenting herself as an all-too-tempting offering.

"There are a lot of things I wish I could do now," he muttered, cursing his sore but mostly healed arm. "What did you like to watch?"

"Sitcoms." She sighed, gazing longingly the dark TV. "I know they were super cheesy, but I loved them."

"Why?" His curiosity was piqued. He'd always like documentaries.

"I like to laugh. And no matter how bad a day you had, watching those shows would make you laugh. I haven't really laughed since..." Her gaze grew just a little bit distant, and the pain in her eyes made his teeth clench.

"What was your favorite show?" Lincoln eased down on the bed beside her, wanting to touch her but hesitating. He'd spent the last few weeks pushing her away because he'd felt weak and ashamed. Now he didn't know how to get back to where he'd been with her. So he did what he and his men did on their downtime: shared stories, memories, talked about favorite foods and favorite movies. It worked well as a reprieve from the fear and anxiety around them.

"There was this one, about an office with all these employees. This one character was super obnoxious, so this other character pulled pranks on him." Caroline was smiling now, and the brightness of it would have knocked him over if he hadn't already been sitting down.

"What kind of pranks?"

Caroline spent the next hour reenacting about a dozen episodes and somehow managing to spoil all the funny parts until they were both laughing. He couldn't help it. She had a sexy, happy laugh. A laugh a man like him never got tired of hearing.

"I guess what I loved most was how the people were normal, like me. They faced normal problems, but the show made it amusing and true. Like the office romances. It's hard not to fall for someone you work with, someone you're close to on a daily basis." Her face reddened and she looked away, and he had a feeling she was thinking about them and how closely intertwined their lives had become since they'd met.

People bonded in times of danger. People became lovers, soldiers became bands of brothers, strangers became parents to orphaned children. It was human nature to take care of each other. But contagious diseases were different. They drove people apart. They were terrifying because they were invisible and could be anywhere, on anyone. He could still hear Adam on the radio in the bunker, giving the last few messages of hope to those still listening.

"We must never forget who we are. We must care for each other. We must put others before ourselves. The nations of the world can survive this if we stay true to the only cause that matters now—the survival of the human race. Together."

Lincoln wasn't sure he believed any of that, but he'd believed in Adam and would have followed him to the ends of the earth. In a way, he had. Now he would follow Caroline. He saw that same hope in her and that belief in humanity in her eyes. It stirred something deep within him, something he had thought long dead.

"Rest and let me get the chickens. I'll put them in the room across the hall."

She stretched and yawned. "You sure?"

Fuck, she was adorable. "Yeah, get some sleep."

She scooted back on the bed and lay down on her side, falling fast asleep. He envied her that. He had a soldier's ability to sleep just about anywhere and anytime, but he never slept deeply the way she did. He woke with every creak and groan of the places where he slept.

Lincoln returned to the car and carried the pet carriers with the chickens upstairs, placing them in a room across the hall, which was also empty. He let them out of their carriers and closed the door to keep them inside. He would check for eggs tomorrow. Then he entered the room he shared with Caroline.

She was still asleep. He pulled back the covers of the other bed, and then removed her shoes and socks and tucked her in. He checked the bathroom; it had running water. Despite his fatigue, he wanted to collect supplies while he could. The front desk's cash drawer had been forced open by a crowbar and emptied. Lincoln slipped behind the desk and reached the shelves of bottles of Tylenol, ibuprofen, and other basic drugs. He grabbed a stack of razors and a couple boxes of condoms and shaving cream. Yeah, he knew he was being presumptuous for getting more condoms, but he never wanted to have an *"Oh shit, where's the condoms?"* moment if something happened between them. The last thing he needed was worrying about bringing a kid into this fucked-up world.

He searched the kitchen and found a large store of powdered eggs, which had a shelf life of five to ten years, and an endless supply of those tiny single-serving cereal boxes. Those were gold. He would have to pack every one of them into the car. It would be a tight fit, but they could eat Froot Loops like kings.

By the time he got back to the room, it was dark. He settled in the bed opposite Caroline. He was afraid if he tried to sleep next to her tonight, he might do something he'd regret. She was so goddamn irresistible, and she had no clue. This wasn't just about them being some of the last people on earth—this was about *her*, who she was, how she reminded him about what was still good in the world. She was like a bottle of hundred-year-old whiskey to an alcoholic trying to make it one day sober.

He swept his small Maglite over their room before he turned it off, wanting to make sure all was well before he let his guard down. Who knew what monsters lurked in the shadows outside, waiting?

10

Here life has death for neighbor,
And far from eye or ear
Wan waves and wet winds labor,
Weak ships and spirits steer;
They drive adrift, and whither
They wot not who make thither;
But no such winds blow hither,
And no such things grow here.

—"The Garden of Proserpine"
by Algernon Charles Swinburne

The chill woke Caroline with cold, creeping tendrils, stealing beneath the thin hotel blankets. Bleary-eyed, she reached for the comforting warmth of Lincoln's body. But he wasn't there. She jolted awake, crying out in fear.

"Lincoln! Lincoln!" Terror shot through her like a shotgun blast. Her lungs seized, her vision blacked out, and she bent double over the side of the bed, dry-heaving.

"Caroline." Lincoln's deep, rumbling purr of a whisper was there beside her, his arms strong and warm as they wound around her, pinning her to the bed, like the roots of an ancient tree. He hadn't abandoned her in the dark. She was safe. She wasn't alone. Great gasping, gulping sobs escaped her with such force, she wondered if her lungs might bleed from the stress.

"Shhh..." His beard rubbed her forehead, and she buried her face against him, needing to be assured by all five of her senses that this wasn't a dream. She couldn't smell things in her dreams.

"I thought you left me...I..."

"Never." He said the word softly, yet it seemed to vibrate through her, echoing deeper than anything else in her life ever had. It seemed to be more than a declaration of love. It was a vow, an unbreakable one. But how could he make such a vow to her? They were strangers, thrown together by circumstances and tragedy.

"I'm sorry," she murmured, her lips brushing his neck.

His arms tightened around her. She realized they were lying down on her bed, his body partially covering hers. He gently cocooned her beneath him, just the way she liked. She couldn't miss his hardened arousal that dug into her hip, but it didn't frighten her. She wanted him—she *needed* him in the most primal way. The fear of losing him had made one thing clear to her. She didn't want to go another moment without knowing the intimate touch of another, and there was only one man she wanted.

The first day they'd met he'd said it would come to this; animal lust and the desire for physical comfort. Damn him, he had been right. She would hate him and herself tomorrow. But right now she needed him.

"Please, Lincoln." She kissed his throat and wriggled beneath him, trying to entice him to slide between her legs.

"No, not tonight," he said, before he stole a slow, drugging kiss that made her body ache and her toes curl.

"Yes. I've been wanting you for weeks," she admitted, arching her hips and curling one leg around his ass. "And you've been avoiding me." God, right now she loved his ass, tight and firm...it gave a girl the best fantasies about digging her nails into it while he fucked her senseless. Not that she'd ever experienced that. Her list of ex-boyfriends was short. She'd cared about each of them, but none of them had really been intense like Lincoln.

He was so physically present, so strong and at home in his own skin. That natural confidence was hotter than hell. When he had kissed her that first time, she'd felt almost as confident as him, because she had tasted that primal hunger on his lips and knew it was for her. He just wanted her the way she was in that moment. Naked, gasping his name, and nearly blacking out with pleasure. She'd tasted all of that on his lips and seen it in his eyes. A girl could get drunk on something that like.

"Please...I'll beg," she groaned and rocked herself against him. "You want that?"

"Caroline, I'm not a gentleman. I'm...I'm rough. I can't always hold back once I get started. I will stop if you ask, but I don't make love—I fuck. *Hard.*"

All she could do was moan at how his low, rough words made her feel. She was in heaven. Rough was what she needed. Something to distract her from her fears for the future.

"Hard is good," she assured him.

He kissed her then, devouring any resistance she might have put up had she wanted to. Their mouths stung each other with sharp need. He bit her bottom lip, then licked away the sting, each kiss more blistering than the last. She was greedy for more, wanting to feel his body and his mouth and hands all over her. His tongue invaded her mouth, dueling with hers before he moved down to her neck, nipping and sucking on her skin in between hot kisses. Her body was on fire, wetness pooling between her thighs. The burden of her clothes was suddenly too much.

She struggled with her sweater. He moved quickly, sensing her goal, and with one easy move tugged her sweater off. Then he slid down her body and removed her jeans just as easily. She was down to her panties and bra when he pounced on her. More kisses followed, hard ones that branded her as his. She scraped her teeth over his shoulder and clutched at him in wild desperation.

"How do you want it?" he growled as he reached for his pants. "Hands and knees or on your back?"

"Stop wasting time and"

He didn't let her finish. He rolled her onto her stomach, then lifted her onto her knees. He jerked her panties down to her knees and put a hand on her back, pushing her so she bent forward and rested on her forearms. Then his shaft was nudging her entrance. She parted her thighs wider, panting as he rubbed her folds, coating himself in her wetness.

"Yes," she gasped, wanting now more than ever to feel him inside her.

He rewarded her by filling her completely, his hips slamming against her ass as he fully seated himself, and she cried out at the shock. She felt speared all the way through to her heart. There was nothing else in her head now, no other thoughts. There was only this, only him with her in the dark. She rotated her hips in slow circles, pushing back against him, his rough chuckle sending shivers of sensual delight through her.

Lincoln grasped her hair, pulling it back so she arched her body, thrusting her breasts forward. There was something erotic about still wearing a bra while being fucked, knowing Lincoln was so desperate to take her that he didn't even stop to remove every last scrap of clothing. He pulled himself almost all the way out and then plunged back in, filling her again. They were one in a way she'd never been with any lover before. She felt attuned to him, and he to her.

Pull, thrust, gasp, moan... They created a symphony of intense sounds accompanied by the *tap-tap-tap* of the headboard against the wall. They moved together as he relentlessly rammed into her over and over. She cried out over and over with animalistic fierceness as she gave in to her most primal urges. He kept thrusting into her, clasping her hips as he pushed her to her limits. His hold would leave bruises tomorrow, ones she'd wear proudly because he wasn't hurting her—he was owning her, and she was owning him right back.

They didn't need sweet words or sympathy right now. They needed this. Dark, primal pleasures, each reminding the other that they were strong and alive. She matched him stroke for stroke, push for push, and when he reached around her and found her clit, rubbing it with his fingers, she was lost.

The orgasm hit her full force, shattering her senses. She surrendered to it, collapsing down on the bed. Lincoln kept her ass in the air as he fucked her hard a moment longer, finding his release within her, and she loved that. His body tensed, and she felt the heat spread deep inside her. A long moment later she lay panting beneath him, and she realized that neither of them had thought to use a condom. He had a whole pouch full, and he hadn't even used one.

Oh God...

Neither of them said a word for a long while. When she thought he was close to drifting off, he suddenly spoke, causing her to tense.

"I'm sorry. I got carried away." He nuzzled her neck and pressed a sweet kiss to her skin. He'd fucked her like a warrior and now cuddled like a tame tiger.

"I got carried away too. We never even had the *talk*, like good adults are supposed to."

His rich chuckle would have made her smile at any other time. "The *talk*? What's that?"

"You know..." She blushed. "Are you clean of diseases? Am I on the pill? Do we need a condom?"

"Oh..." His chuckling stopped. "*That* talk."

She braced herself. "Lincoln, I'm not on the pill, but I'm clean."

"Me too. Clean," he replied, nuzzling her ear. "Now's the part where we talk about the fact that I just fucked you bareback? I wish I could say I regret it, but I sure as hell don't. You were a slice of heaven."

His words made her blush deepen, and she was thankful for the darkness, but it also made her warm and gooey inside. He was certainly no poet, but he knew how to make her feel like a goddess.

"We have to be careful. What if... What if we end

up having a baby?" It was a dangerous question in a dangerous world.

"Then we handle it."

"Handle it?" Her voice pitched up an octave uncomfortably. "You do realize we don't exactly have doctors and hospitals anymore. If things stay like this, the risk factor is going to be high giving birth. Then there's the question of even raising a child in this world..."

"I know."

"And you're the one who keeps talking like it's the end of days."

"I know, but...I want to believe it won't stay that way."

It was the first she'd ever heard him even hint at the possibility of a better future.

"But it's up to you. Like you said, the risks are higher right now. Keep it or..." He didn't finish, and she realized what he meant. She'd always known her feelings on unexpected pregnancies. Despite the world having gone to hell around her, her thoughts hadn't changed. She thought of a child with a flutter of hope. Would it be immune? Would she be forced to watch it perish from the virus?

"I think...I think I'd want to keep it," she whispered, then held her breath to see if he would react badly. "If it happens."

"Then that's what we do," Lincoln replied, his arms holding her closer to him, and he pulled the sheets up around them.

"What do you want to do? It's our choice, one we should make together." While it was happening inside her body, they had done this together, and whatever came of it, she wanted him to know she valued his feelings.

"I...honestly?"

"Honestly," she insisted.

He breathed in her ear, his heart beating faster against her back while she lay against his chest.

"I think we should be more careful from now on, until things improve. I don't want a life on the run with a child. The dangers, aside from Hydra, are numerous. Bandits, murderers, rapists. God knows what's out there. We don't know of anywhere that's truly safe anymore. How can I feel like a good father when all I would do is put my child in danger?"

His honesty hurt, but she needed to hear it because those were his feelings.

"But if I wanted to keep it, you would...want to stay and be a father to it?"

She'd never felt more vulnerable than she did now, laying herself emotionally bare to this man. She was essentially asking for a commitment from him. He could leave her tonight while they slept, and she could be left alone, possibly pregnant. Fear seized her, and she rolled to face him, watching the moonlight hit his face. He looked old, not in years, but in life, like she was gazing upon the statue of an ancient king. Solemn, tragic, mysterious—they all crowned him in the darkness that lay between them.

"If you wanted it, I would find a way to keep you and the baby safe," he said. "No matter what."

She sighed and pressed her lips to his throat in a gentle kiss.

"But we don't have to worry about that now. We won't know for a few weeks. I'll raid the first pharmacy we come across for a pregnancy test." He brushed a lock of her hair back from her face and tucked it behind her ear. "You should get some sleep."

"Could we sleep skin to skin?" she asked, feeling oddly uncomfortable in her bra while he still wore his jeans. He pulled back the covers, and they both stripped down to nothing. He pulled her back into his arms.

"To think this happened because I thought we should be in separate beds to avoid *this*." He chuckled, but she was too exhausted to focus on what he said.

She drifted into a twilight sleep where she was somewhat aware of her dreams of a dark-haired, brown-eyed child running in the woods, swallowed up by darkness while she and Lincoln cried out as they searched for their child. Would any child in this world ever be safe again? Not having an answer to that haunted her, destroying any chance of happy dreams.

———

L incoln listened to Caroline's breathing and knew when she was asleep. He wouldn't sleep at all, however, not after what they had done. They had possibly created a life tonight, and he could barely stomach the violent knotting in his gut at the thought. Had he condemned an innocent child to facing the horrors of their newly changed world? But if Caroline wanted the baby, it would become a part of his mission.

He stretched back on the bed, listening to the heavy silence. People didn't understand silence, not *true* silence. There was no hum of cars on the road, no vibrating of the walls with air conditioners or hissing of water pipes, no sounds from numerous electronic devices, no sizzling of the air with electricity snaking through the power lines. It was all silence. Only the wind made any sound as it raked against branches or pulled bits of trash along the ground. But there was no wind tonight. In the silence, a man could imagine a thousand sounds that weren't really there but would haunt him until he was convinced he was hearing things.

In the last few months, he'd taken to sleeping with a small handheld radio. The white noise static sound of dead channels helped to soften the roar of the silence and the other sounds he dreamed he heard.

The crackle of voices through the radio was one such imagined sound. He had bolted out of his bed a dozen other nights after Adam had died, expecting, *hoping* to hear the last president of the United States say something, anything, even though he knew the man was dead. But always he dreamed it just as sleep began to creep in.

"This is a call for help. Any survivors, please respond."

Lincoln listened to the words his mind must have dreamed up.

"Please respond..." The tinny voice crackled through the radio again. Lincoln was surprised by the realness of his dream and decided to investigate. He tucked Caroline into bed, making sure she was covered. Then he pulled on his briefs and reached for the radio where it sat next to the lifeless TV.

"Please respond. We are calling for all survivors. This is Dr. Erica Kennedy from the CDC. We have power in our headquarters in Atlanta. Please respond."

"CDC?" He uttered the initials like they were a foreign tongue. He'd been at the White House when the director had urged the president to enact the Omaha Protocol...the bunker...the last hope to keep the chain of command alive.

Lincoln's heart began to pound as he reached for the radio. He clicked the talk button and brought it to his lips.

"This is Major Lincoln Atwood, First Special Forces Operational Detachment–Delta. Please repeat your full message." He let go of the button and waited, his heart hammering wildly.

"This is Dr. Erica Kennedy of the CDC. We have power at the headquarters in Atlanta. We are urging survivors to come forward and provide blood samples for testing. Are you confirmed to be immune?"

Lincoln's hand started to shake as a violent surge of emotions flowed through him. Hope, joy, excitement, fear. He hit the talk button.

"I am confirmed immune, and I'm with another immune survivor."

Erica's voice came back on quickly. "Thank God! You're the first person I've been able to reach. Please come to Atlanta. We need you."

Lincoln had the sudden sense he was being watched and saw Caroline was sitting up in bed now, her eyes wide. The moonlight made her pale face glow. They locked gazes, and she slowly nodded.

"Dr. Kennedy, I'm happy to report we will be on our way. We just have to make a trip to Joplin first to check on some family. If we find any other survivors, we'll bring them along." Caroline would want to punch him for leaving Glenn and Joanie in Nebraska when they could be of use to the CDC now.

"Thank you, Major Atwood. We will stay on this channel. Contact us if you can, and keep me updated on your progress." The radio was silent for a moment, and Lincoln wondered if they were done communicating.

"Be careful out there. You could save many lives if you can make it to Atlanta safely."

"Understood," Lincoln replied, then set the radio down.

"Oh, Lincoln...," Caroline whispered, and then she sniffed. Tears streaked down her cheeks. He rushed to her, kneeling by the bed and cupping her face.

"Hey...honey, this is good news."

"I know," she said, still sniffling. "I'm happy. I forgot what hope felt like, you know? Real hope. I'm just a little overwhelmed."

He kissed her forehead. "Me too."

"Come back to bed?" she asked.

"Yes, ma'am." He saluted and won a smile from her. He slid back into bed beside her, spooning her body, holding on to her like a life preserver.

They lay together, sharing body heat and silence. But for the first time in months, he felt like the silence didn't suffocate him. Because within that silence, he had finally heard the radio crackle. He had heard *hope*.

11

Pale, without name or number,
In fruitless fields of corn,
They bow themselves and slumber
All night till light is born;
And like a soul belated,
In hell and heaven unmated,
By cloud and mist abated
Comes out of darkness morn.

—"The Garden of Proserpine"
by Algernon Charles Swinburne

Caroline woke in bed alone, her panic rising again, but the sounds of the shower relieved her fears that Lincoln was gone. After last night's mind-blowing passion, the possible repercussions, and the radio contact from the CDC, her entire world had changed.

She tried to process both the fear and excitement about how she and Lincoln might be more than partners in survival—that they might be parents too. And the thought of a cure? That was news she *never* thought she'd hear. After the world had lost power and communication, she'd assumed the CDC had gone dark like everywhere else. Yet here was the dawn, the actual dawn, with sun streaming through the windows bright and warm in a way it hadn't in weeks. It was so easy in the winter to forget what the sun really felt like, and ever since Christmas, it seemed like the sun had abandoned them.

The water turned off, and she could hear humming from inside the bathroom. She lay down on the bed, watching the shadows and light through the gap between the door and the carpet as Lincoln moved about on the other side.

She closed her eyes briefly, pretending for one glorious moment that life was normal again. Cars were speeding down the highway, the TV would spark to life when she used the remote, and that she'd just had amazing sex with a man after dating him for months. She almost laughed at the silly daydream. For the first time in her life, she'd be bringing a man home to meet her parents, and it was literally because the world was ending. Her sister was going to laugh at the irony.

Lincoln emerged from the bathroom. A towel hung

low over his lean hips, and that taunting group of muscles forming a V on his pelvis made her thighs clench together. His chest was smooth except for that trailing patch of dark hair leading to... She jerked her focus up to his face. Her heart stuttered.

Caroline went slack-jawed as she realized she was staring at a stranger. The man who stood there, water drops clinging to his skin and looking like he'd stepped out of her darkest and most delicious fantasies, was not a man she knew.

"L–Lincoln?" She tested his name as the man stroked a hand over his clean-shaven face.

"What? You don't like it? Did I cut myself?" He stepped back into the bathroom, checking his face in the mirror.

"You shaved. It's just...I guess I didn't recognize you. I'm so used to you being a mountain man." She had started to grow fond of her sexy, intimidating mountain man.

"Given the recent news, I thought cleaning up was in order. You don't like it?"

"No, I do, I do. I was just...surprised, is all." Truth was, Lincoln Atwood was even sexier than she'd guessed. Beneath all that facial hair was a chiseled jaw, a strong chin, and the most sensual lips a man could have. He was perfect. Fitness-magazine-model perfect. And he had just fucked the life out of her last night. She stifled a giggle.

"Caroline?" He spoke her name cautiously, and she

knew how unsettling it must be because Lincoln was normally so self-assured about everything. His confidence had always made her feel safe. Now she saw a suddenly awkward and shy side to him. That shouldn't have turned her on, but it did.

"You're beautiful," she blurted out without thinking.

He chuckled. "Okay...not exactly the word I was looking for."

"I mean I like it, the beardless look. It's hot, but the beard was hot too. But maybe I miss my mountain man a little." She then bit her lip, trailing her gaze down his body once more. He noticed, and his own sweeping appraisal of her set her body on fire.

"Keep looking at me like that and I'll show you your mountain man, honey," he growled. Self-assured Lincoln was back, and she wanted him so much. He took a step toward her, and she had only a moment to remember their mistake from last night.

"Condoms!" Caroline held up her hand, catching his attention. He snatched his backpack and pulled out a fistful of condoms, tossing them on the bed so they rained down around her. Then he ripped the towel off his hips and stalked toward her. He pulled back the blankets on the bed, exposing her naked body. She squealed as he crawled up the bed, caging her beneath him, pinning her arms on either side of her head as he stole her lips in a possessive kiss that made her blood sing.

His body commanded her sensual surrender, and she

was happy to give in to his every demand. He moved down her body, his lips exploring the valley between her breasts, her hard nipples. As he laved at the sensitive peaks with his tongue, she groaned with pleasure. She felt both desperate and at peace as he made love to her.

The raw, aggressive passion from last night was gone, replaced by a slow, deliberate sweetness. He had said he was rough, but this certainly wasn't. He was gentle as he parted her thighs, gentle as he explored her folds with his mouth, licking her until she came apart with exhausted screams. Then he moved back up her body and sheathed himself in a condom before sliding into her welcoming body.

It felt so good to feel him inside her, the connection between them burning so deep. He rode her slowly but with hard thrusts, pinning her beneath him on the bed. She dug her heels into his ass, and their gazes locked as their breath mingled.

For the first time she saw a glimpse of Lincoln without shadows, without pain. There was only hunger and something deeper, something akin to wonder. That sense of awe was growing inside her too. This thing between them had become much more than she'd imagined—it was more than just sex. Right now, they were one body, one heart, one mind, one soul. The past ceased to exist and the future was a bright star in the distance. This moment became their entire universe.

They didn't kiss now; they simply moved together, faces fixed upon one another as they became slaves to that biological need to connect. Softer, sweeter emotions ran like quicksilver beneath her skin as a second climax, not as sharp, but richer, rolled through her. Her body quaked from the force of it. Every nerve ending seemed to come alive, and her legs fell open on the bed as a delicious fatigue overcame her. Every tensed muscle, every flash of anxiety shooting through in the last few months suddenly eased. At least for now. She felt only a quiet, soft joy, like waking to bright sunlight and hearing the chatter of birds outside one's window after a violent thunderstorm.

Lincoln kissed her ear as he left to use the bathroom. Then he dressed and set his bag on the other bed, sorting through the weapons and supplies. Caroline wanted to stay in bed forever, but she knew they had to get moving. They needed to make it to Joplin by nightfall, find her family, and then head to the CDC in Atlanta.

The thought of a cure or a vaccine lifted her weary spirit. The population may be decimated, but a cure was still important. Fear of Hydra-1 was almost as devastating as the disease itself, and until the survivors were sure it wouldn't return, rebuilding on any large scale would be impossible.

She slid out of bed and rushed into the bathroom, still a little shy in front of Lincoln. She was relieved to find the water was fairly warm, almost hot. She lingered in the stall, letting the droplets grow cold on her skin before she got out. Then she wrapped a towel around herself and wiped a hand across the mirror, clearing a path in the slightly fogged-up glass so she could see her reflection. She had avoided mirrors for months, almost afraid to see her face after everything that had happened. But now, now she had to see. Hope burned inside her like a raging fire that she never wanted to go out. She looked like her old self again, the woman who refused to give up.

Caroline was still smiling an hour later as she and Lincoln finished their breakfast in the empty dining hall of the hotel. Then they packed up the car with their supplies and got back on the road. She kept the radio close by so they could hear if the CDC made any more announcements. Even the sight of burned-out buildings, looted stores, and abandoned homes couldn't penetrate the small bubble of hope that now blossomed in her chest.

Four hours later, they were almost at her home, and she fought to control her excitement.

"You're going to love my parents. My father is a sweetheart, and my mom is fierce." She grinned like a fool at Lincoln, but he wasn't smiling. "What's the matter?" she asked. He continued to drive, but he reached out and placed a hand over hers on her left knee and gave it a gentle squeeze.

"I'm worried, that's all," he replied.

"Worried? We haven't seen anyone on the road, and—"

"About your family. Caroline, you need to prepare yourself for the possibility that they didn't survive."

His words filled her mouth with an acidic taste, and she shook her head stubbornly.

"They'll be fine. I'm immune, so they have to be too." She'd secretly been preparing herself for the worst, but she didn't want to act like her family was already dead. She'd cling to her hope until the last possible minute.

"We don't know that," Lincoln said with a sigh. "Back in December, the CDC said they weren't sure how the antibodies form, if any do. It could be genetic, but it also could be environmental. We don't know if something occurred within you, me and the other survivors that creates an immunity. The couple from the sporting goods store were both immune, and they had no shared blood. What does that tell you? A coincidence that two immune people got married? Possibly, but it could be something they ate, took as a medicine or had a vaccine to another virus that happened to work against Hydra-1. We don't know. I just want to make sure you have accepted the possibility that we might find them gone."

Caroline felt a sudden surge of panic bursting in her. They were alive. They were safe. Just like her. They had to be. She wasn't going to think about anything else. She turned her gaze to the window, not wanting to look at Lincoln's face or she might start to think he could be right.

"How much farther?" he asked when he turned onto the street that led to her childhood home.

"The last house on the right, before the street turns left." She sat up, eager to see the redbrick house. The neighborhood looked nearly empty of life, but there weren't any bodies visible anywhere, either. Was that good or bad? They parked in the driveway, and she started to get out, but Lincoln caught her arm.

"Wait. Let me go in. I'll make sure no one else is there. We can't have another incident like Omaha."

It killed her to wait, but she did. He went up to the door, his gun half-raised as he tried the knob. She climbed out of the car and waited, her heart racing. Caroline scanned the street, but she saw no immediate threat, so she started toward the front door. She ran straight into Lincoln's hard body. He caught her by the shoulders.

"Stop," he commanded, his tone firm but soft. It frightened her. She lifted her gaze to his and saw the truth in his eyes. "Don't go in there."

"No..." The word escaped her in a pained moan. Agony tore through her, and she crumpled to the ground. Lincoln caught her in his arms and settled her on his lap as he sat on the steps just outside the front door. She turned to stare numbly at the door, the merry red paint, the Christmas wreath still up months longer than her mother ever would have allowed it.

"Lincoln, I never had the chance to say goodbye to them. I never got to tell them... I..." It felt as though her heart was bleeding out, and she couldn't breathe or move. Lincoln banded his arms around her, holding her tight against him while she succumbed to a grief so overpowering it might have killed her if he hadn't been there. She swallowed thickly, her throat so tight it burned like shards of glass.

They were gone. Her only ties left in this world, her reason for making it through each day. Without them it seemed like everything was at an end. It was as though she'd been climbing the stairs in the dark and miscounted the steps, thinking she had a step to take. Then she'd tripped, her heart leaping into her throat as instinct took over as she tried to catch her balance. The shock of it all slowly bled away, and all the while she clung to Lincoln, his heat keeping her body warm, his scent enveloping her. Only his arms around her kept the shock from fully setting in.

"Where are their bodies?"

"In the backyard. Three graves," he said.

"Three... Wait, three? But my sister was here with her husband...and the baby!" She scrambled off his lap and rushed inside. It was quiet, dark, and musty as she searched every room. Each one was empty. She stared at the glass door leading to the backyard and saw the three graves. The earth was still fresh. How many days had they been dead?

Caroline put her hand on the knob, holding her breath as she prepared to go out and check the graves. A soft, keening whine broke through the darkness which crowded around her heart. She found Lincoln in the front doorway behind her, his gun up.

"Did you hear that?" she whispered.

He answered with a nod. They both waited, listening again for the cry. When it came, she realized it was more of a whine than a cry, and it wasn't coming from upstairs, but the basement. She rushed for the door, but Lincoln blocked her path, shaking his head. He opened the basement door and headed down first, weapon raised, his flashlight in his other hand braced just above the gun. He descended into the darkness, and Caroline followed close behind.

The whining continued, and there was a scraping sound and a muffled groan. Caroline bit her lip to hold back a scream as Lincoln's flashlight swept the room. When she saw what made the noises, she gasped.

"Rick! Oh my God!" She shoved past Lincoln and ran to the man lying on the ground. He was sunken-faced and pale, his clothes covered with sweat. Her nose wrinkled as she approached him and she could smell vomit nearby. Rick blinked against the light of the flashlight as Lincoln joined her and crouched down close to him.

"Caro," Rick breathed her name and coughed weakly. "Knew you'd come. I told Nat you'd find a way."

"Rick..." Caroline couldn't stop the tears that were streaming down her cheeks. "What happened to them?"

"Dead, two weeks ago. Nat, Stephen, and Amelia."

"Ellie?" Caroline asked, her voice breaking as her heart ripped apart with fresh pain.

"There." He pointed to the corner of the basement. A baby carrier sat there, its shade pulled down so they couldn't see clearly inside.

"Oh no..." Caroline couldn't look. "Lincoln..."

"I'll look," he said. But as he moved toward the carrier, a dog lunged out of the shadows, growling. Lincoln raised his pistol.

"No, wait! It's my parents' dog!" she cried out. "Kirby," she told Lincoln. She kept one hand on Rick as she whistled for the handsome Irish setter to come over.

"He won't leave Ellie," Rick whispered. "He's guarding her." He tried to roll his head in the direction of the dog. "Kirby boy... Come..."

The dog whined, and it was then that Caroline realized she must have heard Kirby's whine from upstairs. If he hadn't whined, they wouldn't have found Rick.

Lincoln knelt in front of the setter and held out a closed fist to the dog. Kirby inched his face out, sniffing hesitantly at Lincoln's hand. His tail wagged.

"You're a good boy, aren't you?" Lincoln said soothingly. "Protecting your human pup, aren't you?"

Kirby's tail wagged a little more quickly, but the dog was still uncertain. Lincoln opened his fist slightly and brushed the back of his knuckles along Kirby's shoulder, and the dog calmed. Caroline's heart raced as Lincoln then reached up to push the shade back from the carrier.

"She's alive!" Lincoln hissed. "The baby's alive! We need to get her upstairs, away from him in case she's not immune."

"She is…" Rick choked out. "Safe. Nat got sick and was holding her in her arms the night she died. Ellie was fine. Small fever, but fine." He gripped Caroline's hand. "Take Ellie. Go. There's nothing left for her here."

"No, Rick. We won't leave you."

He squeezed her hand tightly, eyes wide and blood-shot. "I want to die knowing my child is safe with you. You hear me?" His voice was stronger as emotions gave his feeble body strength. "It's my last request." He let go of her and slumped back to the ground, struggling for breath.

"Caroline, he's right. We need to leave." Lincoln stood, the baby carrier in his arms. Caroline could see Ellie's face, cherubic and plump, her little body tucked under blankets as she slept.

"Here." Lincoln handed her the baby carrier. "Take her upstairs, and the dog too."

"What are you—?"

"I'm going to stay here and help Rick. Now go. Wait for me upstairs," he ordered. She obeyed, because she trusted Lincoln.

She faced Rick one more time, knowing that she'd never get the chance to express everything she wanted to say to her family, and there wasn't time now to tell this man what he'd meant to her.

"I love you, Rick." Her voice roughened as she

struggled to speak. "You were my brother, my friend. Thank you for marrying Nat, for..." She closed her eyes and inhaled a deep breath. "Thank you for everything."

Rick's eyes glinted with tears. "Love you too, kid. Just wish I could have stuck around." His eyes strayed to the baby carrier. "Now go on upstairs and take her with you."

Caroline's throat worked as she nodded and tried to swallow her grief. She understood that Rick would have given anything to kiss his child and hold her one last time but the risk was too great.

"Come on, Kirby." She carried the baby up the stairs, her heart growing heavier with each step. She knew what Lincoln was going to do because she'd heard him talking in his sleep last night. She knew now what kept his dreams dark and full of sorrow.

He'd killed Adam Caine, the last president of the United States. But it had been more than that. He'd killed his friend. Caroline couldn't imagine the burden that had placed on his soul.

He was an angel of death, and now he would help Rick. She'd watched men, women, and children waste away over days and weeks. It was an ugly, painful, and slow death. No one deserved that suffering. No one. She reached the top of the stairs, her eyes filling with tears. Her body went rigid when she heard the shot ring out. The baby stirred with a mewling wail and they both began to cry.

12

@CDC: *We are actively working on a vaccine but urge people to stay in their homes and avoid contact with others as much as possible. Hydra-1 is passed by transmission through touch, fluids, and air. Self-quarantine is the best way to preserve your life and the lives of others. If you believe you are ill, contact our hotline, and we will arrange for transport to one of the nine hundred triage locations that are being established throughout the United States. It is crucial to report if you are ill. Hiding your condition only puts your life and the lives of others at risk.*

—Centers for Disease Control Twitter Feed

January 3, 2020

L incoln knelt beside the man who lay slowly dying.

"Rick?" he asked, and the man nodded weakly. "I'm Lincoln Atwood."

"I'd shake your hand, but...." Rick gave a raspy chuckle. Lincoln grasped Rick's hand, ignoring the possibility that the man was infectious. If Lincoln hadn't died by now, he wasn't going to, at least not until the virus mutated.

"You military?" Rick asked as he studied Lincoln.

"Delta Force," Lincoln answered solemnly.

"No shit." Rick laughed. "Boy, Caro knows how to pick 'em. I bet you're one tough bastard."

At this Lincoln did laugh, the sound hurting his chest because he was damned near close to crying. He'd thought he'd had the last of these moments back in the bunker.

"Tough enough." Why he said that he wasn't sure, but he felt Rick wanted to know that Caroline was safe with him.

"Damn, wish I wasn't dying. Would have loved to share a beer, hear your war stories." Rick smiled, the expression softening the pained look upon his face.

In that moment Lincoln glimpsed another life. One where he and this man would have been friends. They would have sipped beers and sat in lawn chairs while Caroline and her sister made margaritas during a lazy summer day, connected in a deep friendship the way two brothers-in-law could. But that was life which would never be, a future that was dying with the man on the floor.

"You going to take care of her?" Rick asked. His eyes

were solemn and focused despite the pain Lincoln knew he was in.

"Your kid? With my life," he promised.

"I figured. But I meant Caro." He closed his eyes for only a second before looking at Lincoln again. "I've known her since she was a kid. She's all heart." He smiled. "Natalie used to say Caro would save the world someday, if we would just let her."

Lincoln smiled too. From the moment he caught a glimpse of Caroline, he'd sensed that same thing, she was his future, and somehow not just his, but possibly everyone's future.

"You've got to protect her," Rick said. "Promise me. She's tough, but she still needs someone to have her back."

Lincoln nodded. "I'd die for her."

"Good." Rick relaxed a little, and then his gaze flicked to the gun Lincoln held. "Don't let me stay down here. Do what you need to do, and bury me beside Nat in the backyard."

"Okay." Lincoln swallowed down the hundreds of other words he wanted to say to this man besides *okay*. But his lips wouldn't form any other words, and his throat constricted. The world was full of silence now, silence like the one that transpired between them in that basement, as Lincoln realized what Rick was asking of him. A silence heavy and aching with pain no man or woman should ever have to feel. A pain of a loss so deep that it burned through a man's bones and left scars. Lincoln was done with being the man who had to take the life of someone good, someone true, someone whose breath meant hope for a better world.

"Fuck..." Lincoln's eyes blurred with tears, and he wiped his forearm across his eyes, trying to clear his vision.

"I'm sorry to ask you to do it," Rick murmured gently, a saintly glow around his face now as he stared up at Lincoln with concern. Taking the life of a good man didn't just leave a stain on his soul—it left him with a burden upon his shoulders that no one could ever help him carry.

"I'd ask the same if it was me." Lincoln's voice broke. "Damn, I wish we were getting that beer." He would have given almost anything for that, for the future neither of them would have. He squeezed Rick's hand, afraid to let go or else he'd break like no man was supposed to.

"I'm ready," Rick said. "Should've died days ago. I think I was waiting for you and Caro to come find us. Now you have. I can rest." Rick closed his eyes, and a hint of a smile curved his lips, and he let out a slow breath.

Lincoln recognized when a man was ready for death. Rick was at peace. It didn't make what he had to do any easier, though. He wished he had something he could give him to make it quick and painless, but all he had was his gun.

"Just think about that beer," Lincoln whispered to

him. "The two of us, watching our girls and the sunset playing off the water of a backyard pool in endless glints of light. Taste the sweet bitterness of a good old IPA beer."

"Yeah...I can taste it," Rick sighed.

For a moment, Lincoln was there with him in that memory of a moment that would never be, and he could feel the sun and see the water sparkling and hear Caroline laughing while he tasted that beer. His throat burned, and he could barely breathe.

His usually steady hand shook as he stood and raised the pistol. The sound of the shot rang out like a cannon in the concrete-walled basement. His ears rang for several long seconds as he looked anywhere but at the body lying still at his feet.

Another life to add to the list of his sins, even though it had been done with good intentions. His road to hell was paved with hundreds of well-intended stones.

He stared at Rick. The man had a name, a home, and a family, all dead save for the two females upstairs. Lincoln was so *tired* of all this, the deaths, the struggles, the hungry nights and cold beds. A perpetual winter had fallen over the world. It reminded him of the stories by C. S. Lewis where four children stumbled through a wardrobe into a land trapped in winter. There was no evil white witch here to defeat in a glorious battle, just an endless fight against invisible microbes that were armed to destroy humanity forever.

Lincoln squeezed his eyes shut, flashes of the desert heat of Iraq and Afghanistan coming back to him, moments when mortars had shelled his location and he screamed the names of his brothers until he lost his voice. Even in those moments, there had been hope. A world away, he had known that the land of the free, *his home*, was safe.

But no one had escaped this hell.

He opened his eyes and forced the spiraling dark thoughts into a tiny box inside his head and buried it.

"I'm sorry we didn't get here in time," he whispered to the dead man.

He shivered as though an invisible touch had landed upon his shoulder. He'd felt that once before, when he'd lost a man in Kabul. He'd felt the boy, barely twenty-two, die in his arms, heard the death rattle in his chest and saw the distant gaze of his eyes as he'd passed away. He'd felt that same gentle touch then, almost a nudge, and then he'd felt that subtle presence that only his most primal instincts seemed to recognize or understand. Then that presence had faded away like mist before a powerful dawn.

He hoisted Rick's body up over his shoulder in a fireman's carry and took him upstairs. He didn't look for Caroline, and he was glad she wasn't in sight.

He took the man outside. They were far enough south that the ground was not frozen now that it was March. He laid the man down on the ground and then picked up a shovel from by the back door. Lincoln dug and dug until his back ached and his palms were raw from the old splintered wooden handle of the shovel. Then he carried Rick over to the shallow grave and buried him.

When he was done, he stood looking down at the four mounds of earth. Caroline's parents, sister, and brother-in-law were all gone. She might have seen them one last time if he hadn't gotten shot back in Omaha. He'd cost her the only thing she'd wanted. Her family. She would never forgive him. Hell, he'd never forgive himself.

Lincoln stared at the gun in his hands, unaware of when he had removed it from his shoulder holster. It would be so easy to... There would be nothing left, no more guilt, no more misery. Only a true silence and true darkness, one he wouldn't mind.

"Lincoln?" The single word shocked him back to himself. He slipped the gun back into his holster with shaking hands and faced her. She was standing half a dozen feet away, her gaze worried and her eyes red-rimmed. She had been crying.

"Sorry. I'm coming back in now," he promised, his voice rough with emotions he wished he could hide from her.

"Thank you. I know what you did...how hard that was. I can't even imagine..." There was no hate in her voice, no fury, not even pity. There was only compassion in her too lovely hazel eyes and...a deeper emotion that scared him more than anything else.

Why was she not condemning him? How could she not hate him right now?

"I..." He didn't know what to say next, and his words trailed off into silence.

Caroline walked up to him and embraced him. She wrapped her arms tight as though trying to crush him, and the pain in his still healing shoulder felt good. Like it was cleansing him somehow. He wrapped his arms around her and embraced her in return. This woman was and would always be the beautiful, bright, lighthouse tower in the storm around him. She cut through his darkness, even the parts he swore would never see light again.

"It's okay," she whispered against his chest. "It's okay..."

He should have been the one comforting her. He should've been holding her in his arms and promising to give her back the life she'd once had. But here he was in a cold, quiet yard, four graves at his back, and all he could do was hang on to her for dear life.

"Do you mind if I say a few words?" she asked, and pulled out a slender old-looking book from her coat.

"No," he replied. "I think they'd all like that."

"I know they would," she agreed with a sad smile. "This was my dad's favorite book of poetry. It has some classics in it, but there's one I think that's the best. It's called Do not Stand at my Grave and Weep by Mary Elizabeth Frye. He read it at my grandmother's funeral a few years back, and it's always stuck with me."

She thumbed through the pages, and he stood silently beside her, one arm around her shoulders, the other gripping the shovel's handle so hard his knuckles were white.

She cleared her throat, trying to smile, but it soon faded as she began to speak.

> *Do not stand at my grave and weep*
> *I am not there; I do not sleep.*
> *I am a thousand winds that blow,*
> *I am the diamond glints on snow,*
> *I am the sun on ripened grain,*
> *I am the gentle autumn rain.*
> *When you awaken in the morning's hush*
> *I am the swift uplifting rush*
> *Of quiet birds in circled flight.*
> *I am the soft stars that shine at night.*
> *Do not stand at my grave and cry,*
> *I am not there; I did not die.*

She was quiet a long moment afterward, but her words seemed to echo in the still yard.

Do not stand at my grave and cry. I am not there; I did not die.

Lincoln struggled for a breath as he watched his

woman stand there and not cry. Her eyes held tears, but she didn't shed a single one.

"They aren't there; they didn't die," she finally whispered and then turned to him. It wasn't a denial of their deaths. Rather it was an acceptance that they had been something more than mere bodies living on this earth. Who they were deep inside, their souls, was all around them, glinting off snow, shimmering in the night sky, or a soft whisper of birds' wings as the dawn broke over the horizon. She was right. Her family wasn't there buried beneath the ground, nor was Adam still lying on his cot in the bunker.

They are not there; they did not die.

The burden crushing him slowly began to ease, and he pulled Caroline into another hug. Somehow she'd done the impossible—she'd shared his burden and given him the strength to go on. He'd been right. This woman was the embodiment of hope.

"Let's go inside. We have a lot to pack. They stocked up on baby supplies. Formula, diapers, all sorts of stuff. Regular supplies and dog food too. They were prepared for the long haul." Caroline's voice held a hint of false cheer, but he only saw her courage. She was strong. How could he ever have believed this woman was weak?

Lincoln followed her inside, and they were both greeted by the excited prance of the Irish setter.

"Hey, Kirby." Caroline ruffled her hand in the dog's fur on the top of his head. Kirby twirled expectantly to

Lincoln, and Lincoln suddenly laughed, which sounded ridiculous at first in the silent house.

"What? What is it?" Caroline asked.

"I've wanted a dog all my life. My dad never let me have one, and obviously I couldn't have one in the service. It took the world ending for me to finally get my childhood wish." He knelt down at face level with Kirby and reached out to pet the dog. Kirby bumped his nose into Lincoln's outstretched palm, then moved in for an excited lick of Lincoln's face.

"You are wrong, you know," Caroline said. Her eyes were soft as she looked at him.

"Yeah? About what?" He straightened.

"The world ending. I've been thinking a lot about it. The world never ended. The wind still moves, and the grass will grow in the spring. The birds still sing. There is still life. This isn't over, Lincoln. *We* aren't over. My niece, Ellie, is in her nursery right now, perfectly healthy. She's alive, we're alive. Joanie and Glenn are alive. That woman from the CDC is alive. There are others. We have to find them, have to tell them to join us. We need to band together." She grasped his face in her hands, pulling his head down to hers. "We can do this. We can rebuild. I know it."

Then she kissed him.

13

@CDC: We recommend that you wear medical face masks and protective eye gear when around infected individuals. It is also greatly recommended that you avoid close contact with other people, even if they do not show signs of infection. The incubation period of Hydra-1 is still unknown.

—Centers for Disease Control Twitter Feed

January 7, 2020

Her kiss was like a damn drug, making his mind go blank of all things except how good she made him feel. It was like feeling the sun on his face after a century of gray skies and endless rain. Her breath was warm against his face and he sighed, wishing he could kiss her for hours. He wrapped his arms around her waist, absorbing the emotions he swore he could almost taste as she met him kiss for kiss.

There were promises of trust, passion, desire, longing, and sorrow. Caroline could fit a universe of feelings in just one kiss. She was the kind of woman a man dreamed about, the kind Lincoln had never believed he would find.

When their lips parted, she stroked a fingertip over his mouth as though trying to memorize the shape. She half smiled, and the expression made her glow somehow, even in this dimly lit house.

"Come on, let me show you everything. I don't think we'll have a chance to come back here anytime soon. I just want to see everything one last time." She checked to make sure Ellie was sleeping in her crib before she took him through the house of her childhood, pointing out room by room, the things that had made it home.

Her father's messy office held the lingering hint of cigar smoke. Her mother's studio had oil paintings of the gardens that she'd created on her free weekends. The cozy sunroom with bookshelves stuffed with every kind of book imaginable. There was the kitchen with its country French colors and welcoming design. The dining room had a large table set for eight. Closets full of board games with worn covers from years of use. The piano in the formal living room had dozens of pages of sheet music piled up on the music stand. Her and Natalie's bedrooms were full of high school photos and college graduation pictures and notes from friends, journals, and travel books. The last room they entered was the nursery. The pink elephants painted on the walls held a personal touch. He thought he recognized the style.

"Your mother painted these?" he asked Caroline.

"Yeah. Natalie and Rick lived close and visited a lot, so they made their guest room into a nursery for Ellie to use when Nat and Rick came to visit."

Ellie lay in her white wooden crib, shifting her chubby legs as she tried to kick free of the blankets. She was so small, so vulnerable. Caroline picked her up and held her out to him. He tried to refuse, but Caroline gave him a firm look that warned him he had to take her. He picked up Ellie and stared down at her. She scrunched her nose and yawned, and the soft kittenish sound she made slipped through a chink in Lincoln's armor and went straight into his heart. He settled her into the crook of his arm and inhaled her sweet baby scent. He'd always wondered if that baby smell people talked about was real. Turned out it was, and it did funny things to him. He wanted to just close his eyes and hold on to her forever.

"I found these in the bathroom." Caroline held a pregnancy test box. "I'll wait a week and try it." She put the tests in a backpack and began to stuff diapers and baby clothes inside.

"I think we'll have to teach Kirby to carry Ellie's emergency go-bag," Lincoln said as he rocked the small blanketed bundle in his arms. She couldn't be more than five months old.

"Good idea." Carolyn took the baby back and placed

her in the carrier. Two hours later they were packing up the car again, this time with the baby and a dog in tow.

"Ready to leave?" Lincoln joined Caroline by the steps to her home. She wiped her tears away, and her expression changed to one of steely resolve.

"Next stop, Atlanta?" she asked.

"The CDC is our best bet. Others will be picking up the transmissions, I'm sure." Lincoln curled an arm around her and pressed a kiss to her temple. It was easier now to touch her, to be affectionate. He'd never imagined he could be what his men had called "domesticated." They'd all joked about being half-wild with the way their lives were and the way they lived. Yet now he was settling down. He had a woman and a baby to look after, and he didn't want to be anywhere else in the world than where they needed him to be.

"Atlanta it is, then." Caroline leaned against him for a brief moment, then pulled away and got in the passenger side. Ellie was already asleep in her carrier in the back, and Kirby thumped his tail as they got inside.

Lincoln said nothing more as he drove them away, but he reached for Caroline's hand and squeezed it tight.

The gray sky seemed thinner now, and the horizon was flushed pink with the sun sinking below the trees. Lincoln prayed for a day with clear skies and sun, just one.

As they drove toward the highway, Caroline pulled

out his phone and connected it to the vehicle's speakers. Bill Withers started to croon "Ain't No Sunshine."

Bill was right. If Caroline went away, she'd take every bit of light with her.

———

C aroline eyed the small house they'd found off the highway for the night. Ellie was restless in her carrier and likely needed a diaper change.

"I wish I knew more about babies," she confessed to Lincoln. He was unloading their emergency packs and heading for the door. He glanced over his shoulder at her, a sweet, amused smile on his lips.

"You'll figure it out," he promised. "If not, I'll find a bookstore and get you some baby books."

She huffed and picked the carrier up from the back seat and followed him.

"You mean *we'll* figure it out. You're part of this now, Lincoln. Ellie, Kirby, and I, we are your new unit." She was teasing him, but when she caught up to him at the front door, she saw he was taking this seriously.

"You're right. You are." Then he focused on the door, using an iron Halligan bar he'd found in an abandoned fire truck earlier that week. It had a forked end to bust doors open.

He was a true soldier, a man of few words, but when he did speak it always had meaning. Sometimes she missed the idle conversations, but other times she didn't mind the silence, not when he was with her.

The door opened, and Lincoln entered first, gun at the ready, but Caroline doubted anyone was alive inside. There were few cars around, and where there were few cars there were usually fewer bodies and likely no survivors. Once Lincoln cleared the house, he left her and Ellie so he could unpack the chickens from the car. Kirby followed him out, a little too curious about the live fowl.

"Come on, Ellie," she said as she took the baby carrier down the hall and found a bedroom.

She pulled the baby out of the carrier and laid down a changing pad on the bed and checked the diaper situation. As she'd suspected, fully loaded. She did her best to clean the baby off and put a new diaper on her. Caroline fixed the little onesie back up and tucked her back in her carrier. Lincoln had found a travel crib in her parents' house that they would be able to leave Ellie in tonight.

Caroline stroked a fingertip down Ellie's cheek, her heart breaking all over again as she watched Ellie's bright blue eyes fix on her. When would she realize her mom and dad weren't ever coming back? Caroline knew that babies recognized the faces of their parents. Would she recognize the fact that she would never see them again?

"I know I'm not your mom and Lincoln is not your dad, but you're ours now, and we will love you just as much as your parents did, okay?" She wiped a tear from her nose and let Ellie grasp her finger tight. The baby made breathless little grunts and exhalations as she tried to communicate to Caroline in return.

"Should we go see what the boys are up to?" She scooped Ellie up, feeling oddly comforted knowing that her talking was welcomed by the baby. They wandered through the house toward the den and found Lincoln setting up lanterns and drawing curtains closed.

He nodded at the baby in her arms. "Is she hungry?"

"Probably." Caroline looked at the baby, who was watching Lincoln with rounded eyes.

"I'll get a fire going in the fireplace. It's too dark for anyone to see smoke. We can warm some water and formula in a pot."

"Okay." She set the baby down on the floor on top of a thick soft blanket, then retrieved Lincoln's satellite radio.

"Can I use this?"

"Sure. What are you wanting to do?" He knelt by the fireplace, arranging logs before he used a paper towel from the kitchen as kindling to get the flames going.

"We need survivors to come to Atlanta, don't we?"

"We do. The CDC will want as many blood samples as they can to figure out what we all have in common."

"I want to find people. I want to remind them that we are all in this together. Anyone who has a radio might hear me. I'll try a different channel each night."

Lincoln stared at her for a long moment. "Don't tell anyone where we are, not specifically. Not until we're in a more secure situation. You could paint a target on our backs."

"I won't," she said, clutching the radio to her chest before she went to the kitchen to retrieve the formula from Ellie's emergency pack.

Lincoln did a good enough job of warming formula and water over the fireplace and then filled the baby bottle after testing the formula on his skin. He stared at her when he caught her watching him, a smile on her face.

"What?"

She chuckled. "How do you know what to do?" She didn't have the faintest clue about taking care of a baby. Whatever other women said, this didn't come naturally, at least not to her. She felt protective, overprotective even, but she didn't have any instincts about what to do, when to feed her, when to check her diapers.

"Haven't you seen *Three Men and a Baby*?" He smirked. "You can learn a lot about babies from TV."

"I forgot about that one." That had been one of her mother's favorites. Three bachelor friends had found an abandoned baby on their doorstep, and they took turns raising it until the mother came back to claim the child. It was a sweet movie and, as Lincoln pointed out, reasonably instructive on caring for a baby.

"You've had her for a while—let me feed her," Lincoln offered, and he took charge of Ellie. The baby stared up into his face, eyes wide and solemn, the way only a baby could be. Lincoln smiled at her, and the baby cooed in delight as he offered her the bottle, which she sucked eagerly. Caroline's heart fluttered. Lincoln was right about ancient instincts taking over. Seeing a man like him holding a baby was stirring all sorts of emotions inside her. She could have taken him right there and then, but she needed to focus on the future. She had to get on the radio to see if anyone else was out there.

"That's a special military-issue radio. You should be able to cut through any signals currently being broadcast to communicate with anyone out there listening."

"I'll be back." She took one of the lanterns and headed into the master bedroom. She sat cross-legged on the bed and turned the radio on. She chose the lowest number channel and then held the button. She felt nervous, talking to no one, or maybe everyone who was left.

"This is Caroline Kelly. I'm hoping someone out there will hear me. If you can, that means you're a survivor, like me. We are the same—we are in this together. The CDC is operational in Atlanta, and they need survivors. With our help, they can find a vaccine. I know a lot of you are scared. There are people out there preying on others because they can, because they think everyone left in the world is looking out for themselves. But if we stick together, if we trust each other to work together, then we can save humanity. We can rebuild.

This is bigger than any of us. Our children and their children deserve a better world, but to do that, we have to stop the chaos, stop the violence and mistrust. So...if you're hearing this, I'm going up to the next channel tomorrow night to find more people and spread the word. Meet us in Atlanta. If we save each other, we save the world. Caroline out." She released the talk button and drew in a deep breath. It was a start.

She found Lincoln pacing across the kitchen, their sleepy ward propped on his shoulder. His eyes were half-closed, and he was humming...Metallica? She bit her lip to hide her smile. Ellie was going to be one bad-ass girl with a man like Lincoln for her father.

"She okay?" Caroline whispered as she joined him.

"Yep. Fed, burped, and out for the count." He nodded at the folded crib. "You take her, and I'll set up the crib in the master bedroom."

Caroline took her niece and followed Lincoln into the bedroom. She set up some lanterns and rubbed a hand up and down Ellie's back while Lincoln set up the crib. Then they set Ellie inside.

"Has anyone talked back to you?" he asked when she handed him the radio.

She shook her head. "Not yet, but it's just the first day."

"You're pretty amazing," he said, catching her hips and pulling her gently against him.

"Yeah?" She curled her arms around his neck. "How so?" There was something about the way he held her, the way he looked at her. She felt like she could do anything in the world so long as he held her and looked at her just like that.

"You believe in everything. I thought you were gullible and foolish at first, but now? Now I understand. Hope is a gift." He leaned down, their lips inches apart. "You're *my* gift."

They kissed, the hungry raw passion of the moment consuming them as they tumbled back onto the bed. *You're my gift.* And hope to him was a gift.

I think I'm falling in love with you, Lincoln.

She kissed him back with desperation, tugging at his clothes even as he was tugging at hers.

They made love hard and slow, as though determined to feel every bit of each other in intimate detail. Lincoln didn't let her once lose focus on him or her pleasure. In the orange glow of the lanterns, they each made silent vows to one another. Caroline would never give up. She had everything to fight for.

14

@CDC: The governors of the following states have declared emergencies and will be closing major highways in and out to prevent the spread of Hydra-1. New York, Illinois, California, Texas, Michigan, Virginia, Massachusetts, South Carolina, and Florida. If you live in one of these states, you are federally mandated to stay in your homes except to secure food and medical supplies. Additional triage stations will be announced shortly in cities in the above listed states.
—Centers for Disease Control Twitter Feed
January 14, 2020

The days passed slowly, the travel arduous and grim as they drove through Missouri. So many of the interstates and highways they would have used were road-blocked or so cramped with abandoned vehicles that they were forced to turn back. Each time this happened, Lincoln's face darkened, and Caroline did her best to ease his worry and frustration. No one was used to this, the end of the civilized world. The only thing that kept Caroline going was speaking on the radio each night, spreading words of hope that she hoped somebody would hear.

Ellie chirped happily in the back seat, growing more each day, and it filled Caroline with quiet joy to see glimpses of Natalie and Rick in her little face. Whatever this new world held for them, Ellie was bringing her parents with her in some small fashion.

Lincoln stopped the car at a mall outside of a small city in eastern Missouri.

"I saw smoke on the horizon, could be wildfires. We need to get our supplies fast and keep moving."

"Got it," Caroline agreed.

Lincoln left Caroline alone with the baby and the dog while he siphoned fuel from the cars. They had used half their extra fuel supply in just seven days due to having to retrace their steps and find new ways to head east.

Caroline picked up Ellie from her car seat and walked around with her, holding her up so she could look about. Kirby didn't stray far; he marked a few trees by the edge of the parking lot before he trotted back to them. The chickens in the back were silent, clucking every now and then from their pet carriers. A breeze suddenly caught some tendrils of Caroline's hair, tossing them around. She laughed as Ellie caught a strand and tugged hard.

"Ow...*ow!*" Caroline winced as she extricated the hair from Ellie's tiny but forceful grip. "You pull hair like your mama does." She laughed again, thinking of all the times she and Natalie had fought as kids. Natalie used to pull her hair, and Caroline had been a shover.

A hint of smoke was carried on the breeze, and she turned her head toward the western sky. Plumes of black smoke were billowing upward, blending deceptively with the clouds. If the wind hadn't changed, she might not have noticed the smoke until it was too late. The sun began to set beneath the layers of clouds, and it looked as if it was wreathed in a crown of fire. The wind must have changed, carrying the wildfire their way.

"Lincoln!" She shoved Ellie back in her car seat, strapping her in. "Kirby, up!" She pointed at the back seat, and the dog leaped inside. Caroline screamed Lincoln's name again, not seeing him. What would she do if the fire reached them and she still hadn't found him? She'd vowed never to leave him, but she had Ellie to think of now and—

Lincoln vaulted over the hood of a Taurus fifty feet away.

"Get the engine started!" he bellowed. Caroline got in the passenger side and started the ignition. Lincoln threw himself in the driver's seat, and they shot out of the parking lot into the streets. Ellie started screaming in distress.

"Lincoln..." Caroline turned around in her seat, watching the houses and businesses half a mile down the road being devoured by the flames. It was a sea of fiery horror behind them.

"I know, I know," Lincoln hissed as he swerved around dead cars on the road. The wildfire raced behind them like a gathering storm. Caroline was torn between trying to keep her eyes on the flames and the now darkened streets as smoke suffocated the last of the sunlight. The car jolted to a stop as they hit a deadlock of cars blocking a tunnel.

"Goddammit!" Lincoln shouted and slammed his hands on the steering wheel. Kirby barked and then whined.

Caroline placed a hand on his arm. "Breathe, Lincoln." She had no idea how she was calm in that moment, but something inside her told her that they couldn't die today, not after everything they'd been through.

"This is not where it ends, or how it ends." She nodded at a side street to the left. It looked wooded, which wasn't good, but it had no sign of cars. Lincoln swerved the wheel over, and they shot down the forested road, bumping over cracked asphalt. The fire was ever closer, pacing its cage like a tiger, seconds from breaking free. Caroline tried not to think about what would happen if the road they were on curved back straight into the blaze.

The fire started to catch up with them, catching

trees along the road on either side. Thick smoke began to cloak the roadway, and Caroline was terrified they would crash into something. But they couldn't afford to slow down. The acrid smell of the wildfire seeped inside the car, and Caroline grabbed a spare coat to cover some of the vents, but she couldn't reach them all.

Orange embers began to shower down like glowing raindrops as the branches above them caught fire and the dry dead limbs turned to fiery dust. The street ahead was now invisible. The smoke was thicker than fog but lit with a dull glowing orange like hot coals in a blackened fireplace. The world outside seemed full of a heavy roar.

Caroline put a hand on Lincoln's arm, and their gazes locked for half a second.

"I love you."

"I know," he growled and slammed his foot on the gas, and they drove into the murky road ahead.

———

Lincoln was sure they were dead. But then the skies cleared, and there was an open road free of cars and fires. They shot across a bridge, and a wide, fast-moving river flowed far below them. He lifted his gaze to the rearview mirror and saw the fire and smoke growing more distant by the second.

What the...?

He jolted out of shock and checked on Caroline in

the passenger seat. Her eyes were closed, and she was whispering a prayer, one hand still gripping his arm. Checking the plastic mirror attached to the headrest of the backseat which reflected against the car seat, he saw Ellie was sitting wide-eyed in her car seat, her little pink cheeks covered with tears. Kirby was panting, his head darting all around the cabin. The two chickens stirred but made no other sounds.

"Jesus...we made it." He stretched his hands along the steering wheel and felt each of his knuckles crack from the tension.

"Honey, it's okay. Open your eyes."

Caroline slowly looked around in shock and then turned halfway in her seat to look through the back of the car window at the inferno far behind them. "How...?"

"A river—we crossed a fucking river." Lincoln let out a pent-up breath, his lungs itchy from the smoke.

"A river," Caroline echoed and then buried her face in her hands. Lincoln wanted to pull the car over and hold her in his arms, but there wasn't time. They had to keep driving. If the embers crossed the river and started a new blaze, they could still be in trouble. They had to keep going. He'd drive all damn night to keep his unit safe. He closed his eyes half a second, hearing Adam's voice in his head.

"You always need a unit, Lincoln. A family to protect. Never let go of that instinct."

He hadn't. Having had a dick of a father and few

friends in the town he grew up in, he'd come into the army unsure what it meant to be a part of something bigger than oneself. Once he'd discovered that higher purpose, he'd known he would be in a unit for the rest of his life. When Adam had fallen ill in the bunker, Lincoln had felt his world ending. The last life he had been trusted to protect had been ended by his own hand.

Now he and Caroline, Ellie, Kirby, and hell, even the chickens fell under his protection. They were his unit now.

"Caroline." He placed a hand on her thigh, giving it a gentle squeeze. She dropped her hands and wiped her eyes. She checked on Ellie again before she looked his way.

"I'm okay," she said, her face getting some of its color back.

Lincoln focused on the road again and then said the words back to her that she deserved to hear.

"I love you too." He cleared his throat and kept his eyes on the road.

He'd never said that to anyone except his mother. He'd been around, but always kept things casual. That had been how he'd lived. But there was nothing casual with Caroline. She was making him break every rule he'd created to survive.

Neither of them spoke for a long while as they drove through the fields and forests of Missouri and entered Tennessee. They passed through small towns, stopping for food, supplies, and gas. By nightfall there were no motels in sight, but Lincoln saw a sign, and he knew Caroline was going to love his choice of improvisation. She was asleep as they stopped in front of the building. When he woke her and she opened her eyes, she grinned in delight.

"A library!"

He nodded. "It's as good a place as any to settle down without a hotel nearby."

"You could literally choose *any* house to stay in, Lincoln." She seemed surprised by his choice.

"Is any house going to be as cool as a library?"

"Touché. I didn't know you were a reader."

He chuckled. "I read. A lot."

"Seriously? What's your favorite book?"

"*The Great Gatsby* by F. Scott Fitzgerald. I thought you would have seen it when you snooped through my go-bag."

She blushed. "I didn't get all the way through your bag, just half of it." Caroline brightened again. "So Gatsby? Really? Why that one?"

"I suppose..." He paused. He'd never before really voiced what drew him so deeply into that particular book. "I feel a bit like Gatsby reaching for the green light at the end of Daisy's dock across the water. The belief in something pure, wishing forever that I could have my deepest dreams come true, yet knowing that in those final moments I'll face reality, that what I long for is forever out of my reach, forever in the past."

Caroline's eyes widened, and her lips parted as she drew in a breath of surprise. "A lot of people think it's a love story, how Gatsby spent his entire life trying to be good enough for a silly woman like Daisy, but it isn't."

"No, it isn't," he agreed. "It's a story about hope, about never giving up on one's dream." He smiled ruefully, realizing only now that perhaps he was more like Caroline than he'd wanted to believe at first. Perhaps he was a dreamer after all, and no matter what, he'd be like Gatsby, waiting by his pool for the phone to ring just as autumn leaves began to fall, signaling his death was imminent. But would he die still full of hope? Or would he live and have that hope whither?

Caroline quoted his favorite passage by heart as though she'd written it herself. "*And as I sat there brooding on the old, unknown world, I thought of Gatsby's wonder when he first picked out the green light at the end of Daisy's dock. He had come a long way to this blue lawn, and his dream must have seemed so close that he could hardly fail to grasp it. He did not know that it was already behind him, somewhere back in that vast obscurity beyond the city, where the dark fields of the republic rolled on under the night. Gatsby believed in the green light, the orgastic future that year by year recedes before us. It eluded us then, but that's no matter—tomorrow we will run faster, stretch out our arms farther . . . And one fine morning— So we beat on, boats against the current, borne back ceaselessly into the past.*"

The fine hairs on the back of his neck rose, and his skin broke out in goosebumps.

"What's your green light, Lincoln?" she asked softly, her gaze so ancient in understanding that he couldn't doubt that his entire life had led him to this moment with her where civilization lay in ruins and he stood on the steps of the library speaking of dreams drifting endlessly back into the past.

"My green light?" He swallowed thickly. "It's you." He wasn't sure what he expected her to say or do after he'd just laid bare part of his soul. Perhaps he expected her to kiss him, or to confess that she felt the same, or that she might laugh it off and speak of his foolishness. Instead, she merely spoke a single line from *The Great Gatsby* to him, the line that had never seemed to make sense to him until she said it right then.

"Life starts all over again when it gets crisp in the fall." Reflected in her gaze wasn't hope this time, but knowledge. Knowledge that whatever the winter had stolen away, spring, summer, and fall would bring back to them. Life, however small and fragile, would still be life, and they would cling to it and defend it with everything they had.

They broke into the locked library by using a pair of bolt cutters to take the chain off the door. Caroline carried Ellie and her crib inside while Lincoln and Kirby explored the rotunda of the library's interior, making sure it was completely empty. Despite the lock on the door, there were plenty of ways someone could have broken in. But all was quiet, all was empty. The sun set, leaving them in darkness except for the lanterns they'd brought in. He used the gas stove top to make a pot of beans and to warm up the formula for the baby.

He let the chickens run about the restroom and scattered the corner of one stall with chicken feed he'd gotten along with the extra dog food. They used the rolled-up sleeping bags from the sporting goods store back in Omaha and made up one large sleeping bag for them to share.

Caroline curled into him, her warm breath on his throat as he wrapped one arm around her. "Lincoln..."

"Yeah?" He waited, feeling her settle against him after a long moment.

"We almost died today."

"But we didn't. Just like we haven't a dozen other times."

"I know... But today was so close. I didn't want to make you say you love me too. I know you thought you had to say it back, and I'm sorry."

He couldn't resist chuckling. "For a brave, intelligent woman, you sure are dense sometimes."

"What?" She pulled away from him, but he dragged her back into his arms.

"I didn't say anything I didn't mean. There's nothing you could do to make me say something like that unless I wanted to."

"You mean that?" she asked.

"I do. You've made me feel love is possible. You are my hope, Caroline. *Always*." He wished he could make her understand what was in his head and in his heart.

"Can we take some books with us tomorrow?"

"Sure, it's not like some librarian is going to get angry if we don't return them," he replied, mentally rearranging the space in their vehicle to accommodate a box of books.

Caroline laughed, and the sound made his blood hum. He'd never considered himself a funny guy, but whenever he managed to win a laugh from her, he felt like a hero.

"Thank you." She kissed him and tucked her head under his chin, quickly falling asleep. He lay there holding her for a long while before he followed her, drifting into dreams. Dreams filled with chaos, blood, and regret.

———

January 2020

He sat in the passenger seat of a Humvee, assault rifle propped against his shoulder as he watched the line of military tanks and vehicles form a convoy on the outskirts of Washington, DC. Congress and the Senate had all been given orders to remain in the Capitol. Families were notified that the representatives would not be coming home until things were declared safe.

"This is fucking messed up, Atwood," Julian Holt muttered from the driver's seat.

"Agreed." Lincoln glanced at his friend. He'd been

with Julian since they were both in their twenties and recruited into Delta Force.

"How long will everything be like this?" Julian asked, his light brown eyes full uncharacteristic worry.

"I have no idea. Adam says it could be months before the CDC works out a vaccine. The army's testing samples from the O'Hare airport victims." He remembered hearing about that one. One survivor after six days. All the other passengers trapped in the quarantined terminal had perished. One out of so many.

"I've got a bad feeling about this, man. A real bad feeling, you know. Like when things went to hell in Syria. I still have nightmares about Cruz and Ross."

Julian's dark skin and soft eyes made a contradiction of solemnity and playfulness that Lincoln liked, but not today. Julian had the look of a man who'd seen death up close and personal.

Haven't we all? Lincoln stared out across the sea of the military forces on the move. He and Julian were under strict orders to protect the president and vice president. Lincoln would be boarding a military transport flight to Omaha tonight. At least, that was the rumor. Julian was supposed to return to the Supreme Court and act as the justices' protection detail.

"Fucking Omaha," Lincoln muttered. The end of the line. The last plan during a national crisis. They watched as a civilian tried to escape by driving his car at the barriers in the distance. The soldiers guarding the barriers opened fire on the vehicle, but it kept coming until it crashed into the barriers and the car crunched like a tin can before exploding seconds later.

"Shit," Julian cursed. "They should know there's no way out."

"There's always a way in and out. Just a matter of finding the weak spot," Lincoln reminded his friend.

Julian was silent a long moment. "You know, I gave up smoking for my girl. But man, I would do anything for a drag right now. I'd even take a fucking e-cigarette."

"Me too." Lincoln had never smoked before in his life, but now seemed as good a time as any to start.

"Delta Two to Delta One. Major Atwood, come in." A voice came over the radio, and Lincoln picked it up.

"Delta One responding. Atwood here."

"Major, we have a situation." Lincoln recognized the voice as one of the newer members of the force, Jesse Poole.

"What is it?"

"Satellite footage is being sent to your phone, Major."

Lincoln pulled out his secure phone. A video clip was uploading on the screen. He clicked on it, and Julian leaned over to watch. It was satellite footage of Russia, or what was left of it. Moscow was in ruins. Smoky black pits were all that was left.

"What the fuck?" Julian grabbed the radio and responded.

"Poole, what the hell is that?"

"Russia went nuclear to try to cut off the infection. Millions are estimated dead. *Millions*."

Lincoln's blood ran like ice water in his veins. This really was the end of the line. They were done. They were all done.

———

L incoln jolted awake, his heart racing and his throat tight. He reached for Caroline.

She wasn't there.

He scrambled to his feet, shoving the sleeping bag down his body. He scanned the dark library and saw a distant lantern light deep in the fiction section. Creeping closer, he heard Caroline speaking. When he saw the satellite radio in her hand, he knew what she was doing. He lingered in the shadows, listening to her speak.

"This is Caroline Kelly. I'm just outside Memphis. Still headed to Atlanta. Please join me there. The CDC needs blood samples to find a way to stop Hydra-1. I need you to join me. We are better than this. We can put aside our fears and distrust. We can work together to save each other and ourselves. I don't know if any of you have ever read this, but there's a poem called *If* by Rudyard Kipling that my father used to read to me. It's gotten me through dark times, and I want to share it with you. It gives me hope. I hope it gives you hope too." Then Caroline began to read:

. . .

If you can keep your head when all about you
  Are losing theirs and blaming it on you,
  If you can trust yourself when all men doubt you,
But make allowance for their doubting too;
If you can wait and not be tired by waiting,
  Or being lied about, don't deal in lies,
Or being hated, don't give way to hating,
  And yet don't look too good, nor talk too wise:
If you can dream—and not make dreams your master;
  If you can think—and not make thoughts your aim;
If you can meet with Triumph and Disaster
  And treat those two impostors just the same;
If you can bear to hear the truth you've spoken
  Twisted by knaves to make a trap for fools,
Or watch the things you gave your life to, broken,
  And stoop and build 'em up with worn-out tools:
If you can make one heap of all your winnings
  And risk it on one turn of pitch-and-toss,
And lose, and start again at your beginnings
  And never breathe a word about your loss;
If you can force your heart and nerve and sinew
  To serve your turn long after they are gone,
And so hold on when there is nothing in you
  Except the will which says to them: "Hold on!"
If you can talk with crowds and keep your virtue,
  Or walk with Kings—nor lose the common touch,
If neither foes nor loving friends can hurt you,

If all men count with you, but none too much;
If you can fill the unforgiving minute
    With sixty seconds' worth of distance run,
Yours is the Earth and everything that's in it.

C aroline wiped her eyes, but her voice never faltered.

"This is what we're fighting for. The nobility inside all of us, the purity of our purpose, which is to save each other. I'm Caroline Kelly, and I'll be speaking tomorrow on the next channel up. Caroline out."

She clicked the radio off, and it was Lincoln who noticed the small book of poetry she held. Her father's.

Lincoln slipped back into his sleeping bag, not wanting Caroline to know he'd woken and worried about her. Then he waited until he heard her light steps on the tile floor as she padded over to him. She climbed back in the sleeping bag and cuddled against him again. The words of Kipling's poem ran through his head as he drifted back to sleep.

 nd so hold on when there is nothing in you
    Except the will which says to them: "Hold on!"

237

15

Excerpt from the private journal of Dr. Erica Kennedy, interim director of the CDC:

November 11 – We have sent an agent into the field to investigate rumors of a virulent new disease. The agent has failed to report. I am now on site in China to follow up on the situation. These are my findings:

The virus started in a wet market. Bats were caged too close to civet cats. An apartment owner fell ill while tending to the animals he was selling. The virus jumped from the civets to the human, and the virus entered his skin presumably through a minor cut. This man fell ill seven days later and was taken to a nearby hospital.

While waiting for treatment, he collapsed on the floor. He suffered internal bleeding, liquification of his liver, and his intestines shed their lining, producing a bomb of lethal infectious bacteria. He was rushed into an emergency room, where he vomited blood and bile. After this, he slipped in and out of consciousness as his body began to expel all moisture. Over the course of a week, he became fully dehydrated, a process that continued even after his death on day nine, ending up as what the staff translated to me as a mummy. His remains were sealed in a plastic waterproof bag and stored in a hospital freezer rather than the morgue.

I examined the remains in a sterile setting, taking full precautions. But I admit, I felt terrified, and it was not just the usual bout of nerves when entering a hot zone. This was true terror. I saw what this virus did to him, what he looked like...

I took blood and tissue samples from the victim and examined them with the equipment they could provide. The structure of the virus formed a strand like a piece of string with a knot at the end. If I had to guess, it may be part of the family Filoviridae, or filoviruses that form infectious viral particles. They encode their genome in the form of single-stranded negative-sense RNA, most commonly associated with diseases like Ebola or the Marburg virus.

This virus starts out with a similar form of viral hemorrhagic fevers before it dehydrates the body faster than the body can be replenished until the host dies. What's most unusual is that this process somehow continues past death, but this is not caused by the virus itself, but rather the conditions created in the cell left behind. I am unable to determine how long the virus stays alive once the host is dead, but that is a crucial question. Will the bodies carry the disease, like other viruses, or do the host remains seal the fate of the microbes inside it?

. . .

Caroline watched the sunlight illuminate faint freckles on the bridge of Lincoln's nose as he lay sleeping beside her.

Sunlight. The brightness of the glorious sun filled the room, warming everything, including the sleeping bags she and Lincoln were cocooned in. Caroline held her breath, counting the freckles, so faint, but visible there in the light of the sun. It made her think of Tyler, her first crush. She'd been in middle school, and he had been the playful redhead with cinnamon-hazel eyes and a wicked smile. He'd had freckles like these, though more of them than Lincoln. Seeing them now on Lincoln made her smile, and that love she felt swelled inside her, like a building tidal wave, strong and unstoppable.

I love you, Lincoln Atwood, and I'll never stop. Even when my last breath is gone. You're mine and I'm yours. She exhaled slowly as time seemed to freeze, and he slowly opened his eyes.

"Morning," he said. His sleep-roughened voice filled her with a feminine awareness that made her blush.

"Morning," she replied, content to watch motes of dust catching the beams of light streaming through the windows.

"The sun's out," he murmured, childlike wonder striking him the way it had her a moment before.

She lifted a hand to touch his lips, and he kissed her fingertips. "Beautiful, isn't it?"

"Best thing I've seen in months, aside from you." He rolled her beneath him in their large sleeping bag, and she laughed softly.

He settled into the cradle of her thighs. Their mouths met in slow, sweet kisses that turned hot and intense. She let his tongue explore her mouth, and she reached between them, pulling her panties down a little. He chuckled and gave one hard yank, ripping them off. Then he shoved his pajamas down and retrieved a condom from his bag close beside them. It was a little difficult to get in a comfortable position in the tight confines of the bag, which made her laugh. It took him a few times to get it right. When he buried his shaft inside her, she arched her back at the sensation of being filled by him. There was no point where she could feel an end to her and a beginning to him.

She moaned against his conquering lips as they moved together, making love. Each time he sank inside her, that burning core of love within her seemed to burn even brighter, like the birth of a new star that would burn for millions of years, maybe longer. The pleasure between them built until they came together, shivering and shuddering as ecstasy rippled through them like rocks dropped into a still pond.

"I love you," she whispered as the sunlight turned his dark lashes a softer burnished gold.

He stole a sweet kiss that melted every bone in her body into a delicious puddle beneath him. "I love you too."

Ellie gave a little wakening cry from her travel crib. Caroline and Lincoln shared one more kiss.

"I'll be right back," Lincoln murmured, he headed to the restroom to dispose of the condom.

Caroline climbed out of the sleeping bag and found a spare pair of underwear before she went to retrieve Ellie. She bounced the baby in her arms, murmuring a gentle lullaby her mother used to sing to her and the baby gazed up at her with wide eyes. Ellie stretched her tiny hands up, touching Caroline's cheek. Caroline gently caught one of the baby's hands and pressed a kiss to the little palm. The baby cooed, gasped and squirmed in response. When she looked up she saw Lincoln had returned from the restroom and stood there in nothing but pajama pants, watching her with a stark longing in his eyes. She understood that look all too well and it made her heart quiver like notes upon a harp.

"My turn to feed the little tyke." He gently took Ellie from Caroline and carried her around, whispering softly to her while he prepared a bottle for her. Kirby watched them, his tail wagging, sending small clouds of dust up from the floor.

Caroline gazed at them a moment longer before she took some fresh clothes to the ladies' room, along with one of the boxes of the pregnancy kits. It was time she tested one out. She followed the instructions, then got dressed while she counted the minutes. Then, with a shaking hand, she retrieved the test from the counter and looked at it. A single blue line. She checked the symbol against the box. Negative. Not pregnant. She was torn between relief and disappointment.

We have Ellie. Her niece would be a delight to them, always and forever. No matter what happened in the future. She dropped the test in the trash and came back into the center of the library.

"She's fed but needs a change," Lincoln said, handing Ellie to her. "Your turn."

"Thanks." Caroline changed Ellie's diaper and put her back in the crib so she and Lincoln could eat.

"So...I used the test," she said quietly as she took a bite of the canned peaches they'd brought in from the car.

Lincoln watched her intently. "And?"

"Not pregnant," she said.

"Are you okay?" Lincoln covered her knee with one hand.

"Yeah. It's probably for the best. I guess I was excited about the idea of a baby, but right now? We have Ellie, and until we figure out a vaccine, I don't want to risk another innocent life."

Lincoln nodded. "Agreed."

They packed the car, and she took a moment to collect a few books. Classics by Dumas, Brontë, Austen, some modern ones by Graham Greene, J. K. Rowling, and C. S. Lewis. She took books that meant something, books that were part of humanity's legacy, a legacy she would fight with her last breath to preserve for Ellie and future generations to come. When she carried the box up to Lincoln, he couldn't hide his smile.

"Only one box? I was convinced you'd try to sneak another one."

She chuckled, but her heart ached as she faced the library again.

"I wish we could stay here forever." Safe, surrounded by the stories of people long dead. The place of the written word had become more of a sanctuary than a tomb. No one would come back here, not for a long while. She sensed it deep inside her bones, and it filled her with sorrow.

We were your last visitors, and I'm sorry we couldn't stay. She bid farewell to the library and tried to ignore the pain in her heart that stung sharply for having to leave it all behind.

"You sure you're okay?" Lincoln asked as he curled an arm around her waist and pulled her into his embrace.

"Yeah. I will be," she murmured. For the hundredth time, she marveled at the thought of their chance meeting, of how they'd almost killed each other, and how he had casually stated he'd have her in his bed. He had been right, damn him. But she had no regrets in letting fate or instincts make that choice easier. Lincoln was her man, now and always. Just as Ellie and Kirby were hers, in a different but equally important way.

"How far to Atlanta?" she asked once they got back to the road.

"Maybe two days if we don't have any more major issues on the highways and if we continue to stop for supplies."

They drove for three hours before Ellie's cries made it clear she needed a change, and Kirby took to whining as well. Lincoln found a shopping center not far off the highway, and they piled out. Kirby ran to the nearest bushes, and Caroline took Ellie into the burger joint they'd parked next to. She used a lantern to illuminate the dark women's bathroom as she changed the baby's diaper.

Ellie kicked her chubby legs and squawked loudly for such a tiny creature. Caroline laughed and tickled her tiny feet, playing peek-a-boo with her. Then she fixed her onesie and tucked her back in the portable car seat and opened the door to leave the restroom.

She froze as she stared down the barrel of a gun.

She knew only what Lincoln had taught her about weapons, but she recognized the extended barrel of a silencer. Her gaze went from the gun to the man holding it. He was dressed similar to Lincoln when she'd first met him, wearing black military pants and a dark sweater. Another gun was tucked away in a shoulder holster. He wore a backpack, and his eyes were cold and expressionless. Military? The three men in Nebraska who'd tied her up had dressed like it, but according to Lincoln they hadn't been. But something about this man was different. He held himself still, utterly calm, not high from a killing spree. He was a true soldier, like Lincoln was.

Caroline didn't move, but when Ellie sighed and wriggled in her car seat, Caroline wanted to push the baby carrier behind her. Where was Lincoln? Or Kirby?

"Please... Don't hurt my baby," she said, keeping her voice calm. "Let's talk it out. Tell me what you want." She nodded at her backpack. The man's eyes didn't leave her face. "Please. She's innocent. We need to band together, not hurt each other."

The man's eyes widened. "It's you, isn't it?" He suddenly grinned, but that smile terrified her. No one smiled like that now, not unless they found something they wanted. That wasn't a good sign. She slowly set the carrier down behind her. The man was still grinning, and he started to lower his weapon.

Caroline struck. Lincoln's lessons paid off. She kicked out in a martial arts move that would have made Lincoln proud and knocked the gun from his hand. It hit the floor and slid far out of reach. Then she grabbed her own gun from her hip in a move she'd practiced a hundred times until she could do it without thinking. Just because she believed in hope for all mankind, it didn't make her an idiot. She would hear these men out, but she wasn't going to do that by giving up a safety advantage.

"Don't fucking move," she growled, aiming the gun at the man's head. Lincoln had said never aim for the chest on anyone who looks military. They might be wearing protective Kevlar. A head shot at close range was easier to pull off.

"Easy." The man wasn't smiling anymore. "I just want to talk. No one is going to hurt you or the kid."

"After that little greeting of yours? Yeah, right." She scowled at him. Every protective instinct she had seemed to have tripled with Ellie nearby. Her hands didn't even tremble as she held the gun, and she knew they wouldn't shake if she pulled the trigger.

"We are better than we think we are," the man said. "This is what we are fighting for, the nobility inside all of us, the purity of our purpose, to save each other." He repeated her words from her broadcast back to her, the ones spoken into the satellite radio. "You're Caroline Kelly."

"I... Yes. I am."

"We found you." He was still smiling. "I can't believe it. We've been on your trail for three days. We were in Kansas City," he explained, still keeping his arms in the air in surrender.

"*We?* There's more of you?"

"Three. We left from Fort Riley in Kansas. We were headed back to Fort Benning in Georgia when we heard you on the radio. I'm Sergeant Miles Jackson, Army Ranger, at your service, ma'am." He snapped to attention and saluted her.

She stared at him, still too afraid to lower the gun. "I'm Caroline, but you already know that. This is my niece, Ellie. Where are your men, Sergeant?"

"Miles, please," he corrected, still grinning. His smile seemed less threatening now, but she still didn't trust him. Now he reminded her of a golden retriever, with his happy smile, boyish good looks, and blond hair. The military demeanor had vanished.

"They're scouting the area. We saw your vehicle pass ours on the highway and hoped it was you, so we tailed you to this area."

"My dog... Have you seen him?" She prayed they hadn't done anything to Kirby. She might still shoot this man if he had.

"Dog? I didn't see" Kirby leaped through the open door, startling her as he skidded to a stop in front of Caroline. Lincoln was on his heels, gun raised.

"Down on the ground!" Lincoln bellowed.

"Lincoln, wait!" She tried to step between the two men, but Miles instantly blocked her from danger. He glared at Lincoln.

"Don't hurt her," Miles said to Lincoln.

Lincoln glared back at Miles. "She's not going to be hurt. She's *my* woman."

Miles relaxed slightly and glanced her. "He's with you?"

She nodded. "Everyone calm down. Lincoln, Sergeant Jackson was looking for me. He heard me on the radio. He said he and his friends were headed to Fort Benning."

Lincoln kept his gun raised as he watched Miles. "You're not alone?"

"Nope, he's not," another man said as two armed men stepped through the doorway of the restaurant, crushing broken glass between their boots as they came up behind Lincoln. They both aimed their guns at Lincoln.

"We found her." Miles nodded toward Caroline.

"Sergeant, tell your men to back off and lower their weapons. Now. Lincoln will hurt them if they don't," Caroline said.

"Lincoln?" one of the men by the door said. He was an attractive black man with a sternness about his lips and eyes. "That you, Atwood?"

Lincoln's hand stayed firm on the gun. "Holt?" He kept his eyes fixed on Miles and Caroline.

"You made it out of Omaha after all?" The man Lincoln called Holt lowered his gun, and the second man followed suit, albeit a little slower.

"Omaha was boring as fuck." Lincoln laughed and lowered his gun. He shook Holt's hand before pulling him in for a hug.

"So now you've gone domestic? Woman, baby, family dog?"

Kirby seemed to sense that the danger had passed and was now tentatively waving his tail and looking between the four men.

"They're my unit," Lincoln assured him. "But you could say I'm starting to settle." Caroline blinked. She'd never seen Lincoln so calm or playful before. He was almost a stranger to her, not that she minded the change.

"Caroline, come over here. You've got to meet Julian. Julian Holt, this is Caroline Kelly." Julian bowed like a gentleman and smiled broadly.

"Lincoln, this is Sergeant Miles Jackson and Lieutenant Jason Huang." The Asian man who was the third in their party nodded in greeting. "Airborne Rangers."

"So you're Caroline. We've been listening to you every night for the last week. Been trying to track you down," Julian said.

"Really?" Caroline picked up Ellie's carrier and move closer to Lincoln, not out of fear, just nerves. She felt outnumbered by all these military men, regardless of how nice they might be.

"Yeah, you're famous. We've run into some survivors on the roads. All of them are headed to Atlanta. They want to help." Jason held out a hand to shake hers. "It's a real honor to meet you, ma'am."

Her heart fluttered with joy and hope. "People are really going? How many have you seen?" She couldn't help but wonder why she and Lincoln hadn't seen anyone themselves, but perhaps it was because he'd been keeping them on smaller highways, avoiding places he worried scavengers might be lurking in wait for innocent travelers.

"We've seen maybe two hundred or so in the last six days," Jason said. "Probably more out there. We had a ton of extra radios, so we been passing them to anyone we can and telling them to listen for you. We managed to organize a couple of caravans out of the survivors so they had safety in numbers while heading south to the CDC."

"Why didn't you go straight to Atlanta?" Lincoln asked. "They could probably use the help."

"We didn't know you were with her. We were hoping to offer a military escort, but looks like you've got it covered." Miles chuckled.

Lincoln met Holt's gaze. "We can still use your help. We don't know what lies between us and Atlanta. If all those people heard her broadcast, I fear some lowlifes might smell an opportunity."

"I hear that. We'd be glad to tag along," Julian confirmed. "You need help with supplies?" He looked at the baby carrier with curiosity. "You actually have a baby with you?"

"Yes, we do," Caroline admitted and faced Ellie toward the men. "This is my niece, Ellie."

"Cute kid." Julian shot an amused look at Lincoln. "Nice to see you playing daddy."

"Shut the fuck up," Lincoln snapped in a mocking tone. Kirby bounced around, only knowing there were more people around to play with, and barked as everyone moved back out to the street.

"Julian, Huang, check the mall for baby supplies. Jackson, you're with me. We'll get food and gas," Lincoln ordered. Caroline realized that Lincoln must have outranked all of them. Or maybe it wasn't about military rank, but because he had been with her longer. She honestly had no idea, but watching them made her think of nature documentaries about wolf packs. Lincoln was clearly the alpha.

She carried Ellie out to the car, and Kirby stuck with her. She removed the baby from the seat and held her, letting her twine her tiny fists in Caroline's hair as she watched the weak spring sun stretch the shadows of lampposts and the occasional abandoned car over the parking lot.

People were listening...to her. A girl from Missouri who had once worked in internet advertising. Hundreds of people were on the way, ready to help each other, all because she had tried to remind them what it meant to keep hope alive.

She stroked Ellie's pale blonde hair and breathed in the child's clean scent. This was what she was fighting for. Ellie's future. These days of darkness, of shadows, fear and death... They had to end. The legacy of humanity was not going to be extinction, not on her watch. She knew what she would say tonight. While the CDC worked on the blood, she was going to get the power back on. After that she would find a way to reestablish law and order and find a way to assign people new jobs based on their skill sets so they could all work together to rebuild. She just prayed everyone would be willing to listen.

———

I n just two days, Lincoln and Caroline reached the outskirts of Atlanta. Julian, Miles, and Jason were on their tail in the armored Humvee they'd taken from Fort Riley. Lincoln felt the hope that Caroline had created in him grow even stronger. He had assumed Julian was dead like all the rest when they had divided up before he'd accompanied Adam and Whitaker to Omaha. But Julian was immune. Ninety-five of a hundred people died, Julian had said, but still that was five men or women the virus hadn't been able to take down, for every ninety-five who crashed and bled out. That meant there were a hell of a lot of survivors out there they needed to find and help.

"We're close now," Lincoln said.

Caroline was watching the window, silent and focused. Ellie and Kirby and even the chickens were asleep. Last night, he and Caroline had slept without any bad dreams, knowing that others now watched over them.

"I hope Erica Kennedy is still okay. We haven't heard from her except that first time," she said.

"I know." He hadn't wanted to worry Caroline about that, but it was possible the CDC had been compromised or that men who wanted access to a building with power had taken over. It had been risky to announce that the Centers for Disease Control had a backup power source in their building.

Lincoln turned down CDC Parkway and then hit

the brakes when he saw the building and what was in front of it. A tall glass building created a shadow over the parking lot, which was full of hundreds of vehicles. A small town seemed to have popped up in front of the building.

He started to drive a little slower. "Holy shit."

"They came," Caroline whispered.

"Yeah, they did. You helped make this happen, Caroline," Lincoln said, completely in awe of his woman and what she had done.

"There has to be more out there. Think of all those people who don't have satellite radios. God, Lincoln, we have to get the power back on and the cell towers... maybe we can use the emergency broadcast system..."

"Easy, honey, we'll find a way. One step at a time." He cupped her shoulder and gave it a squeeze. They would have to see what the situation was before he'd let Caroline go running across the US trying to save the world. It was still a wilderness out there, and it would be a long time before it was safe. But this was a start.

A group of armed men stopped their vehicles before they could reach the makeshift village. A man in a sheriff's uniform stood at the front of the armed group. He looked to be in his midfifties, but he was fit, and Lincoln would bet anything he'd be a bear in a fight.

Lincoln stopped the car. "Stay here. I'll talk with him. If it starts to look like it's going south, get in the driver's seat and get Ellie out of here."

"But" Caroline opened her tempting lips.

"Don't worry. It'll be fine, but I have to plan for every possibility. Do it for Ellie." He waited until she answered with a nod, and then he walked over to the sheriff and his men.

"Welcome to Atlanta," the sheriff said. "We are running a safe camp here, so if you have a mind for trouble, you can go back to where you came from." He rested his hand close to his gun, and the men flanking him all eyed Lincoln with open distrust.

"I want no trouble. I'm Major Lincoln Atwood. My girlfriend and I need to see Dr. Erica Kennedy, the interim CDC director." He couldn't help but wonder if Caroline heard him from inside the car.

"Is that so? What for? There's no vaccine yet," the sheriff pointed out.

"I know. That's why we're here, isn't it? To all give blood samples? I am immune, and so is Caroline." He jerked his head toward the SUV.

"Caroline?" The sheriff's eyes widened. "You don't mean Caroline Kelly?" The sheriff was staring at her now with a look of wonder, like she was a Hollywood celebrity, and her name rippled through the men behind him like a wildfire.

"Yes." Lincoln finally understood.

These people came here to help, which he had expected, but he had not thought about the fact that Caroline might become something more, something bigger than herself every time she talked. In delivering her messages of hope, she had become humanity's beacon in their darkest hour, a voice that spoke to something deeper than any current of fear or self-interest. She spoke to a person's soul. Just like she had done for him, she had done for everyone here.

"Could we meet her?" a man behind the sheriff asked, his face bright with eagerness.

"Sure." Lincoln looked over his shoulder at the SUV and waved for Caroline to come over. She retrieved Ellie from the car before she came to stand at Lincoln's side.

"You're a mom?" the sheriff asked, bending over to look at Ellie.

"She's my niece. My sister and her husband didn't make it." Caroline set Ellie down and held out her hand. "I'm Caroline"

"I heard." The sheriff enveloped her hand in both of his, almost hugging it. "I'm Pete Andrews, the sheriff of this little unofficial camp."

"Hi." Caroline smiled at him. "You guys heard me on the radio?"

Pete nodded. "We did. You..." He cleared his throat and removed his hat, holding it in his hands respectfully. "You've helped a lot of people, Ms. Kelly. Me among them." He looked to Lincoln briefly. "I was one minute away from calling it quits, ma'am. Then I heard you, like the voice of an angel." The group of men behind Pete were nodding in agreement.

"I...wow, I had no idea." Caroline turned bright red and leaned instinctively against Lincoln. He instantly curled an arm around her shoulders, drawing her closer. He was so damn proud of her that he was almost shaking. He had to remind himself why they were here.

"Is Dr. Erica Kennedy here?" he asked the sheriff again. "We haven't heard from her in almost a week. We're worried something might have happened to her."

"She's inside. She's fine. She's been overloaded with all the samples. We have over two thousand people here in the area who came to give blood."

"Two thousand?" Lincoln stuttered over the numbers.

"A little more than that, but yeah. We've only been here two days, but we've managed to organize a small tent town. We're working next to move people into the nearby housing divisions for long-term residences." Pete grinned. "Come on, let's get you inside to see Dr. Kennedy."

Lincoln and Caroline followed the sheriff inside. Lincoln noted that their escort had remained behind to keep watch over Kirby and the cars. Then they headed for the glass building. He was too afraid to believe in good news, but he so desperately wanted to believe they had a fighting chance.

Please... God...if there was ever a time to answer the prayers of a sinner like me...

16

Excerpt from the private journal of Dr. Erica Kennedy, interim director of the CDC:

I feel like I am chasing a ghost. Everywhere I turn in these wet markets I see places where the virus could linger and grow. Stagnant pools of water, the droppings of birds mingling with pigs. The sharp claws of monkeys who bite and scratch anyone who gets too close to their cages. The filth and the mix of animals is everywhere, and I feel the seeds of mankind's destruction being sown and brewing like a deadly apocalyptic storm upon the horizon.

I've taken dozens of samples and found no trace of the virus as of yet. Where is it hiding if not in plain sight? This morning, I received an urgent call to visit an apartment, one I suspect our previous field agent visited. But when I arrived, no one was there to let me in. I used an old spare hotel key card to pick the lock of the squalid residence. I entered with caution, wearing a mask and two layers of gloves. I kept my sleeves and pants taped closed. It is not my best improvised protection, but it is all I've had time to arrange.

The home was quiet; the silence was like a tomb as I entered. It was dark and dusty, with the smell of death, that sharp, pungent scent that makes every instinct inside me scream out to run away. The deeper I moved into the residence, the heavier the smell became.

"Hello?" I called out in both English and Mandarin. No answer. I walked into the next room, a storage room, and froze. Hundreds of cages were piled up on top of each other, a veritable menagerie. Each creature inside was dead. A lifeless crab monkey stared blindly at me with milky-white, glassy eyes rimmed red. Its body was coiled tight, as if whatever had killed it made every muscle seize up. Its tiny clawed paws were curled into fists, and its face was uncharacteristically stoic. No death grimace, no silent scream. Like Marburg or Ebola, whatever this virus was, it killed parts of the brain, liquefying the tissue until the creature lost control of its facial expressions entirely. But there was something different about this virus. It did not leave the bodies to melt and decay. No, this monkey's body was clearly starting to harden, to mummify.

What on earth was this thing? I wanted to take samples, but this was a hot room, one that was brimming with hundreds of millions of virus strands. It was possibly even airborne. The thought strangled me, and I rushed from the room, trying to resist the urge to rip my mask from my face to breathe easier.

Something grabbed me, and I screamed as a man with bloodshot eyes shouted at me in Mandarin.

"Go, save yourself!" But his hand curled around my upper

arm, and I could not get free. Then the man gargled, and his eyes rolled back in his head as he vomited all over my face and chest.

Black vomit. Terror the likes of which I have never known swept over me. I kicked the man in the stomach, and he released me. I ran from the apartment and stopped in the front yard, gasping as I dragged the mask off my face and stripped off the protective gear. I tossed the contaminated items on the ground and started weeping. Protocol didn't matter anymore. The damage was done. He had vomited in my eyes, and I hadn't worn any protective goggles. I knew what would happen now. I was among the dead, and my days were numbered.

Caroline stared up at the pristine interior of the CDC lobby as she and Lincoln followed Sheriff Andrews through the maze of the expensive light-gray leather chairs and the clean white tables at the café in the main waiting area. They caught an elevator up to the third floor, and Caroline couldn't believe she was surrounded by electricity.

"They really do have power?"

The sheriff nodded. "There's a generating station a few miles away that we've been able to keep running. It's powering this area and extends for about a hundred miles. The CDC was running off gas generators until a month ago. Then Erica was able to figure out how to get the station running. We have men and women working shifts to keep things operational."

"Do you know where the other generating stations are in the area?" Lincoln asked.

"No, but city hall would still have paper records. What are you thinking?" Andrews asked.

"Caroline thinks we need volunteers to start moving out to the areas where the stations are. We need to expand the grid. It may take a few years, but we could get the whole state back up and running with some effort and coordination," Lincoln suggested.

Caroline's heart swelled with pride as she watched him get involved. He'd been listening when she'd talked the other night about how she'd try to get the power back on.

"We can start talking about that tonight, especially with the people who've already given samples. They're looking for something to do to help."

The elevator opened, and they stepped into a laboratory.

"Dr. Kennedy, we've got visitors," the sheriff called out.

"What?" A dark-haired, Indian woman emerged from the nearest closed door with a hazard label on it.

"Caroline Kelly and Major Lincoln Atwood are here to see you."

"Oh my God!" Erica rushed to embrace them as though she'd known them all her life. "Sorry," she said with a laugh, eyes bright with emotions. "I can't believe you're actually here."

"It's okay." Caroline's eyes stung with tears as well.

"We were worried when we didn't hear any more broadcasts from you after that first time."

"I'm so sorry. I was listening to you every night. Then people started arriving by the hundreds, and I'm down to two lab technicians aside from me who can handle the level 4 hot zone viruses. I'm trying to train the remaining staff of eight that we still have. We'll need all the help we can get once we have a working vaccine."

"Level 4 what?" Caroline asked.

"Level 4 hot zone is a certain level assigned to severely dangerous viruses. Viruses like Hydra-1 are so dangerous that they require special training for those who come in contact with them, or else the technician can spread the virus by accident and cause a fresh outbreak."

"Okay... But all the people outside are immune, right?" Caroline was worried about all the people she'd seen outside.

"As far as I can tell. Most of them explained during their blood draws how they had come into close contact with some of the infected Hydra-1 victims and they didn't contract the disease. Like me—I had one of those early victims vomit on me. I survived, by the sheer grace of God, I'm sure." Erica's gaze grew distant for a moment, as though she was plagued by dark memories. She shook herself out of it. "Sorry. Why don't you come this way, and I'll get your blood samples and your medical histories."

Caroline went first, sitting in the sterile plastic chair of the exam room while Erica withdrew a vial of blood.

"Now, Caroline, what was your exposure?"

"Well, I was at the O'Hare airport—"

"What?" Erica gazed at her, stunned. "You were the sole survivor who was quarantined, weren't you? I thought you might have been a rumor. I wasn't high up enough in the CDC at the time to be at your location when you were discovered. I heard about you in a briefing, but I couldn't believe it. I wanted to try to find you, but the papers regarding your information were lost, and the hospital was abandoned. We all thought you were dead."

Caroline shivered, and Lincoln wrapped an arm around her waist and leaned in, kissing her temple. "I survived the terminal and the hospital. By the time I escaped, I didn't fully understand the chaos around me. Everyone was panicking. I returned to my apartment and hid for a week. By the time everything went quiet, I realized what that meant..." Her voice broke. She didn't want to ever relive those days, the bodies everywhere, the danger and the fear. And that awful silence, so loud that it seemed to roar like a jet engine.

"I know." Erica's voice was dead and world-weary. "Everyone is gone. I lost my husband and my two children."

"I'm sorry," Caroline whispered.

Erica nodded and took a deep breath, focusing on

her work. "You're next, handsome." Lincoln sat down and offered up his arm without a word.

"I'll get this tested right away," Erica said as she finished.

"Doctor, are we any closer to developing a vaccine?" Lincoln finally asked.

"We think so," Erica said. "I'm trying to replicate the rVSV–ZEBW vaccine, which was in trial testing for Ebola. It is a recombinant, replication–competent vaccine. There's some promise the same process will be compatible with Hydra-1."

"What does that mean?" Caroline asked.

"Think of it like this—it's how we use a dead flu virus vaccine to inoculate people against live versions. The vaccine, if done correctly, can be engineered to express a glycoprotein, which is something that helps your cells interact. The vaccine would make that glyco-protein come from Hydra-1, so the person's cells would then be provoked into neutralizing an immune response to the virus. It's like injecting a tiny portion of the strand of a single virus rather than a complete strand. A full strand can replicate—a full strand can kill you. And it only takes one strand to do it."

Caroline felt dizzy at the thought of something so tiny having such devastating power.

"But the more blood samples I have, the better I can focus on the way the virus interacts with immune people versus someone who is susceptible to infection."

Erica finished collecting a sample from Lincoln and

then looked them both over in concern. "You two look exhausted. How much sleep have you had?"

"Not much," Caroline said. Lincoln merely grunted.

"Why don't you sleep in one of our guest rooms tonight? We have places where our staff can stay overnight. You will be safe here," she said, and by the look she sent them Caroline knew that Erica had some understanding of what they had both been through in the last few months.

"This way." Erica led them to the elevators and down to the second floor. There were two halls on either side of the elevator bay that had real bedrooms, no hospital rooms, and a bathroom complete with a shower.

"We usually have dinner around seven if you want to come down to the café. Pete finds food, and we usually make a decent meal."

"We have chickens!" Caroline offered. "They lay great eggs. We would be happy to start filling the kitchens with them."

Erica grinned. "Real eggs would be a treat. We've been going off of powdered eggs for a long time. I know that Pete and the others have been working to find any livestock nearby to get a farm up and running, but we aren't located near much farm land."

Erica left them alone in the room while Caroline checked on Ellie. Holt and the others volunteered to take care of Kirby for a while. The baby was still fast asleep in her portable crib. Caroline collapsed onto the bed, covering her face with her hands as she tried to come to terms with the fact that she was here in Atlanta, at the CDC. And there was hope, real hope, all around them. It felt impossible, yet here they were. She looked up at Lincoln with tears in her eyes.

"Honey, you're killing me." He knelt in front of her, cupping her face in his hands, and then he leaned in and kissed her.

And just like that, her love for him burned away all fear and doubt. She wrapped her arms around him, pulling him closer. They moved without words, shedding clothes until they were skin to skin. Lincoln pushed her flat on the bed and settled into the cradle of her thighs. He thrust into her, and she threw her head back, closing her eyes as exquisite pleasure began to build with every thrust.

I'm alive... There's hope... There's us. She dug her fingers into his back, moaning as he moved within her, over and over, his steady rhythm fast and glorious as he reminded her how good it felt to surrender to instinct and emotion.

Lincoln knew just the way to master her body, to control it and gently demand her surrender to his dominance. He nipped her neck and then captured her hands, pinning them to the mattress on either side of her face as his body rocked into hers, their hips colliding.

Gazes locked, they didn't look away, didn't kiss for a long minutes as he circled his pelvis, finding a new spot to hit deep within her over and over. Her breasts rubbed against his chest, sweat dewing upon their bodies as they moved in time.

She couldn't forget how much she'd claimed to hate him and how she wouldn't sleep with him even if were the last man on earth. How wrong she'd been about him...but she knew it was because he was the man for her, not because he'd been the only man there. Destiny...fate, whatever you wanted to call it, had brought them together that night at the grocery when he'd captured her. And now she was completely his and he was hers.

"I love your eyes when you start to come," he growled low, the rumbling sound making her even wetter. She wriggled her hips, urging him to fuck her even harder.

"I love everything you do," she panted back, grinning at the look of primal delight on his face.

"Then you're going to fucking love this, honey." A second later, he unleashed that raw, almost violent passion that drove her into new heights of ecstasy. He fucked her like there was no tomorrow, like it was the last few precious seconds they had on earth together. She was going to scream his name in a second and she didn't care. It was worth it to feel him inside her, driving in and out endlessly.

The climax hit her, and she could only gasp his name aloud. He slammed a hand against the headboard and growled, his eyes fixed on hers as he followed her into bliss. They collapsed together in a tangle of limbs and sleepy shared smiles. Neither of them moved for the longest time. There was something undeniably intimate to lay together like that, their bodies still coming down from the sexual high and feeling the invisible bonds of love only strengthening between them. He cupped one of her breasts, gently stroking the pad of his thumb over a nipple and she shivered in delight.

"I love when you touch me," she whispered. Whenever his hands were on her, she felt cherished, even when he was making love to her like a wild animal.

"One of these days, I'll make love to you slow," he whispered. "Soft, sweet, like a proper gentleman."

Caroline giggled, her face flushing as she looked up at him from beneath her dark lashes.

"I don't know...I like how you do it now. It's really... hot." She felt embarrassed admitting that she liked him fucking her like that. Her old boyfriends had all been so polite, so very missionary and gentle. But when a man lost control, when he wanted her so much he lost his mind, that...that was hotter than anything in her wildest dreams. And that's how it was when Lincoln made love to her.

The bed creaked slightly as they shifted a little. Caroline threaded her fingers in his hair, playing with the silken strands and lightly scraping her nails against his skin on the back of his neck. His eyes almost rolled back in his head and his cock jerked inside her.

"That feels good," he whispered. "So fucking good."

Caroline continued to touch the nape of his neck and he lowered his head to kiss her. Their mouths moved slowly, languidly. He tasted her like he was sampling a fine bottle of whiskey and the following groan that escaped him echoed on her own lips. That single, long kiss erased the world around them, leaving her in a private cocoon of warmth with just Lincoln, their bodies connected as tightly as their hearts.

She looked up at him after their mouths broke apart. There were a thousand things she wanted to tell him, but she couldn't seem to find anything that truly expressed what lay in her heart.

"Thank you for finding me, Lincoln, for believing in me."

He nuzzled her cheek. "Thank you for finally sleeping with me." He cracked a wolfish grin and she smacked his chest, laughing.

"I'm serious!" she said.

He sobered. "I'm the thankful one, honey. You're something special and I was the lucky man to stumble upon you first. And there's no way I'm letting you go now." And then he kissed her again and for a long while later neither of them thought of anything else except that single, potent love spell sort of kiss that everyone dreams about having some day. It was the kind of kiss a person built dreams upon.

Finally, Lincoln pulled the covers up around them as she lay close against him, feeling his heart beat against her cheek. She could almost set her own heart to the steady rhythm of his. Caroline drifted to sleep, and for the first time in months she wasn't plagued with night-mares, not at first.

She was back at home, eating dinner with her parents, laughing as Natalie and Rick teased each other. Ellie tried to communicate in her own baby babble way, and her little blue eyes were full of mischief and wonder. But then Ellie coughed, and her eyes were suddenly wreathed with a strange red color. Then blood trickled down her tiny nose, and she coughed again.

"Ellie!" Caroline bolted upright in bed. For a moment nothing around her was familiar. It took her a moment to back away from the panic she felt.

"Caro..." Lincoln tried to draw her back down in bed, but she didn't let him. Something had woken her. Something was wrong.

A tiny cough came from Ellie's crib. Caroline leapt out of bed, throwing her clothes back on before she rushed over to check on the baby.

"No!" The word was a strangled cry as it escaped her. Blood had clotted around Ellie's nose, and her face was pale—too pale.

"Caroline?" Lincoln got out of bed, pulling on his pants and boots. He knelt down beside her.

"I thought she was immune. I was sure. How else could..." Caroline was numb. Frozen. What could she do? An awful roar seemed to fill her head like the sound of a tornado, a deafening noise that made it impossible to think.

"Hang on, I'm going for help." Lincoln's words seemed to come through the vast distance of a tunnel submerged with water.

She reached out and lifted the baby into her arms, cradling Ellie against her chest. At that moment she would have given anything for the child to take her strength, her immunity. Tears fell onto the baby's blanket, one that Caroline's mother had stitched by hand with the kind of love only a grandparent could have.

"You are our hope," she whispered to Ellie. "You're the last of the Kellys." The baby blinked slowly, and her blue eyes were glassy. "Don't you die on me, do you hear?"

Lincoln burst into the room with Erica right behind him. Caroline held out the baby, her body shaking. Erica carried the baby away, and Caroline stayed on the floor by the crib. Lincoln lifted her up into his arms and carried her back to the bed. They didn't speak. He understood her, understood that she needed the silence, needed to wall herself off from everything or else she wouldn't survive the grief that was laying siege to her heart.

Nat, I tried. I tried to take care of her. I loved her as if she were my own. I'm so sorry.

She closed her eyes, but she only saw her sister's face there waiting for her. Not her sister all grown up, but when they were little.

Nat leaned over the bathtub while Caroline bathed, sharing her favorite rubber ducky, which wore a black top hat. Nat turned the flashlight on as they giggled inside a blanket fort. Nat tossed Caroline the keys to her car so she could take her driver's test in Nat's vintage red Mustang. Now she saw her sister's face in her dying baby, and it was like seeing Nat's grave all over again.

She'd had hope, hope that had been crushed right in front of her. There would be no coming back from this grief if Ellie didn't survive.

———

L incoln watched night fall outside their small guest room in the CDC headquarters. He didn't want to leave Caroline alone, but he had to see Dr. Kennedy, see if there was any news on Ellie's condition.

"Caroline, I'll be right back," he murmured and kissed her temple. She didn't move as he left, didn't acknowledge him. She was in shock. He tucked her under a few extra blankets and left the room. Outside, his three friends stood facing him, their expressions grim.

"We heard. How is she?" Julian asked.

"Bad. She's in shock."

Miles and Jason stared down at their combat boots, wordless. They no doubt felt the same as him. Fucking useless. Even on the worst days of his job, when he was pinned down, the enemy surrounding him, the crack of gunfire and the explosion of debris around him, he still felt like he could fight back. Even his fists would be left if he ran out of ammo. But this? The invisible monster lurking in a space so small, dormant until a susceptible host came along? He couldn't put a bullet in the head of a microscopic strand of Hydra-1. Razor-sharp rage cut through him, and he surrendered to the wrath.

With a roar, he swung his fist into the nearest wall, and pain exploded up his arm to his shoulder.

Julian put a hand on his arm, but Lincoln nearly shrugged him off with a snarl—almost. He wasn't a wounded animal; it wouldn't help to lash out at his friend.

"Let's go see the doc," Miles suggested.

"Yeah, she may be close to a vaccine, assuming it can help someone who's already infected," Jason agreed. Julian gave Lincoln a gentle nudge as they headed down to Dr. Kennedy's lab floor.

One of her technicians, a woman named Isabel, met them at the entryway to the labs.

"Can we speak to the doc?" Miles asked.

"Only if you suit up." She nodded at the door behind her. It had a sign that said "Decontamination Area."

"I'll walk you through the procedure. You won't be near the hot zones. But you'll be next door, so it's an extra precaution."

"But we're immune," Jason pointed out.

"Yes," Isabel said. "But you could still take the dormant hot agent outside with you. We want to keep the CDC clean. If we ever find a way to stop this, we don't want an immune person years from now to walk through and touch a doorknob or an elevator button and give the virus a new home. Or God forbid, a chance to mutate into something that could kill even those of us who are naturally immune."

"You heard the woman," Miles said. "Suit up, guys."

Lincoln donned the suit as instructed and taped up his wrists and ankles before he followed Isabel inside. They were showered with chemicals and their suits inflated with air. The sound of the air filtration was loud.

"Can you hear me?" Isabel's voice came through a comm in her helmet. Lincoln flashed her a thumbs-up. She laughed a little.

"I can hear you if you talk."

"Oh." He felt a bit like an idiot. Of course these suits had microphones.

"Follow me, gentlemen." She led them down the hall and through another pressurized zone before they found Dr. Kennedy and Ellie. The baby was in an isolette incubator, to keep her body temperature maintained. Several little, flat, white pads with wires were taped on her chest, monitoring her vital signs.

She's so small. All this time, he thought Ellie was a fighter, this little bundle of strength, but now he saw how very small and delicate she truly was. Her breathing was shallow, and her temperature was at 101 degrees.

"Dr. Kennedy." Lincoln joined her at her desk, where she was peering into a microscope. Her clear face mask on her helmet was pressed against the eyepiece.

She waved him over and vacated the stool. "Come take a look at this." He looked into the microscope and saw several strand-like shapes wrestling with red blood cells.

"What is it?"

"The enemy. Hydra-1. The strands of the virus attacking Ellie's blood sample."

Lincoln's entire body went rigid with primal fear for the child he'd come to see as his own in the last week. To see what was happening to her, to see the devastation the virus wreaked upon her cells was horrifying in a way that would haunt him for the rest of his life. He focused on the microscope again, watching the most ancient battle play out. Deadly virus versus living cells.

"I injected a test vaccine into the cells. Normally, a vaccine works only to prevent falling ill, but I think what I've been creating so far may be a dual cure and vaccine, which means if it works, it could stop the progression of the virus already present in a person's system. So far the virus is fighting it but not succeeding in breaking the cells to replicate. If they were, we would see tons of bloated cell membranes exploded into a gooey gray residue."

"Is that the medical term for it?"

"You don't want the medical terms, trust me."

Lincoln peered hard at the virus in the cells. He didn't see any gray residue.

"So...is this the cure?" he asked, too afraid to hope.

"It *might* be," Erica said. "The virus takes a few days to manifest itself inside cells normally, so I can't say for sure."

Lincoln's breath shook as he glanced at the baby inside the incubator. "How long does Ellie have...before?"

"Before she crashes and bleeds out?" Erica said and blushed. "Sorry, that's the medical term. I didn't mean to—"

Lincoln shook his head. "It's fine. You warned me. But how long does she have?"

Erica looked to the bassinet.

"A day, maybe less. She's so small, the virus can destroy her much faster than it would an adult."

"Give the vaccine to her. *Now*."

Erica hesitated. "I plan to, but you have to realize, it could behave differently inside the human body. She could worsen and die even sooner. Caroline should be the one to—"

Lincoln turned to Julian. "Get Caroline in here." Julian nodded and left the room. Lincoln refused to leave Ellie and he knew Caroline would understand.

Erica and Lincoln watched Ellie silently while they waited. Ten minutes later, Caroline, fully suited up, came into the lab. She went straight to the baby, her face wet with tears. She splayed her gloved hands on the plastic case. Lincoln's vision blurred, and he had to remind himself to breathe.

"Julian said there might be a vaccine that could also be a cure?" she said.

"It's far from certain, but it's our best shot yet," Erica explained. "We won't know right away if she will survive. It's possible it can even speed up the virus."

Caroline stared at Lincoln and then at Ellie, her face pale as alabaster.

"Dr. Kennedy, if Ellie were your child, what would you do?"

Erica's eyes brightened with tears. She had to be thinking of her own children.

"I...would take the chance. She's already close to crashing. She can't survive if we do nothing. If she were an adult, she'd have a five percent chance of surviving. We don't have any records on infant survivors."

"We need to try." Lincoln could hear Caroline suck in a shaky breath through the radio.

Erica went to a lab station and prepared the vaccine. She came over to Ellie and opened the bassinet. Caroline reached down and carefully grasped one of Ellie's small hands. Lincoln took Ellie's other hand.

Caroline met his gaze and mouthed the words *"I love you."* He managed a nod back as Erica injected the needle into the baby's tiny thigh. Ellie twitched, and her small mouth opened with a startled cry.

"I'm sorry, sweetheart," Erica breathed. She wiped the injection site. No blood welled up. "Now we wait."

"Can I stay with her?" Caroline asked.

"Yes, but the battery on your suit will die in a few hours. I'll go get a replacement battery ready."

Lincoln pulled up a pair of stools by the baby's bassinet. "Grab two." He and Caroline both sat down to wait.

"Anything we can do?" Julian asked. He, Miles, and Jason still stood in the back of the room, wearing their spacesuits.

"Pray." He'd never been much of a believer, not in the churchgoing way. But there had been moments of his life, times when the darkness was ready to take him over, that he thought he could sense something, a peace and tranquility that came from an unknown place outside him. Whatever that was, he did believe in it.

Don't let Ellie die. We need this hope more than you can know.

❧ 17 ❧

Final radio broadcast from Adam Caine, the last president of the United States:

I know you are afraid. I know it feels like darkness is all around you. But you must remember that you are not alone. We are all in this together.

We have faced war, natural disasters, times of true crisis. This is no different. But this time we risk losing ourselves to the madness of our own fears. We must stop ourselves from falling apart. We must come together. A dozen sticks bound together are stronger than a dozen sticks alone. Trust each other, move past fear, leave behind hate.

We face hard times ahead. But if we work together, we will save each other. We will not go quietly into the night, we will not vanish without a fight. We will survive if we believe in each other. Do not give up that which is our greatest strength.

Do not give up our hope.

• • •

Caroline was exhausted, but she kept herself upright on her stool, her hand clasping Ellie's. From time to time, she would drift into a near sleep state and see flashes of memories of her family, both painful and beautiful. Like finding an old photo of lost loved ones hidden at the back of the drawer. She embraced the pain and the longing for what she had lost and poured that blend of emotions into her heart. Tears dropped down her cheeks inside her spacesuit.

She kept her vigil all night. By two in the morning, she jolted when the baby in the bassinet stirred and started to cry.

"Ellie?" She and Lincoln tensed, afraid they were seeing the spasms of death, but then Caroline really looked at the baby. The pallor of her skin was gone, replaced by a healthy peachy color. Ellie squirmed and fussed in a way Caroline had come to recognize.

"I think she's hungry. Dr. Kennedy, can we feed her?" Caroline asked.

Dr. Kennedy came over to check Ellie's vitals and take a blood sample. "Yes, if she's wanting food, we definitely should."

Lincoln left and returned with a bottle of baby formula. He handled it to Caroline, who picked the baby up and held her against her spacesuit-covered chest. The baby drank greedily from the bottle, and Caroline felt like she could finally breathe a sigh of relief, at least for the moment. Caroline waited for Dr. Kennedy's results, her heart pounding.

"The virus doesn't seem to be replicating. Ellie's system is fighting back. A few more days and her immune system might be able to remove the strains of the virus from her body altogether." She paused a moment before feeling confident enough to add, "I believe we have our cure."

Caroline bit her lip to hold back a sob of relief. Lincoln put an arm around her, their spacesuits crushing against one another.

"She's going to be okay, Caroline. Now you need to rest," he said.

"You both do," said the doctor. Caroline met his gaze. His brown eyes were dark and stormy with emotions, but he was just as exhausted as she was.

Jason entered the lab, grinning. "Lincoln, you and Caroline need to see this."

"What is it?"

"Just come."

"You know, at some point I'm going to have to remind people what the chain of command is," Lincoln muttered. They followed him out, careful to follow the decontamination procedures. Then they went to a tall bank of windows that looked out over the CDC courtyard.

"There," Jason said, his voice soft and reverent. "Take a look."

Caroline stepped up to the windows and looked

down. Hundreds of candles and lighters filled the night as a thousand people held a silent vigil below.

"My God..."

"They heard about Ellie. They've been there since midnight. Men, women, children. Praying for and believing in you. Caroline, you did this." Jason paused before he continued. "We were broken, a nation scattered on the winds, and you brought us back together. You made us one people again. A nation to fight for." Jason paused again. "You weren't simply just giving us hope. You spent the last week sharing ways to rebuild, safe zones, how to find supplies, blocked roads, the locations of wildfires. You told us what to do. You gave us a blueprint to come back to ourselves as a community."

Caroline stared speechless at the dots of light, and she remembered a poem her father used to read to her.

Out of the night that covers me,
Black as the pit from pole to pole,
I thank whatever gods may be
For my unconquerable soul.

"William Henley?" Jason asked, still smiling.

She nodded. "'Invictus.' My dad loved poems. He used to read them to me and Natalie all the time."

She looked out once more at the sea of candles, her heart bursting with hope and pride. Lincoln wrapped her tightly in his arms.

"Ellie is safe. You're safe," he whispered.

"*We're* safe," she corrected.

"What do we do now?" Jason asked him.

"What I've always said we'd do. We rebuild," Caroline said. "We make a list of the survivors, find out their knowledge, skills, and former jobs. We get the power on, we get farms going, we start searching for other survivors, the ones who didn't hear the broadcasts. We rebuild."

Miles joined them at the windows. "Finally, some orders we can follow."

Caroline leaned her head against Lincoln's shoulder and drew in a slow, deep breath.

"I love you," she whispered quietly enough so that only he could hear. His arms tightened around her, and he rubbed his cheek against the top of her head.

"I love you too."

But the words bore so much more than a simple declaration. They were vows that went deeper than blood, deeper than the necessities of survival. They were vows whole new worlds were built upon.

———

South Carolina, three months later

"How much farther?" Caroline asked. Lincoln turned their car up the wooded dirt road toward a distant cabin by a shimmering lake.

"It's over there." Lincoln nodded at a small log cabin, his heart hammering. Ellie sat in the back seat in her car seat, making small random chirping noises that made him laugh most of the drive to his parents' cabin. Now he was too nervous to think beyond what lay in that cabin.

"Stay in the car. Kirby and I will take a look around. Odds are..." His voice roughened suddenly.

Caroline reached over and covered his hand where he rested it on one of his thighs.

"We know the odds," she said. "But a little faith doesn't hurt, either." Her lips curved in a hopeful smile. How could he not have faith when he looked at her? In the last three months, Caroline had helped get the power back on around Georgia, and now they were looking toward the surrounding states. Lincoln had organized an effective security force, making Julian, Miles, and Jason team leaders. They had kept her people safe from any dangers still lurking out there, but there were fewer and fewer crazed bandits every day it seemed. Many tried to come in from the cold, so to speak, hoping to make amends.

They'd found another ten thousand people in the last couple of months, and all were now connected on the CB radio system until the cellular network could get back up and running. Caroline and the others sent out daily broadcasts, bringing together news to connect survivors, create supply depot stations, and a way to gather information about those who were ready to join society again. Caroline had the only radio that could reach the entire United States on the emergency channel, the one that Lincoln had carried out of the bunker from Adam's last moments alive. But Holt and the others had worked extensively to get the CB radio system up despite the limitations of the range. So far, the plan was working.

It was a start. A good one.

"Go on, we'll wait here." She nudged him, and he slowly climbed out of the car, the Irish setter quickly following him out. The dog kept sniffing the air and clung to his side as they walked the last fifty feet.

The oak trees around the cabin had grown taller and thicker since he'd last been there. How long had it been? Lincoln couldn't remember, maybe when he was twelve? The lake just beyond was small but always well stocked with fish, and a person could survive here for a long time if they had to.

Lincoln reached the front steps of the cabin and looked up toward the open screen door. A woman stood there, staring at him with wide, tearful eyes.

"Mom?"

"Oh my God. Lincoln! Harry, Lincoln's here!"

Lincoln winced when she said his father's name, but she shoved the screen door open and rushed into his arms. He caught his mother, her body still slender and delicate. Once a dancer, always a dancer. Her gray hair was cropped short, and she still smelled of lavender. The scent brought back a wave of memories, good memories, ones he'd sometimes thought he didn't actually have. Then she pulled back and looked up at him, smoothing her hands over his chest and then touching his face tenderly, her lips quivering.

"I knew you'd be alive," she whispered. "I knew it."

A shadow darkened the doorway of the cabin, and Lincoln looked past his mother to see his father. His old man was now indeed old, his hair completely silver and his eyes softer than Lincoln remembered them being.

"Sir," he said stiffly.

His father looked from him to the dog wagging his tail beside him. "So you finally got a dog, huh?" There was a twitch to his lips that made Lincoln think the old man was on the verge of smiling.

"Yeah...and a wife and a kid." He nodded toward the SUV at the edge of the clearing.

His mother almost shrieked. "What? Don't make

them stay in the car! Get them inside! I want to meet them!" His mother rushed back into the house, muttering frantically about guests, where her tea bags were, and for Harry to get the coffee brewing. Lincoln stood there on the porch, the scent of the woods and the lake wrapping around him as he stared at his father and his father stared back at him.

"I..." his father started. "I'm glad you're here, son. We've been worried sick, gave up hope, really." He leveled his gaze at Lincoln. His chest ached as he stared at the man he'd hated for so many years. "The world ending makes a man realize how many mistakes he made, you know?" Harry said quietly. "How many times I let you down, hurt you. I..." Harry cleared his throat and looked away. Lincoln did too. He could barely breathe, so he turned to wave Caroline inside. She was already halfway out of the car, carrying Ellie in her arms.

"Mr. Atwood?" Caroline greeted him, all smiles as she stepped onto the porch. "It's so nice to meet you. I'm Caroline."

For a second Harry just stared at her, and then he looked between her and Lincoln. "You're not...not Caroline Kelly from the radio?" His voice deepened as he struggled to contain himself.

"I guess I am." She blushed a little. Lincoln knew she'd never get completely comfortable with people recognizing her.

"Son, you married *her*?" Harry asked, mystified.

"I did," Lincoln said. They had stood in a small church in Georgia last month with a pastor, who'd married them. It had been one of a long list of best days of his life since he'd found Caroline all those months ago.

Harry stepped aside, and Lincoln led Caroline inside. "Glad to see you have your mother's good sense." Ellie fussed a little in her arms, and Lincoln reached for her, giving Caroline a break. When his mother came back into the living room with a tea tray, she nearly dropped the tray on the coffee table before she rushed over to coo at the baby and demand to hold her. She bustled Caroline off to the kitchen, leaving him and his father alone again. Just what he didn't want.

Harry shifted restlessly as he sat down on the couch. "So...you've been busy." His father might have asked him how he wanted to take his tea, the question was so mundanely spoken, yet Lincoln knew what his father was asking. How the hell had he survived?

"We've *all* been busy. I found Caroline, and we... well..." He wasn't used to talking this much, not to anyone but Caroline, and certainly not about what he was doing. "We've found so many survivors. Most of them were able to get to Atlanta, but we've got nearly forty states with listed survivors who have reached out. We're getting the power up and running, and we have a vaccine." He patted his pocket and pulled out a vial from the stash Erica had given him before they'd left

Atlanta, plus a couple of syringes. He and Caroline had been working their way through the small towns on their way here, providing the combination cure and vaccine to anyone they encountered in order to prevent a secondary outbreak.

"This is for you and Mom. It works." He didn't tell his father about how they'd almost lost Ellie, or the pain he'd felt as he realized he was a father watching his child suffering and fighting for her life. Instead, he simply handed over the vial and syringes.

"Thank you." Harry took them and remained silent until Caroline, Ellie, and his mother came back in.

"Rachel, the boy has vaccines for us." He used one on himself before he sat Lincoln's mother down in a chair and administered it to her arm.

"Lincoln, what's going to happen now? We've only heard the radio broadcasts," his mother said, looking to Caroline briefly. "I mean, you make things sound very positive and hopeful...but is it really?" Her face was lined with worries he wasn't used to seeing since he'd left home.

"Everything is going to be fine," he promised her.

"I understand your concerns," Caroline said as she helped his mother pour tea. "Am I just trying to keep hope up in a hopeless situation? Let me just say that things have changed a lot these last three months." She spoke to them about the future she was helping to build toward, and how they'd organized survivors across the country, setting up CB relays to keep people in touch and to organize food and supply transports. Her next project was international contact, to find out what had happened farther north and south and across the oceans. If they could get a few of the big cargo ships running, things could really start turning around.

His heart was so full of pride that he could barely hold it in. He glanced at his father once and saw tears in the old man's eyes.

A while later, his parents were settling Ellie in for a late-afternoon nap, and Lincoln walked Caroline out to the shore of the little lake. She reached for his hand and curled her fingers around his, giving him a gentle squeeze.

"You okay, mountain man?"

He laughed and reached up with his free hand to touch the beard he'd started to let grow again. It had been amusing to learn that his rugged look turned his little spitfire on more than anything.

"I'm okay, honey." He stared out at the beautiful view, the wilderness all around them, and for the first time he didn't feel so lost within it. The trees creaking in the breeze, the whisper of leaves, and the splashes of fish jumping to catch dragonflies hovering just above the water's surface...he felt at home.

He turned Caroline's face toward his so he could lean down to kiss her.

"I love you," he said, amazed at how easily those three little words came to his lips now, yet how the emotion behind them had such force he often thought his heart would shatter.

"I know." She gave him a mischievous look and then took off running down the shoreline. He raced after her, their laughter echoing off the water and the distant hills.

EPILOGUE

You are a child of the universe,
No less than the trees and the stars;
You have the right to be here.
And whether or not it is clear to you,
No doubt the universe is unfolding as it should.
—"Desiderata" by Max Ehrmann

Three years later

Caroline walked up to the palatial mansion, passing through the tall wrought-iron gates. She entered the house, the dust catching beneath her fingertips as she touched a banister leading upstairs. Dawn was breaking over the horizon, and beams of sunlight broke through the windows as she walked ahead. Lincoln followed, carrying Ellie in his arms. She was a bright-eyed, beautiful toddler full of mischief.

"Mama?" Ellie called out, her voice echoing in the grand hallways.

"Yes, honey?" Caroline kept moving, searching for something.

"Check the dining hall," Lincoln suggested as they walked deeper into the house. Kirby stayed close to Caroline as she entered the dining room. She pulled back some tall brocade curtains and light flooded the room, illuminating the portrait of a solemn, wise-looking man seated in a regal but practical red velvet chair. He leaned forward, one hand braced on the arm of the chair as though he meant to stand. He seemed to be in deep contemplation.

"Who dat?" Ellie pointed a tiny chubby finger at the man in the portrait.

"This, Ellie, is President Lincoln. A very good man. Your father was named after him." Caroline winked at Lincoln. He didn't resemble the president at all, except for the beard, which Caroline adored. The reminder of her mountain man who'd rescued her always made her heart race.

"Let's go find your office." Lincoln led her this time, showing her the way.

Even after all these years, he remembered the way. He reached the door to the office and opened it for her. She went inside, and Lincoln tested the light switch. There was a hum of electricity above them, and beautiful bright lights came on. They illuminated long yellow curtains and three windows behind a large ornate desk. Two couches filled the rest the room, and a grandfather clock sat dormant against one wall. At least eight flags were resting in stands around the room, three of which were American.

Caroline's hands shook as she touched the fabric. "I can't believe we're really going to live here."

"I can." He chuckled. "Now sit down at your desk so I can take a picture of you." Lincoln sat Ellie down on one of the couches, and Kirby hopped up next to her. The girl buried her face in the dog's fur, giggling, and Kirby took it all in stride, like he always did.

Lincoln held up the smartphone as Caroline sat down in the leather chair. They'd gotten the cell networks up a year ago, and they were close to restoring the internet since they'd gotten in touch with fifty other countries, which were all working together.

"Well? How does it feel, Madam President?" he asked, snapping a picture.

Caroline laughed, but she soon sobered. "I still can't believe it."

"I can," Lincoln replied. "You got the power back on and food back on shelves in stores, and you reestablished law in the cities—you did all of it."

"Now I just have to set up a new Supreme Court and try to get a government running that won't spend all its time playing politics."

"Couple of amendments might help in that regard,

but I think we've got a few generations before you'll need to worry about lobbyists and whatnot."

She made a note. "Yeah, well, best to get to work on that before it's a problem down the road."

Lincoln smiled. "See? Already thinking like a president."

"I still don't know if I want the job." Her gaze darted around the room in awe, and he saw clearly how intimidated she was.

"Best qualification I've heard yet."

She flushed. "All those things you said? It's not like I did them myself. I had tons of help."

"It doesn't matter. You were the catalyst, the leader to all of us."

"But you should have been—"

He shook his head. "Honey, I'm just a glorified bodyguard."

"Correction, you're the First Man," she said with another giggle.

He rolled his eyes. "Julian and the others are going to give me shit about that. But if I'm being honest, I like it. I'm not just the First Man—I'm your *only* man."

He came around the desk and leaned over, kissing her so that she forgot about being the leader of the United States. She touched his hand, stroking his wedding band. Then he reached out and caught her hand, lacing their fingers. They had been married almost three years ago. Back when everything had seemed dark and hopeless. Back when they had almost lost Ellie. But the darkness was gone. Now there was only light, only hope.

Lincoln removed Adam's radio from his waistband and held it out to her. It was hers now, her special beacon of hope, the way to reach the nation, even now after three years had passed. She took it with a smile and turned it on. Lincoln leaned against her desk, staring down at her with love in his eyes. She turned it on and began to speak.

"This is President Kelly. I am addressing you from the Oval Office in the way our forefathers had fireside chats over the radio long ago. We are once again a united people, bound by the goodness in our hearts. We're in this together, and I promise you, there is hope. We are a brave nation, and we have emerged from this crisis stronger and more united than ever. I will be conducting my first live television broadcast tomorrow night, which will also be shared on the radio for those who don't have TVs. We will talk about the way to move forward, what our next steps will be to find our way back to the safety and comfort of the world we once built. We can do it again, I know it. I believe in us. I believe in the power of our spirit and the purity of our hearts, so long as we trust each other and care for each other. I'm Caroline Kelly, a survivor just like you. We are in this together. Caroline out."

. . .

Thank you so much for reading *A Wilderness Within*! I hope you enjoyed Caroline and Lincoln's story!

Have you read the first story in my Unlikely Heroes series, *Midnight with the Devil*? Diana, the heroine falls in love with Lucifer, the very devil himself. Can she save his soul and her own before it's too late?

Turn the page to start reading Diana and Lucifer's story! Or buy it HERE!

- Sign up for my newsletter to get new release alerts, exclusive bonus scenes, contests and more here: https://landing.mailerlite.com/webforms/landing/i1j5n9

- Join my Private Facebook Group Emma Castle's Crew, for exclusive Giveaways and sneak peeks of future books here: http://bit.ly/2FqxHGu

Turn the page to read the beginning of ***Midnight with the Devil***!

MIDNIGHT WITH THE DEVIL - PROLOGUE
WHAT TIME HIS PRIDE HAD CAST HIM OUT FROM HEAVEN, WITH ALL HIS HOST OF REBEL ANGELS. - JOHN MILTON, PARADISE LOST

"How you have fallen from heaven, Morning Star, Son of the Dawn!"

"Favorite son no more!"

"No longer will you shine!"

The taunts from his brother angels filled his head as he fell through the clouds. Light and darkness consumed him in flashing turns as he passed through the stars, into the clouds, and toward the earth. The air cut him, and the wind roared around him so deafening that his eardrums burst. Dawn was on the horizon, and he would die before he saw it fully claim the skies.

"You, my brightest star, my favorite among the angels, how you have disappointed me." Father's voice was the hardest to bear.

Lucifer closed his eyes, welcoming the end, the death of light, the death of life.

"You were to bring light into the world, inspire my

creations, not corrupt them with your jealousies. Now you will rule the corrupted who follow you and become the king of hell."

The earth rose up to meet him, and he embraced the pain. His angelic heart shattered at the same moment his body broke upon impact. Everything went dark around him. Then bit by bit he became aware of himself, feeling every muscle, every bone, every atom that made up his body, screaming with pain. He hadn't died?

Lucifer gazed up at the endless clouds above him. The rift in the sky that would have let him back into the heavens was closed. He drew in a breath, the air like knives in his lungs. Something was different. He felt... empty. White feathers floated around him, their heavenly luminescence glinting in the sun.

My grace...it's gone.

It seemed like a millennium passed before he realized he lay upon the broken, cracked ground of the earth. His naked body hurt all over, but the pain was greatest along his shoulder blades. He was glad he could not see his back. There would be two terrible wounds replacing his snow-white wings. He reached out and grasped one of the remaining feathers that floated along the ground close to him and slipped it into the folds of the white tunic he wore. He needed that one bit of heaven, that one bit of *home*, or else he might go mad with grief.

The light inside him—the glowing essence that had once brought him only joy—was gone. There was nothing left inside him, nothing but darkness. He was in a crater in a desert land. Lucifer struggled to roll onto his stomach, his body too weak to stand.

He lifted his head, hearing the distant sounds of birds. Beyond the wasteland he'd fallen to, a beautiful Eden lay ahead, a land of green, full of beautiful beasts and flowers. Father had spoken so often about the world below the clouds.

Rage flooded through his body, giving him new energy and strength. Somewhere in that Eden were his father's favorite beings—*humans*. A vile word for vile beings who were no comparison to angels. But he was no longer an angel. He was fallen. A being without wings, without grace.

What am I now?

The question had no ready answer, and he cringed. For the first time in his existence, he didn't know what he really was.

He dug his hands into the arid dirt, clawing his way toward the garden ahead of him. At the center of the beautiful world, a single tree stood tall among the rest. Amidst its branches hung gleaming red apples. Father had spoken of this tree, the one that bore knowledge for the ages. Humans had free will, which angels did not, and if those humans dared break their promise to stay away from the tree, Lucifer would have his revenge and watch his father's favorite creations fall from grace.

Lucifer's lips twitched. He would not have long to wait to get his revenge. He could see the weakness and frailty in humanity. Bringing down the humans, one by one, would break his father's celestial heart, just as he had broken Lucifer's.

The wind carried away the feathers of his once angelic wings. He was glad he had caught one and tucked it safely near his heart. Paradise was lost to him, and he would make sure those damned humans would never reach it either.

CHAPTER 1

BETTER TO REIGN IN HELL THAN SERVE IN
HEAVEN. - JOHN MILTON, PARADISE LOST

Hellfire Rising was a den of corruption.

A hotbed of sin and scandal.

Here hearts were broken, dreams destroyed, and dark fantasies realized.

It was the closest thing to a home Lucien Star had. He leaned against the balcony overlooking the dancers below, and with a snap of his fingers he held a glass of brandy. He took a slow sip, savoring the dark, hard flavor of the alcohol.

Two years ago, he had left behind the devil that his father expected him to be and remade himself into a different devil. Lucifer—the Morning Star, the once favored angel, the ruler of hell who never left the darkness—was gone. He was done spending the majority of his days in the dark abyss and the fires of hell in the realm of the evil and the damned. He stopped calling himself Lucifer and instead became Lucien Star. He used his powers to create a world that catered to his own desires, Hellfire Rising, a club in downtown Chicago.

He returned to the abyss, to the darkness, only when absolutely necessary to see to his duties. The gates of hell needed guarding, or else they would break and demons would flood into the world, destroying it. That was not what Lucien wanted. Contrary to popular opinion, he rather liked the human realm the way it was. He didn't want to see it destroyed by flames and left in eternal darkness.

A woman below him on the stairs glanced up, flashing him a sultry smile in open invitation. He raised his brandy glass in salute, but he wasn't interested. His mind was on other matters, like the strange preoccupation with deep, troublesome thoughts. It was so unlike him that it rattled the bars of the hellish emotional cage he felt trapped in tonight.

He wished hell could run itself, and it did...*mostly*. The damned didn't need him there to continue their suffering at all times, which was a relief. He despised hell. But he couldn't avoid his job completely. He had to watch out for stray demons that wandered into the paths of mortals, then catch and destroy them. That didn't give him joy either.

He preferred the mortal plane, watching humans make decisions that put them on the path to sin. He loved the secret language of hidden smiles, seductive glances, exploring hands as they gave themselves over to their darker desires. He craved corruption, not evil.

"Lucien." The smooth, dark voice caught Lucien's attention. He still stood at the edge of the balcony on the top floor of his club that led to his private office. From the relatively secluded spot, he could see the club patrons below him dancing wildly.

"Yes?" He turned away from the smoky haze of the strobe lights that lit the club below and faced Andras, one of his fellow fallen angels. The blond-haired man had the palest blue eyes, like frozen glaciers. They had once been brothers in the glittering city of clouds, but now they were brothers bound in darkness.

"You asked me to bring you a list of the deals made on crossroads this month." Andras walked over to Lucien and held out his palm as though to shake his hand.

Lucien put his hand into Andras's, and his head suddenly filled with a flood of images. A hundred souls, a hundred deals made. Deals made out of anger, greed, and lust.

How utterly dull and predictable.

Lucien released Andras's hand and sighed as he turned back to face the crowd below. Andras joined him at the railing and remained quiet for a moment. Lucien again fixated on the feeling that had increasingly haunted him the last few years. He wasn't content. There was a cloying emptiness that seemed ready to strangle him, and he couldn't shake it. He was no stranger to that hollow feeling, but it seemed worse of late.

"Sir, you seem...unsatisfied."

Lucien nearly denied it, but he *never* lied. The devil only ever spoke the truth. Everyone painted him a liar, but it wasn't true. They lied to themselves and each other in his name.

"I am unsatisfied," he finally admitted. From the moment he'd been cast out of heaven, he had been restless and full of rage. The rage had faded over the many years he'd been in hell. Corrupting souls was too easy. A hint here, a little nudge there, and these mortals fell into sin so easily. He craved a challenge. The gates of hell required pure souls to be corrupted in order to stay strong. The more souls he took below, the stronger the powers keeping demons in hell were. In a strange way, corruption of a few protected millions. And it had been a long time since he'd focused on pure souls as targets. The gates were starting to crumble.

Nothing like a challenge when hell itself needed saving.

"Are there not any good, incorruptible souls still out there? The gates are weak. I can feel it," he muttered. It was a rhetorical question, but Andras straightened.

"There must be. Shall I find one for you? I too have been worried about the gates. It's been a long time since we've gone in search of pure souls to power the portal."

Lucien crossed his arms over his chest, frowning at the crowd below him. He hadn't expected Andras to offer to find one. He'd been thinking aloud more than anything, but Andras was a loyal soldier and clever. If anyone could find what he needed to protect the gates, it was Andras.

Do I want that? Would the challenge sate my emptiness? Or should I leave it up to Andras to secure the safety of hell?

No, he had to be the one to do it. When he corrupted the soul and secured it in hell, it kept the gates strong and the demons where they should be— locked away in crushing darkness.

If there was even the smallest chance of relieving himself of that awful ache, he had to try.

"Find me a pure soul. One that will be a true challenge. The gates need one that will truly test me if we are to secure the portal."

"Understood." Andras vanished, and the flutter of his invisible shadow wings was the only proof of his ever having been there. When Andras fell, he too had lost his snowy white wings. In their place, the scars had formed what were called shadow wings, and those were all that remained.

Lucien turned his back on the club and returned to his office. He closed the glass doors to his balcony and sat in his black leather desk chair. Taking a cigar from the cherrywood box, he removed his silver cigar cutter and cut the tip. Then he snapped his fingers, and a flame blossomed from his fingertips to light the cigar. He drew in a slow breath, relishing the rich, sweet aroma of the smoke, and blew the air back out. The smoke escaped his lips in tendrils that coiled into the air to form a slithering snake.

Andras would find him a soul, a perfect one to corrupt, and it would restore Lucien's purpose and keep the gates of hell intact.

It's time the devil got back in the game.

———

L *ife isn't fair.*

Diana Kingston knew that was the truth, but it didn't stop her from hoping for fairness every day. She sat by her father's hospital bed, helplessly watching him fight for life. He'd slipped into a coma early that morning as the final stages of cancer took hold. Her mother, Janet, held his hand and was talking softly to him about her day, hoping he could hear her. It had been a part of their normal routine before he'd slipped into the coma. When Diana got home from her college classes, she and her mother drove to the hospital to keep her father company while he underwent radiation and chemotherapy for colon cancer. She couldn't get past the pain of watching her mother lose half of herself with the impending death of the man she had deeply loved for more than thirty years.

Most days Diana kept herself together, but today was possibly the end. The doctor had called her mother early this morning to say that her father, Hal, had slipped into a coma. Only yesterday, her father had been glassy-eyed and exhausted from fighting the inevitable but still awake and talking. The machines beeping beside his bed showed his life ticking away, slowly fading bit by bit. Her heart was breaking, fracturing like a mirror into a thousand shards. She could see herself in her father's face, reflected a thousand times over as he gave in to death inch by inch. Would her mother look at Diana and see that reflection of her father? Would it cause her mother even more pain? Diana bit her lip hard enough that the metallic taste of blood surprised her. She licked her lips and rose from the stiff wooden hospital chair.

She was a coward; she was weak—she could not sit there and watch him die. It hurt too much.

"Mom, I'm going to get some air, okay?" She hugged her mother's shoulders and kissed her cheek before she headed to the door.

"Okay, hon," her mother murmured absently.

Diana paused at the door to her father's room, drinking in the sight of her parents. Hal was a handsome man with soft gray eyes, eyes that would likely never open again, and brown hair feathered with gray. Her mother, Janet, had been a real beauty in her youth and was still stunning with blue eyes and raven hair. But her father's illness had aged them both over the last two years, stealing time like fall leaves scattered upon the wind.

When her father died, the blow would crush her mother. They were soul mates. Diana had grown up in a house filled with life and laughter, songs sung in the sun, and dancing in the moonlight. Her parents had a peaceful life, but now life seemed determined to claw back some of the perfection it had given away too freely.

Tears welled up in Diana's eyes as she stepped into the hallway of the oncology wing at Saint Francis Hospital outside Chicago.

Just breathe, she reminded herself. She wiped her eyes, smearing the tears across her cheeks. She'd been raised Catholic, but her faith had never been that strong, not until her father fell ill. Now she prayed like the world was ending, because for her, part of it was.

"You okay?" A nurse came over and gently touched her shoulder in the nice way people do to strangers in pain.

"Yeah," she whispered. "Just a bad day for my dad." The words "he's dying" couldn't come out. She didn't want—and frankly couldn't handle—anyone's pity right now.

The woman nodded in immediate understanding. "Everyone has those bad days here, but they're usually followed by good ones. Hang in there, sweetie." The nurse's brown eyes were tender as she smiled.

"Thanks." Diana tucked a lock of hair behind her ear and glanced around, wishing she could get outside fast, but the hospital was a labyrinth of wings, elevator bays, and nurses' stations.

"Why don't you take a break in the chapel?" The nurse's suggestion sounded good.

Diana thanked her again and walked toward the end of the hall. She reached it and glanced at the door with a little plaque that said "Healing Chapel." As she entered, she held her breath, but the chapel was empty. A stained-glass window of Saint Francis of Assisi standing in the woods surrounded by animals was at the back of the chapel. She'd come here often these last few weeks, and while she was a lapsed Catholic, she knew enough of the saints to know Assisi. He'd become a quiet comfort to her.

The pews gleamed with a splash of colorful light pouring in from the stained glass. Diana walked to the first row and sat down, then closed her eyes as more tears trailed down her cheeks. Two years ago all that had mattered in her life was college. She would be a senior at the University of Chicago this fall, majoring in architecture. When her dad fell ill, her mother had done her best to hide it from her.

Part of Diana was angry that her dad was ill, angry that he was putting her and her mother through hell. And she was angry that she wouldn't be able to fix her mother's broken heart. She was angry most of all at herself for not being able to do a damn thing to help him. Anger felt good, and it made her feel strong, even if only for a short time.

She wasn't sure how long she sat there before she realized she wasn't alone. The fine hair at the back of her neck rose as she had that eerie sensation of unseen eyes gazing upon her. Some ancient instinct warned her that she was in the presence of a predator.

Turning slowly, she looked over her shoulder, near the dimly lit entry. She saw a figure that was wreathed in shadows. For a second, she couldn't breathe. It was as if every nightmare she'd ever had about shapes in the dark, choking, suffocating, and endless nothingness buried in layers of smoke were all there in that doorway. Then she blinked and the shadows vanished.

Instead, a man stood framed in the doorway. His black suit and red silk tie were strangely intense for a hospital setting. She was so used to seeing people in casual, comfortable clothes while they spent long hours at the bedside of a loved one. He held himself in a confident, dominant manner that made her shiver. Gazing upward, she gulped when she realized he was staring at her with the same intensity. The instant their eyes locked, her breath rushed out of her and all the thoughts in her head rattled around. Those eyes—fathomless twin pools of deadly intent that she couldn't understand—caused fear to sink its claws into her as every basic animal instinct in her shrieked to run. She blinked and the strange, frightening spell was somewhat broken, and she was able to take in the rest of his face.

He was frighteningly attractive, like a model from a fashion magazine. He had dark hair, not quite black, and his eyes were just as dark. She could see no hint of warmth there. His features were perfect, a straight nose, chiseled jaw, and full lips that a girl could get lost in daydreams about kissing. There was an edge of danger about him, something that warned her deep down to be careful, to not run, because she was prey and he was a predator. As silly as the thought was, she sensed it was true on some level. She had to be careful.

Yet Diana couldn't help but wonder about this man and who he might be. He was fascinating to look at. She had dated her fair share of guys, but this man...he made the whole world fall away. He was completely absorbing in a way she couldn't explain.

Silence stretched between them. She wanted to wipe away the tears drying on her cheeks, but she couldn't move, frozen by both fear and enchantment.

"I hope I didn't disturb your prayers."

She shivered at his low, silken voice. That voice could tempt a woman to think of her darkest fantasies. Fantasies she fought every day to ignore, yet she couldn't stop her body's reaction. She pulled her control together and forced herself to finally move. She had to get out of this room. Her instincts still screamed at her to get the hell out of there.

"Er...no, I was just leaving." She stood and exited the pew.

He took a step closer, sliding his hands into the pockets of his black pants. The light from the windows moved over him in the strangest way, as though he was bending the light to move away from him, leaving him more in shadow.

Was that even possible? Diana glanced around, very aware that she was alone with this man, and the cold, emotionless faces of the occupants of the stained-glass windows weren't there to help her.

"Visiting someone?"

"My...dad." Just saying it dispelled the fear and desire that this man created inside her. She wiped at her eyes, making sure he couldn't see any fresh tears.

"I'm sorry." He took another step closer, his gaze sliding from her to the stained-glass window behind her. He stared at Saint Francis with an odd, knowing smile as if he were intimately familiar with the saint, which of course wasn't possible.

"Thank you." She grappled for something polite to say. "Are you visiting someone here too?" She studied his profile and the way the light from the stained glass fractured over his features in dozens of colors.

His lips curled in a ghost of a grin. "Not exactly."

"Are you a doctor?" If he wasn't there visiting, he had to be there for some reason, right?

He suddenly chuckled as if at some private joke. "Do I look like I save lives?"

"I...I'm sorry, I just assumed." She started for the door again, disturbed and way too interested in the man.

"Diana, wait."

Her name upon his lips stopped her dead in her tracks.

"How do you know who I am?" Terror clenched her throat so hard the words barely escaped her mouth.

The man turned to face her. His head inclined toward her, his body moving with a slow grace, his eyes pinning her in place as he came closer.

"You sent a prayer out for your father."

Stunned, she nodded.

"I'm here to answer your prayer."

His dark eyes seem to swallow her whole as his words punched her gut. Was this some kind of cruel joke? Was he a doctor playing a game? Or worse, just some creep who lurked in hospital chapels to prey on emotional women?

"I'm not a creep lurking around waiting to prey on emotional women."

He chuckled again, the darkness edging the sound giving her chills. He'd heard her thoughts. "But...how? You're not a doctor. You said you don't save lives. I don't understand—"

He raised one hand, his index finger pointing up to command silence. She closed her mouth. The man drifted closer step by step, and she still couldn't move. They were now only a foot apart, and she could feel that awful, crushing darkness rolling off him in waves.

"I'm not a doctor, and I only save lives when there's something in it for me."

Diana wrapped her arms around herself. "I still don't understand."

"Of course you don't. You're a sweet, innocent

mortal. No need to worry. I am happy to spell it out for you." He reached out to touch her cheek.

Suddenly the chapel vanished around them and they were in front of her father's room, peering in at him and her mother from the doorway. Her father lay still, his face waxen with approaching death, and the sight tore at her heart so fiercely she nearly cried out. The man from the chapel was right behind her, his warm breath fanning against her neck. She shivered.

"I make life-changing *deals*."

"Deals?" She didn't understand how they'd gotten from the chapel to her father's room.

I'm dreaming. That has to be it. No one around them moved. The nurses at the station were frozen, her parents too. The multiple monitors connected to her father were still and silent. This was how all her nightmares went. She couldn't move, couldn't scream, she just had to face whatever was happening. This was most definitely a dream.

"Yes." The man's voice was low, seductive, like a lover. "You want your father to be well again, don't you?"

"Of course I do." Diana stared at her father, his face a mask of pain and exhaustion.

"What would you give for him to be healed?"

She spun to face the dark-eyed man and came face-to-face with his red necktie. He was towering over her; he had to be at least six foot three. She barely came up to his shoulders.

"I..."

"Think now, think hard." The man's dark eyes lowered to her lips as though he was thinking about kissing her. A wild flush rippled through her.

"I would give anything."

"*Anything* is an awfully dangerous word." His dark eyes were like fathomless pools, but in them she saw her father walking, laughing, alive. The hunger for that moment, to see her father healthy and happy, was so strong that she was able to shed her fears of this man and bravely speak the truth.

She pursed her lips for a minute but then nodded. "Anything."

He studied her, and she refused to flinch beneath his assessing gaze. She straightened her back and lifted her chin, wanting to project confidence. The man seemed amused by her sudden change, and a slow, seductive smile lifted the corners of his lips.

"Would you give yourself to *me*? Sell your soul?" the man asked, his voice hard-edged beneath that layer of silken seduction.

"Sell my..."

"Soul." He opened his palm, holding it flat as though waiting for her to take his hand.

"What do you mean, my soul?"

"I'll show you." He extended his hand closer to hers. She reached out, hesitating, but then finally placed her hand in his. The second his fingers curled around hers she was swallowed by darkness.

Fluttering sounds like the rush of a raven's wings in the night made her shiver, and she clung to his hand, which still grasped hers. All around her was nothingness, and she couldn't seem to get any air into her lungs for a long second. Then finally she was able to speak.

"What is this?" she whispered, fear choking her.

"The end of everything you know and love."

"Hell," she breathed. Where were the fires and the evil souls?

"Hell is different for everyone. It's not all fire and brimstone." His chuckle curled around her, hot and seductive.

"I see only darkness," she gasped.

"Because your hell is one of *nothingness*."

Suddenly they were back in the chapel, and Diana fell to her knees, shaking violently. He stood above her, hands tucked in his trouser pockets, waiting patiently.

"You agree to make a deal with me, and I will give you something in return."

She put a hand to her chest as she looked up at him.

"You can...save my dad?" Part of her wondered if she was dreaming. She had to be. There was no way she was talking to the devil about making a deal to save her father's life.

"I can."

"But you said you don't save lives."

The man—no, the devil—slowly smiled. "I said I don't *look* like I save lives, and as a general rule I do not."

"Then why help me?" Diana got to her feet but sat down on the nearest pew. The devil strode to the stained-glass window, tilting his face up, the light playing upon his skin.

"Because you are a pure soul and I hunger for corruption. I need to *corrupt* you."

"Corrupt me?" She shuddered at the dark word. When she thought of corruption, she thought of stealing, of hurting people, of unlawful things she'd never do.

The devil turned to face her again, and the shadows pooled around him, his eyes suddenly glowing with a soft ruby-red gleam.

"I want to own your body, your soul, to show you the pleasures of the dark side. I want you to tell me every wicked fantasy, the worst ones, and I want you to let me act them out with you. When I claim a pure soul through pleasure and bring it to the darkness, that soul then belongs to me in every way."

Her darkest fantasies? She struggled to think, but she didn't have any fantasies.

"*Everyone* has fantasies, Diana. Even pure souls like you."

"You...you said you make deals, right? What would our deal be?" She couldn't believe she was considering this, but if it meant saving her father, how could she not listen to what the devil offered? He would own her soul. Was her father's life worth letting him drag her down into eternal darkness?

"You will come to me every Friday night at

midnight. I can do with you as I please until dawn, then you can leave."

"For how long?" She tried not to think about what the devil would do with her.

"Three months. It will be a delightful gift to myself to celebrate the anniversary of my fall from grace. When you die, whenever that may be, your soul will be fully mine, trapped forever in that nothingness I showed you."

Twelve Fridays? She could survive whatever the devil wanted for her father's sake. She wouldn't think about what would happen when she died someday and how she'd be trapped—in hell—with him. "How...how do I know you won't let him die after you're through with me?"

The devil's grin was scary, not because *he* was scary but because that sexy grin promised all sorts of sins, ones she didn't think she could handle. "I may be the devil, but I'm not a liar. I get what I, and I promise on my black heart you'll get what you want."

She didn't immediately respond. Diana wasn't stupid. She'd seen movies about deals with the devil. There was always a catch, and the trick was finding out what it was.

"What about my mom, or any other friends or family? You'll save my dad but let someone else that I love die instead, right?"

His eyes widened the slightest bit, and then he smiled as though pleased she wasn't simply agreeing.

"That is called cosmic balance, you clever child, and no, I do not have to bend to the will of cosmic balance. You won't face anyone else's death because of our little deal."

Diana couldn't ignore the possessiveness that seemed to emanate from him as he gazed at her. Was her soul really worth it to him? If so, then she had one heck of a bargaining chip, and she refused to waste it.

"I want you to promise that *no one* I love gets hurt and my dad gets totally healed forever."

He waved a finger at her. "Now, now, you can't demand—"

"Do you want my pure soul or not?" The second she issued her challenge, invisible electricity sparked between them. The heat burning through Diana held a promise of what was to come, and it scared the hell out of her. She had to make this deal, but only on *her* terms. If he didn't agree, she still had the power to walk away, and she would.

When he didn't respond, she stood up and started toward the chapel door.

"Fine." He growled the word as he came up behind her. She turned to look at him, stepping back instinctively as he came too close. "I can give your other loved ones extra protection, but if the other side makes a decision, that's on your precious angels, not me. I don't have control over what those winged idiots do. But I swear that nothing I do will cause them harm."

"Okay, so three months of my submitting to you and you heal my dad."

"Submitting?" He laughed. "That's a rather interesting word. Is that one of your fantasies? To have me dominating you?"

Diana shuddered at first, but then an inner voice whispered, *"Yes. Dominate me."* A voice she'd buried every time the desires surfaced, because it filled her with shame "Is that the deal?" she repeated.

The devil grinned. "Yes. That's the deal."

"Do we...shake on it or something?" She held out her hand. He eyed it and then took her hand in his and tugged. She fell against him, surprised at the feel of his warm body against hers.

Before she could push him away, he bent his head and whispered, "You *always* seal a devil's bargain with a kiss." And then he slanted his mouth over hers, burning her lips with his as he ravaged her mouth, his tongue seeking hers. She was too stunned at first, but as his mouth softened on hers, she melted into him.

A frightening sense of falling forever in the darkness and fluttering black wings surged through her, but he held her, banding his arms around her and tethering her so she wouldn't vanish in the nothingness.

She tried to banish her fears, praying for one spot of light in the darkness as they kissed. There was a brilliant flash of bright light, the feel of soft downy feathers brushing against her cheek, and then she glimpsed a shining city in the clouds.

Then it was gone. The nothingness remained.

His lips left hers, and the warmth of his body faded. Dimly, she heard his silken whisper in her mind. *"You are mine now, Diana."*

When she opened her eyes and jolted awake, she lay on one of the pews in the hospital's chapel.

She'd only had a wild dream. Her father wouldn't get better. A tear rolled off her cheek onto the fabric of the seat beneath her. She sat up slowly, combed her fingers through her hair, and tried to compose herself. Then she left the chapel and returned to her father's room. As the door to the chapel closed behind her, she swore she heard a faint, low masculine chuckle.

"I'm going crazy. The stress of all this is getting to me."

As much as she would've done anything to save her dad, there was no such thing as bargaining with the devil. Because she didn't believe in the devil.

CHAPTER 2

BUT HIS DOOM RESERVED HIM TO MORE
WRATH; FOR NOW THE THOUGHT BOTH OF
LOST HAPPINESS AND LASTING PAIN
TORMENTS HIM. - JOHN MILTON, PARADISE
LOST

Lucien stood in the chapel, invisible to Diana, watching her wipe away her tears and leave the room. She was a beautiful woman, with dark-brown hair and dove-gray eyes that reminded him of lightning in winter snowstorms. He'd seen lovelier women, yet there was something about her that drew him in, a natural beauty that seemed to come from within. It was possible that her pure soul was calling to him, but the longing to thread his hands through the straight waterfall of her hair...that was pure lust on his part.

"You don't believe in me yet, but you will." And by the time she realized what bargain she'd made, it would be too late. Her soul would be forever trapped in his clutches, corrupted by his darkness, and that soul would keep the gates of hell strong and secure.

After she left, he raised a hand to his lips, brushing the tips of his fingers over them, wondering.

It had been a most curious thing. When he'd kissed her and sealed their bargain, he had thought he'd seen something, just a quick second of a young girl's hand brushing over cool blades of grass on a summer morning, the chilly drops of dew tickling his fingers as they tickled hers. It had felt...*heavenly*. He'd convinced himself that he didn't want to remember what heaven felt like, how it tasted, how it looked, but kissing Diana had brought back forbidden memories. He buried the rush of pleasure that thoughts of heaven brought because it always brought back the pain of his fall. Instead, he focused on why he would experience that with Diana when he never had with any other mortal before.

He normally saw people's darkest desires when he sealed their bargains. He exited the chapel and moved unseen through the hospital until he reached the room where Diana and her mother were saying their goodbyes for the night and going home. After they had left, he walked over to where Diana's father lay breathing softly, his eyes closed. Lucien stared down at him for a long minute. The man was deep in a coma, wouldn't last the night, not that Diana or her mother knew that. They only knew that time was limited. The doctors had assured them they would have another day or two to say goodbye and take him off the machines. But even the machines couldn't stop the death that was creeping through Hal's body.

Lucien reached out and woke Hal from the coma.

Diana's father's eyes slowly opened up, and he had the look of a man lost, a man who'd begun his travel to the other side but had been pulled abruptly back.

"You've come for me?" The man opened his eyes, and they were soft gray just like Diana's.

"I'm not Death. He's the one who pays house calls," Lucien said with a sardonic smile.

"This isn't a house call?" Hal coughed and winced, and then he relaxed, his eyes starting to close as he struggled to stay awake.

Lucien watched all this in fascination, strangely reminded of his own fall and the struggle to go on. The human will to survive, to overcome any obstacle, even one as painful as death, was so strong.

"So if you aren't Death, and there's no way you're a doctor, then who are you?" Hal asked. Pain filled his voice, but he sounded strong now too. Lucien felt a stab of pride in knowing a man like this had fathered his newest pet, for that was what Diana would be: his pet, a plaything, one he would take good care of even while corrupting her with her own forbidden desires.

"I don't think you want to know who I am." Lucien picked up the charts at the end of the hospital bed, flicking through the complicated pages.

"Try me," Hal challenged.

Lucien put his charts down and walked around the side of the bed, offering a hand. Hal placed his hand in Lucien's just like Diana had, and he showed Hal exactly who he was by letting Hal glimpse his own personal hell just as he had shown Diana hers.

Hal's face paled even more. "You're the...the..."

"Yes." Lucien didn't bother to say the word. He'd never been overly fond of *devil* or *Satan*. They were such negative words for a being who'd once been named heaven's brightest star.

"That's not...you can't be..." Diana's father struggled to accept the truth, but after a long moment, he seemed too tired to fight.

"I am. You'd better believe it," Lucien replied.

"But why are you here?" Hal asked, eyes wide. "I've tried to be a good man."

"And...luckily, you succeeded."

"I don't understand."

"I'm not dragging you down to hell. Scout's honor." Lucien chuckled, but Hal didn't laugh.

"I'm here because your daughter just bought you the winning lottery ticket."

"What are you talking about?" Hal blinked in shock as Lucien placed a palm on his forehead.

"Don't worry, you won't remember any of this."

Hal's eyes closed, and white light went from Lucien's hand into Hal's head. The last vestiges of his angelic powers—oddly the ones the heavens hadn't taken from him when they'd taken almost everything else—still worked.

Lucien dropped his hand from Hal's face and

glanced toward the machine that now beeped in a steady rhythm.

Come dawn, the doctors would be baffled by Hal's quick recovery, and they would send him home, declaring it a miracle.

But for Diana it was to be a debt. A debt he was very interested in collecting. There was a momentary flicker of guilt at knowing he would be Diana's destruction, but he buried it deep inside. The devil couldn't afford to feel guilty, not when the universe's very stability relied on him remaining a selfish bastard and stealing pure souls. For Diana it meant surrendering her pure soul to the realm of darkness so that it could fortify the gates and keep all hell from literally breaking loose.

————

D iana slept in, not wanting to leave the comfort of her warm bed in her little apartment. If she was being honest, she didn't want to face today. She and her mother had spoken to the doctor, and today they would take her father off the machines keeping him alive. The doctor wasn't certain how long it would take for her father to die, but Diana knew it could be a few days. He was so damn strong, had always been strong, and he would cling to life while she and her mother watched in agony.

I can't face that, not yet.

Outside the sun was up, light peeking in through the pale-blue curtains on her bedroom window. For a long moment she lay there, thinking about the frightening dream she'd had when she'd fallen asleep in the chapel the day before.

A deal with the devil.

She sighed heavily and forced herself out of bed. Diana couldn't put off the visit to the hospital any longer. Her mother would need her there, and it would be one of the last times she would get to see her father before...before he was gone. She trembled, and a chill stole through her, settling deep into her bones. Whenever she thought of her dad being gone, it left a burning, hollow ache inside her chest. It would only get worse once he was really gone.

She picked up her cell phone from her nightstand and checked the time. It was nearly noon on a Sunday morning. She'd missed several calls from her mother. Heart pounding, she called her mom back. Something had happened to her dad before she'd had a chance to say goodbye? She tried not to think about it, about how pale he had been last night.

"Diana! Thank God!" her mother gasped when she answered the phone.

"What is it? Dad?" Diana's voice broke, and she was seconds away from crying.

"Yes, but I think it's good news. He came out of the coma. I think..." Her mother choked on a sob. "I think he might be in remission."

"What?" Diana wiped the fresh stream of tears on her cheeks. She didn't understand.

"It's a miracle! Your father called me at around nine. He woke up at six this morning feeling better than he's been in a long time. He called the nurses to have the doctors come see him. They ran some tests and biopsied his colon." Her mother took a deep breath before continuing. "They didn't find any cancer cells."

That couldn't be possible. Yesterday he had been mere days away from death.

"Mom, they made a mistake," Diana said. "They had to."

"They tested him several times on several different machines to be sure."

Diana bit her lip so hard she tasted blood. It was too dangerous to let hope take over. Far too dangerous.

"So what does this mean?" she asked her mother.

"I think he can come home in a few days. I'm headed to the hospital now."

"I can meet you there."

"No, no," her mother said. "Let me go. Just in case." The words she left unsaid were loud in the silence between them. In case it really was a mistake. Better to have only her mother's hopes broken than both of them. But Diana didn't want her facing that news alone.

"I'm coming." Diana hung up on her mother before she could protest, and she hastily dressed and grabbed her keys. Her orange tabby cat, Seth, was perched on the arm of the couch in the small living room, purring as she walked by.

"I'll be back later," she told the cat. He lowered onto his stomach and tucked his paws under his chest, watching her as she slung her purse over her shoulder and slipped outside.

By the time she reached the hospital, she was a nervous wreck. Her hands wouldn't stop shaking. She parked her car and headed toward the oncology department, but when she got to the hall leading to her father's room, the hairs on the back of her neck rose and she had that eerie sensation of someone watching her.

Just like in my dream.

Diana glanced about but didn't see anyone except for the nurses at their stations.

"We made a deal. Don't forget it." The soft, seductive voice slithered inside her mind, and she froze a step away from the door to her father's room.

No. It had been a dream. Their encounter hadn't been real. The man, the devil, that kiss—it had all been a dream.

"You promised me your soul, and I will collect."

Diana shook her head, trying to banish the voice, and she rushed into her father's room.

Hal sat in bed, his face full of color and smiling. Her mother spoke to a doctor who was showing her some lab results. It all seemed so surreal. Last night he'd been still and pale as death, his hands clammy to the touch and his chest barely moving with shallow breaths. The man in the hospital before her now was healthy and bright-eyed. Her heart stung with an overwhelming rush of joy.

"Hey." Diana greeted her father and kissed him and hugged him. He returned her hug, and she was startled by the strength of his embrace. The last few months he had been too weak to do anything but squeeze her hand.

"Hey, kiddo. I think I might be going home in a few days. Can you believe it?" Her father's eyes sparkled with life in a way she couldn't remember. He had been ill for two years now, and she had started to forget the man he had been before the cancer.

"Yeah, Mom called me. I can't believe it." She hugged him again, her heart clenching in her chest.

"It could be that the treatments really worked and we are just now finally seeing the results," the doctor explained. "Either way, I think this is good, Mrs. Kingston. We'll continue to run tests for a few more days to be sure, but I'd like to plan on sending him home on Wednesday."

Her mother beamed at the doctor. "Wednesday?"

"Yes." The doctor smiled. "I try not to let patients get their hopes up, but in this case, things look very good."

"Thank you." Her mother hugged the startled physician and then returned to her husband's bedside.

"I'll leave you all to have some time with him, but make sure he has plenty of rest."

Diana pulled up a chair by her father's hospital bed and grasped one of his hands between hers, squeezing it gently.

She stayed at the hospital for two more hours, her mind reeling as her father got up on shaky legs for the first time in weeks. She didn't understand how this was the same man from the day before—the man who had lain on the bed, so close to death that it hung around him like a shroud. Could her strange dream have been real? Was she actually considering that she'd made an actual honest-to-God deal with the devil? She turned on her laptop and googled "deals with the devil" first thing after she arrived home. As the search history revealed information, she held her breath and read on.

She found several articles about the mythology behind making a deal with the devil. There were even descriptions of rituals for summoning a demon at a crossroads to make the bargain. Seth perched on the edge of her desk, his face alert on the front door, his tail flicking back and forth.

"It's Sunday. No mail today," she reminded the tabby and stroked a hand down his spine. He arched, encouraging her to scratch his lower back right above his tail. Suddenly the mail slot on her door opened, and a letter dropped onto the floor.

Diana stared at the letter. She hadn't heard anyone come up the stairs. She always heard steps on the stairs.

Seth's ears flattened, and he let out an eerie meow. He only made that noise when she vacuumed too close to him under the bed.

Unease prickled along her skin like thousands of invisible spiders, making her shudder. She set her laptop aside and approached the letter cautiously. It was made of expensive crisp white card stock and bound with a red satin ribbon. She picked it up off the carpet and turned it over. There was no return address, only her name, *Diana Kingston*, scrawled on top in flowing cursive.

Diana tugged on the ribbon until the bow fell apart, and then she unfolded the letter to read it.

Ms. Kingston,

You have recently completed a transaction with His Majesty, the king of hell. You are hereby to give yourself over to his desires for three months in exchange for your father's life. You will be ready each Friday night at half past eleven. A black sedan will pick you up. It will bring you to a place where you will fulfill your obligations. If at any point you wish to rescind this contract by invoking the free will clause specified in the attached contract article 2 section 1, then you must face the immediate death of your father.

Any questions regarding your contract with Lucien Star, a.k.a. Lucifer Morningstar, a.k.a. the devil, can be written and directed to Mr. Star's counsel, Lionel Barnaby, Esq.

Sincerely,

Mr. Barnaby

Diana read the letter over several times, unsure

whether she wanted to laugh or cry. "I really made a deal with the devil?"

Something brushed against her leg and she jumped, her heart jolting into her throat as she almost screamed. Seth hissed and bounded away from her, upset that he had scared her enough that she jumped.

"Jesus, Seth." She stared at the vanishing tail of her cat as he whipped around the corner and into her bedroom.

She glanced back down at the letter and then turned the page to see a few more pages of intense-looking legal terms. "Terms and conditions." She scanned the frighteningly long list that made very little sense to her. But she searched for the clause about free will.

"In accordance with the ruling laws of heaven and hell, a human shall *always* have free will, even during transactions with the devil. Any sale of the soul, permanently or temporarily, to the devil to receive benefits is valid and binding unless the mortal exclaims, 'I invoke my right of free will.' At such point the transaction is broken, and the benefit conferred upon the mortal will be undone or taken away."

Diana stared at the contract and read the signature lines at the bottom where her name had been written in her own hand. She brushed her fingertips over the signature to feel the ink, and the memory of kissing the devil flooded back. The heat, the sensual dominance, the feel of wind whipping around her all swept through her like a roaring wave. Gasping, she struggled for air.

She'd sealed her deal with a kiss. In some of the cross-roads mythology articles she'd read, that was how bargains were made.

It is real.

She set the contract and the letter down on her desk, returned to her couch, and picked up her laptop once more. She had no idea what she was looking for. Answers, maybe? But even the internet was no help. She searched for books about the devil and the occult, and a psychic bookshop popped up in the search results. She clicked on the address and saw that it was only two miles away and was open until ten.

Diana cast a look at Seth. He lay on his back in the middle of the floor, his tail twitching.

"Should I go?" she asked. Seth's tail stilled. "Is that a yes?" she confirmed, half smiling as Seth rolled onto his side and looked up at her.

"Fine. I'll go." She closed her laptop and fetched her purse. She exited the apartment and typed the book-store's address into her phone. By the time she reached the bookstore, the sun hung heavy in the sky. Diana parked her car and faced the shop.

A small sign dangled off the metal pole above the door. Its painted black lettering stood out against the pale gray background: *The Occultist's Apothecary*. The shop was surrounded by a coffee shop on one side and a consignment clothing store on the other side. Only the coffee shop was open, but it had few customers.

Diana adjusted her purse on her shoulder and

headed toward the bookstore. A small bell tinkled above her head as she entered. The musty smell of old books, candles, incense, and spices filled the air like an invisible cloud.

There was part of the shop that had a counter with bottles and other ingredients. A beautiful dark-skinned woman stood behind the counter, sorting out receipts. She flicked her gaze up and then returned to her task.

"Excuse me," Diana said uncertainly. "I'm looking for some books."

God, she's going to think I'm crazy.

"Books about what?" The woman's voice was soft and deep, lovely. Her dark eyes lifted again and held on Diana's face. Her expression was unreadable.

"Um..." Diana had to stop herself from glancing around. "The devil. Specifically about making deals... like at a crossroads."

"A crossroads deal," the woman said slowly, her gaze sharpening.

"Yes, or something like that," Diana added. She and the devil hadn't really been at a crossroads. Or had they? The hospital was at an intersection of two streets. Maybe that qualified?

"You're making deals with the dark one, child?" the woman asked.

"I'm twenty-one." She wasn't a kid.

The woman's lips twitched. "What's your name?"

"Diana."

"The Huntress, a goddess's name. It's good to have a

strong name from the old gods." The woman held out her hand over the counter. Diana reached out to shake it, but the woman caught her hand and turned Diana's palm face up, peering closely at it. Then she ran a fingertip along her skin, tracing lines.

"You..." The woman's brow furrowed, and she held out her other hand. She examined both of Diana's palms, frowning.

"What's wrong?" Diana peered down at her own hand.

"A person's palm should have heart and lifelines that are similar but not exact. Yours...*match*."

Diana had never really thought about her palms, but she did know the lines didn't match. Yet as she looked at her hands now, they were exactly the same.

"Oh, child, what have you done?" the woman demanded in a soft, breathless voice, her brown eyes heavy with worry.

"What do you mean?"

"Come and sit." The woman motioned for Diana to follow her back behind a black curtain. She hesitated a second before following. There was a small table covered with a dark-purple cloth and a tea tray. The woman poured two cups of tea and handed Diana one.

"Drink it all." The woman waited while Diana drained the small cup of tea. The woman took the cup and overturned it on its saucer for a moment, then turned it back over. She peered into the bottom of the teacup and frowned.

"You wanted to save your father?"

"Yes." Diana stared at the woman. *How could she know?*

"The dark one came to you and made a deal for your father's life?"

Again, Diana nodded and whispered, "Yes."

"You gave him your body, not just your soul." The woman pursed her lips, turning the cup a little. "He's going to break you, child. No one ever survives a deal like that."

"Break me?" Diana wrapped her arms around her chest, a chill slithering down her spine.

"You are not the first woman to catch his eye. He loves pleasure in all forms."

The woman set the cup down and gently touched Diana's shoulders.

"Is there anything I can do?" Diana asked. She wouldn't rescind the contract because her father's life was at risk, but if there was anything she could do to protect herself, she would.

"Come with me." The woman escorted her back to the front of the store, and she retrieved a small box behind the counter. She sat down and opened it.

A small wooden cross on a leather cord sat inside the box.

"This is a talisman that has been blessed by a saint. Take it. Though I do not know what good it will do."

"I thought crosses only worked on vampires?"

The woman laughed. "Child, crosses do not work on vampires. Vampires are not demons."

Diana blinked. "Are you saying vampires are real?"

"You made a deal with the devil, and you don't believe in vampires?" The woman laughed softly. "Child, the dark is full of monsters, human and other."

"Vampires..." She didn't know what to say. Her world, or what she knew of it, was vanishing overnight. She slipped the cross over her neck and tucked it beneath her sweater.

"How much do I owe you for the reading and the cross?"

The woman held out a hand. "Nothing. My name is Amara. You may come back anytime you need me."

"Really?" Diana wanted to hug Amara and did so, ignoring the woman's outstretched hand. Amara patted her back before they broke apart, but her eyes were serious as she looked at Diana.

"You must be careful. The more you surrender to the dark, to him, the more you will lose yourself. You must find the light inside you and hold on to it. Do not go into his darkness—it will destroy you."

"Thank you." Diana touched the cross hidden beneath her sweater and waved goodbye to Amara before she exited the shop.

A bitter wind curled around her, icy fingers teasing her hair and digging into her clothes, making her shiver. She rushed to her car and got inside. She turned on the lights and thought—for just one second only—that someone was in the back seat. She spun, gasping, but the back seat was empty. She turned back to the steering wheel, her heart pounding and her blood roaring in her ears. She could have sworn there'd been a flash of light, like the yellow of an animal's eyes in the rearview mirror.

"I'm going crazy. I just need to go home and rest."

"Rest." A deep voice laughed in the back of her mind. *"You'll need it."*

Diana closed her eyes, breathing in slowly.

Stay calm. You have to stay rational. I will face this devil and the deal and save my dad. I won't let him break me.

When she opened her eyes again she felt better, more clearheaded, until she heard the voice one last time.

"I will have you in every way I desire."

CHAPTER 3

CHAINED ON THE BURNING LAKE, NOR EVEN
THENCE HAD RISEN OR HEAVED HIS HEAD,
BUT THAT THE WILL AND HIGH PERMISSION
OF ALL-RULING HEAVEN LEFT HIM AT LARGE
TO HIS OWN DARK DESIGNS. - JOHN MILTON,
PARADISE LOST

Amara Dimka locked the door to her shop and flipped the Open sign to Closed. After reading that poor girl's palm and tea leaves, she didn't want to face any more customers. She needed to recover from the rush of premonitions. Touching the other side always took a toll on her. She'd caught a glimpse of a shining city, heard a flutter of wings in the dark, and then her stomach had dropped to her feet as she'd sensed the *end*. The end of everything. Amara paused and leaned against the counter for a minute, catching her breath.

That young woman was in danger, but there was no way to help her. One did not simply defy the dark one.

She put a few books back on the shelves, then fetched a broom from the storage closet and made a quick pass through the shop, collecting a small amount of dust. She leaned the broom against the counter and bent to retrieve a dustpan on a shelf away from where customers could see it. She gripped the handle and froze. *Something* was in her shop.

A chill trickled down her spine, and she suppressed a shiver. She stood slowly, and it took every ounce of her self-control not to flinch when she found herself face-to-face with one of the most beautiful men she'd ever seen. He wore a tailored black suit and a red tie. His dark hair was a little long, and it gleamed as if lit by sunlight although the sun had already set. His eyes were obsidian and eerily unreadable of any emotion.

"Can I help you?" she asked carefully. There was no doubt who this man was.

"I think you can, Amara." His voice was silky and low, like a lover's voice.

She waited, her heart racing.

"You can stay out of my business." His dark eyes flashed with red fire.

"With the girl, Diana?" Amara's heartbeat felt heavy in her chest because she knew her words might sound like a challenge. She didn't want to bow down to him. She was a white witch, not one who followed him. She believed in helping people.

"Yes." The dark one trailed a finger along the counter as though checking for dust, but his finger left a burning path on the counter with a charred black line in the wood.

"I don't hear about *you* making any deals these days." She couldn't help but wonder what had changed for him that he would make this deal personally. "People usually visit me after signing up with a crossroads demon. What's so special about this one that you did the deal yourself?" Amara tried to act casual, as though she wasn't having a conversation with the king of hell. She bent down to retrieve the dustpan and picked up her broom. Then she finished sweeping up the dirt and dust bunnies.

The devil followed behind her, pausing at a shelf of books on witchcraft and plucking a title off to flip idly through the pages.

"She's...pure," he finally said.

"Nobody is pure," Amara replied without thinking.

"I don't mean pure as in free of sin. Everyone makes that mistake." He paused in the study of a book on the Salem witch trials and smirked. Then he waved the book at her. "Poor women, white witches, not dark ones, yet they were killed all the same." He put the book back and crossed his arms over his chest and leaned against the edge of the bookcase.

"If you do not mean sin, then what do you mean?" Amara carried her dustpan to the garbage bin, pretending to ignore his remark about her fellow sisters from centuries ago who'd been condemned to die. No doubt he wanted to hurt her, but she refused to let him see her pain.

The devil watched her, his dark eyes hot and dangerous.

"A soul can be pure when a mortal loves another

more than his or her own life. Diana is the only soul to ever make a deal with me to save someone else."

That surprised Amara. "Surely there have been others."

"I'm sure that people exist who would die for the ones they love, but giving oneself to me? No one has ever done that before. I find her...interesting." He paused at the counter and looked at the glass display cases. "The little present you gave her was charming. Ineffective, but charming."

Amara's face heated. "It won't work?"

"No, not on me. Lower demons, of course, but fallen angels? Never. We Fallen may be barred from heaven, but part of our grace is still there—not the part that allows us back through the pearly gates, but enough to fool little party tricks like the kind with blessed talismans. When I lost my wings, I thought it was all gone, but it turns out that there's a tiny bit still inside me, alive and kicking." He held up his thumb and index finger as he spoke, pinching a tiny portion of the air together.

Grace. Amara couldn't believe it. The devil still had some small bit of the grace of God inside him?

"I will let you keep your life, Amara. I find you delightful. You're terrified of me, but you haven't shown it once. Humans like you are good to have around. It's no fun to play chess with heaven when the other team has only pitiful pawns."

Amara kept her mouth shut. She would not thank the devil for sparing her life.

"If Diana does visit you again, you may ease her concerns. I don't tend to break my favorite toys." He removed a beautiful crucifix from the glass case and examined it in the gold lights of the chandelier hanging above her counter. Amara held her breath.

"As long as she does not rescind the contract, nor does she resist my demands, she will be released from our deal in three months' time. Of course, when she dies, her soul is mine. Forever. But we mustn't let her worry about that, not when she's got about seventy or so years to enjoy life."

"But she will be changed, won't she? When you're done with her?"

The devil smiled, his eyes now cold and black as obsidian. "Oh yes, most certainly. She'll be corrupted, a soul destined straight for hell when the time is right. But you may pick up the pieces of whatever is left if you feel particularly noble."

"I will," she promised.

With another smirk, he walked toward the door and left.

A sigh of relief escaped Amara. "Oh, Lord." She muttered a soft prayer. If the devil planned to visit her more often, she'd have to think about relocating. She paused as she replayed the conversation in her head. Two things about their encounter felt off. The devil had seemed concerned about Amara, a mere mortal, interfering with a contract. He'd also agreed to let Diana go after three months, at least until it was her time to die. That was...*merciful*.

The last time she checked, the devil was not supposed to be merciful.

———

"Y ou didn't kill her?" Andras asked as Lucien walked into the shadows by the closed shop and left.

"No," Lucien said. "She is more useful alive."

"How so?" Andras kept pace with him as they walked toward the parking lot. Lucien felt like moving at the moment, not flitting about with a flick of his thoughts.

"I want Diana to come to me willingly. I do not want her becoming frightened and revoking the contract. Having the pure soul we need is too important. The more she wants me and the darkness, the quicker I can claim her for the gates. If she feels she can run to Amara and find some comfort, then she will be ready to face my desires rather than run from them. So Amara is not to be touched. I want you to ensure her protection."

Andras let out a sigh. "If word gets out we're protecting a white witch..."

"All hell would break loose?" Lucien joked.

"Possibly." Andras frowned.

Lucien slapped him on the back. "Lighten up, old

friend. After millennia, I have finally found something that interests me again. This is a cause for celebration. Meet me at the club in half an hour. We will find some succulent humans to slake our lust."

At this, Andras smiled. "It has been too long since either of us indulged."

"Indeed." Lucien could spend days in bed with women, taking them over and over, never tiring of it. Every position, every toy, every fantasy—he'd done it all.

Andras vanished.

Lucien slid his hands into his pockets and walked along the darkened streets. Night was a time of beauty, a time when shadows ruled and the chill of the breeze rustled the limbs of trees in a way that made one's hair stand on end. Midnight was his favorite time, even though it was a few hours away. When clocks chimed away the twelfth hour, the battle between night and day was completely equal, giving the world a sense of balance, a sense of beauty, a sense of peace.

It had been so long since he had felt peace.

After the fall, he'd mistakenly thought that he would find it, but he had not. His shoulder blades itched, the knotted scars the only imperfect part of him. They always ached when he thought too long about the wings that had once been there.

You can never taste heaven again, not fully. He knew that, yet as he sealed the bargain with Diana he had tasted heaven. *Her* heaven. And he wanted more, was desperate to feel that peace, that bliss her lips had given him. If kissing her, merely kissing her, had been that strong, bedding her would be explosive. There was an irony to it all—the more he would take her to see heaven again, the more he would be condemning her to hell. But that was the bargain, and she had agreed.

He knew Andras would be waiting for him, but he didn't return to the club right away. First he closed his eyes and honed his focus on Diana. He could see inside her apartment, her...cat? The white-and-orange creature stared at him, his ears flattened. People assumed cats were evil, familiars of the devil, but it wasn't true. Cats were a bane to a demon's existence, and they often didn't like fallen angels. They could see and sense the unnatural presence of creatures like him.

"Seth, what's the matter?" Diana came out of her bedroom dressed in boxers and a loose T-shirt.

The cat ignored her, his feline glare still on Lucien. Lucien flipped his middle finger at the cat, and it hissed and sprinted into the bedroom. Diana shook her head and sighed before she went to the kitchen. Lucien followed her, an invisible undetectable presence.

Diana put a kettle on her stove and prepared a tea bag in a mug. As she waited for the water to boil, there was a stark loneliness to her face that puzzled him. He honestly didn't spend much time around mortals, not like this. He was either torturing them, making deals, or banging them in his bed.

She is to be my toy. I am allowed to watch her, to see what she's up to when I'm not around to pull her strings and make her dance like a marionette.

The kettle whistled, and Diana turned off the stove and poured a cup of tea, and then she took the cup to the couch and settled in with a blanket and a book. He eased down onto the edge of the couch arm and leaned over to study the book she opened. He frowned. A vampire romance.

Ugh. There was nothing romantic about those bloodsucking, brooding immortals. Fallen angels were far more interesting. When they bit a lover in bed, it was for fun and not for sustenance.

"Don't worry, Diana. I'll show you how much fun we can have in bed," he whispered. She shivered and pulled the blanket up tighter. She had heard him, the barest hint of his sensual promise.

"Sleep well," he added with a low laugh and left her to dream about him.

———

He was there, in her room. A dark shadow in the corner with glowing red eyes. Diana tried to open her mouth to scream, but nothing came out. The shadow moved closer, manifesting itself into him, Lucien Star, in his black suit with a blood-red tie. He stared down at her on the bed, and then very slowly he reached for the covers, drawing them back to expose her. She was naked, her pajamas gone, and he was looking over her body with a satisfied smirk.

It was a dream, she knew it was, had to be...yet it felt all too real as his hand gripped her throat tightly enough to send new shivers of dread through her.

"Such a pretty little thing, and all mine." Still grasping her throat, he leaned down and brushed his lips over hers. Heat exploded from that kiss, burning her up with an inner fire. Wetness pooled between her thighs.

"How will you resist me when I fuck you into oblivion, little mortal? Will you shriek my name as I thrust my cock deep into you? Will you moan when I take your ass? I have a thousand ways I want to take you. And you will enjoy every second of it, won't you?" He sank his teeth into her bottom lip hard enough that she tasted blood. He tugged on it while he continued to squeeze her throat just enough that she feared she wouldn't be able to breathe.

"No!" she screamed and jolted up in bed. The covers fell down around her, and she reached to cover her naked body...but she wasn't naked any longer. She was clothed again, and the shadow Lucien was gone.

I was dreaming. It was all a dream. She winced as she licked her lip and tasted blood.

Want to know what happens next? Read the book HERE!

EMMA CASTLE
Dark and Edgy Romance

Unlikely Heroes

*can be read as standalones

Midnight with the Devil - Book 1

A Wilderness Within - Book 2

Sci-Fi Romance - The Krinar World

The Krinar Code

ABOUT THE AUTHOR

Emma Castle has always loved reading but didn't know she loved romance until she was enduring the trials of law school. She discovered the dark and sexy world of romance novels and since then has never looked back! She loves writing about sexy, alpha male heroes who know just how to seduce women even if they are a bit naughty about it. When Emma's not writing, she may be obsessing over her favorite show Supernatural where she's a total Team Dean Winchester kind of girl!

If you wish to be added to Emma's new release newsletter feel free to contact Emma using the Sign up link on her website at www.emmacastlebooks.com or email her at emma@emmacastlebooks.com!

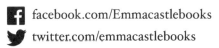

facebook.com/Emmacastlebooks
twitter.com/emmacastlebooks
instagram.com/Emmacastlebooks
bookbub.com/authors/emma-castle

Made in United States
Troutdale, OR
08/03/2023

11780338R00224